# The
# ICARUS
# PROTOCOL

## KEVIN JOHN DOHM

# ICARUS

Greek Mythology teaches us Icarus was the son
of Daedalus, a master craftsman. The story tells us
of Icarus' attempt to escape from Crete using wings
constructed by his father made from feathers and wax.
Ignoring the instructions from his father not to fly
close to the sun, the wax began to melt and Icarus
fell into the sea and drowned.

The myth demonstrates a tragic example
of HUBRIS……..

"I CAN FIGHT OFF
MANY OPPONENTS,

BUT AGAINST THE
GNOMES OF ZURICH

I HAVE NO DEFENSES."

*BRITISH PRIME MINISTER HAROLD WILSON*
*Circa 1960*

# CHAPTER ONE

The sun began its morning assent in the Eastern sky. Hesitating momentarily, giving the appearance of being severed at its equator by the Atlantic Ocean, the red and orange sphere paused and then continued skyward. A warm reddish glow began to bathe the southern tip of the Florida peninsula while the morning fog caressed the low-lying areas of the Everglades. This was one of those mornings when the perfectly clear sky allowed the coexistence of a fiery orb in the east welcoming a new day while the full moon slowly disappeared in the western sky over the Gulf of Mexico bidding adieu to the night.

This mystical morning, only a few weeks from the summer solstice, marked a change in seasons for the local Floridians. Life in general was returning to its regular pace now that the "snow birds" (northerners wintering in the south), retreated to their summer homes. The air was quickly reaching its maximum saturation of moisture. Temperature and dew point readings were identical and without a hint of breeze, the perfect recipe for early morning radiation fog that soaks everything with heavy dew. The rainy season would begin soon.

As the sun continued to climb, a warm, gentle glow stretched completely across the narrowing peninsula, bringing the new day to Marco Island. The small but beautiful tropical isle located on the far southwest side of the state, identifies geographically the beginning of the Ten Thousand Islands that hug the coastline from just south of Naples to Florida Bay and the start of the Florida Keys.

Marco Island prides itself for its manicured white sand beaches, gourmet restaurants, expensive boutiques, and the best game fishing in the United States. This small island (approximately six miles long by four miles wide) is home to some of the wealthiest individuals in the world. Old-family-money types grudgingly shared space with the nouveau riche, dotcom techies, former heads of large publicly held corporations, and courageous entrepreneurs. Many of the so-called captains of industry were now enjoying obscene retirement or severance packages, and in some instances, a combination of both, purloined at the expense of employees and shareholders. Surprisingly, everyone somehow seemed to amicably coexist in this tiny corner of paradise.

The population of Marco ranges from eight thousand full-time residents during the off-season—just after Easter through mid January—to thirty thousand plus during the on season. Most of the transient populations migrate from states in the Midwest with just a touch of New England influence. The Midwesterners give the island a friendlier atmosphere, unlike that of the frantic overcrowded East Coast megalopolis of Miami, Ft. Lauderdale, West Palm Beach, and Boca Raton.

The morning routine was about to begin. Caravans of construction laborers, landscapers, and other service-oriented workers crossed the Judge Jolly Bridge in trucks and vehicles of all types. The local breakfast haunts had the coffee and eggs ready to fuel this hard-working army of mostly Hispanic and Haitian immigrants who could only dream of living in this Garden of Eden. This time of year, the work started early, everyone hoping to avoid the sweltering afternoon heat and daily afternoon deluges.

The charter fishing fleet captains used the off-season to repair their boats and replenish their fishing tackle. A few of the good captains managed to stay busy during the summer months, catering to annual repeat customers—the real fishermen—those who understood the best fishing is when the Gulf waters warm to a consistent eighty degrees Fahrenheit.

A loud thump announced the arrival of the morning newspapers as the awkward bundle came to rest at the entryway to the front doors of the anxiously awaiting homeowners.

Mr. Samuel Sumner III, a retired chief executive officer of a Fortune 500 corporation, was eager to start his daily activities. Sumner's palatial home resided in the very exclusive Estates Section on Marco Island, overlooking Caxambas Pass on the southern tip of the island. Approaching the Sumner estate from Caxambas Court, visitors were greeted with a spectacular view of a long driveway lined with royal palm trees accented by neatly trimmed hibiscus shrubs blooming in an array of explosive red, yellow, orange, and pink flowers. The hibiscus formed a natural outline to the driveway and guided visitors to the circular drive that lead to the castle-like entrance of the home. The average home in this section boasts at least fifteen thousand square feet of living area, a separate coach house to store the numerous exotic automobiles, and a private yacht tethered to the dock in the rear of the home on a secluded waterway.

Sumner was a beneficiary of the lucky sperm club, born and raised in a family supported by old money. Neither Sumner nor his siblings could explain how the family amassed their fortune, nor did they care. They became adept at flaunting and spending their trust funds. Understanding the complexities of making a living and creating wealth escaped him. Samuel Sumner III used his trust fund to stay in school, where he felt safe and unthreatened by the outside world. He frequently joked about becoming a professional student. However, at the age of thirty-five, he actually began to take home a paycheck in return for teaching economics at a prestigious Ivy League school, his career spanned over two decades. During his tenure, he was selected to sit on the board of directors of numerous Fortune 500 companies. He wasn't selected for his business acumen, because he had none. Large corporations like to round out the board of directors with someone from academia in order to appear enlightened, intellectual, and fashionable. His family lineage helped pave his way into the good ol' boys club.

On this particularly beautiful morning on Marco, Samuel Sumner III, a recent retiree, poured his first cup of coffee and asked his housekeeper, Esperanza, to bring him the morning newspaper. Dutifully obeying the order, she fetched the morning paper from the driveway and reappeared moments later with paper in hand.

"Thank you. I'll be out on the dock if you need me," said Sumner. He liked to read his paper sitting in his lounge chair overlooking Caxambas Pass, a perfect location for watching the boats as they headed out to the Gulf of Mexico.

Esperanza knew exactly when to bring Sumner his first refill of coffee. Along with the coffee, she delivered two mechanical pencils with erasers so Sumner could start the daily crossword puzzle. He was surprisingly inept at completing the puzzles, in light of his extended academic history.

"Señor Sumner, is anything else I get for you," asked Esperanza, speaking in her clearest Spanglish.

"No, that will be all for now," Sumner replied. Esperanza retreated to the house to start her cleaning duties.

Sumner looked forward to his *Naples Daily News*. The crossword puzzle in the Neapolitan section was easier than most other papers. Just before starting the puzzle, a noise startled him. He looked out to the water and was delighted at the source of the distraction: a pod of dolphins with their calves splashing in the shallow turquoise waters. Life was good for the dolphins. Food was plentiful and easily acquired.

Taking a sip from his coffee mug, Sumner picked up one of his pencils and began his puzzle for the day. He was again startled by another noise. This one similar to the thud one hears when fluffing a large feather pillow. A great burning sensation quickly followed the sound. Sumner looked up to see a large man standing a few feet away.

"Who the hell are you?" Sumner asked.

He immediately located the source of the burning. A small hole over his left lung was oozing blood. As Sumner began to call for help, the large assassin emptied his silenced revolver. The shots came quickly—thud-thud-thud—striking center mass of Sumner's chest in a grouping of no more than a two-inch diameter. The last two shots, the *coup de grace*, was for insurance—thud-thud—penetrating Sumner's cranium directly between and a half inch above his eyebrows. Samuel Sumner slumped over dead, as the newspaper and pencil dropped from his lifeless fingers.

# CHAPTER TWO

A pproximately one thousand miles northeast of Marco Island, a young, very attractive reception-ist placed her cup of Lipton green tea out of sight and made herself comfortable, preparing for the start of a new day. For the next eight hours, her ability to multi-task would be continually tested as she monitored an impressive array of communication equipment. The horseshoe-shaped instrument panel resembled some-thing you would see on the flight deck of the Starship Enterprise; yet, it allowed her an unobstructed view of the entry vestibule.

She strategically positioned her chair, assuring she was within comfortable reach of all the dials, knobs, flashing lights, and the telephone switchboard. Overly conscious of her hair and makeup, she gently inserted the soft foam rubber earphone into her right ear canal while adjusting the boom microphone, not a hair dis-turbed. The wireless remote headset was ready for action. Reaching over to the far left side of the elec-trical console, she activated her headset with a quick flip of a switch. Initiating a brief test count—1-2-3-4-5, 5-4-3-2-1—she could hear her voice clearly through a small set of Bose loud speakers used mainly for checking the equipment. Almost immediately the phone began to ring.

"Good morning, Industrial Relations Consultants. How may I direct your call?"

After a momentary pause, a deep, guttural, tired voice on the line requested, "Extension forty-five please."

Equal parts of instinct and experience told her to forgo the usual polite inquiry of "who may I say is calling please," immediately directing the call as requested. Extension forty-five rang twice.

"Delasandro here, what the hell's happening down there? I just got to my office and my phones are ringing off the wall."

"Check your computer. I sent you a secure copy from our surveillance equipment; you should have it by now. It appears someone took care of business for us, definitely not one of ours, but it's done. What do you want us to do now?"

"What about the surveillance gear; any chance the local gumshoes might stumble over it?"

"Not to worry. I got there just in time for the show. At first I couldn't believe my eyes, but after it sunk in, I grabbed all our stuff, swept it clean, and beat feet out of there. No signs we were ever there."

"OK, that takes care of our exposure, but who the hell is this guy? I'm just starting to watch the instant replay. He appears confident the way he casually walked up to Sumner, but am I seeing this clearly? It looks like he fires once and then hesitates. What about the noise; is that a silencer on the gun? If I didn't know better, I'd swear he waited for Sumner to look up at him. This smells more of revenge than business."

"I agree on all counts, but whoever he is and whatever the reason, there is no doubt he was motivated. The last two shots to the head were for emphasis. He wanted to leave a message."

"Get back here as soon as you can. I want our people to dissect the post-game highlights, see if we can pick up anything on this guy."

Joseph Delasandro could pass for a grandfather in a Norman Rockwell painting. Grey, thinning hair, neatly groomed, always wearing a cardigan sweater with a heavily starched shirt and perfectly knotted tie, accessorized by a pair of almost round, rimless titanium Italian-made Dolomiti Panto frames with transitional and progressive lenses.. He was the kind of person you could trust with the lives of your loved ones, at least that was the appearance.

For the next half hour, Delasandro played and replayed the video of a textbook assassination, if there is such a thing. Each time he watched the series of events unfold, a nagging visceral feeling came over him. The shooter looked vaguely familiar. The physical appearance, the fluid, purposeful way the assassin moved, energized Delasandro's eidetic memory. His ability to recall images sounds, and objects with great detail had served him well throughout his career.

Unfortunately, it would be some time before the actual video got into the hands of the forensic teams for their expert frame-by-frame breakdown of the action.

"Mr. Delasandro, you have another call on line forty-five. I believe this one is from overseas, Europe I think."

"Thanks, Karen, can you tell if it's our friends the chocolate makers?"

"I'm sorry, Mr. Delasandro, *the chocolate makers*?"

"Karen, you know, Willy Wonka and the Oompa-Loompas…our friends from Switzerland?"

"Mr. Delasandro, I wish you wouldn't refer to them like that. One of these days I'm going to slip up, and we'll all be looking for work."

"OK, Karen I'll try to grow up. Just tell Willy I'll call 'em back on a secure line."

Taking the necessary precautions, utilizing a secured phone line, he pushed the number one on his speed dial. One ringtone later, a voice with a combination of French and Austrian accents answered.

"Mr. Delasandro, we are perplexed. I hope you can shed some light on today's breaking news."

"I'll give you what I have for now. Our people aborted the assignment and immediately pulled out to avoid any embarrassing questions should anyone find our surveillance gear. Our sources close to the scene are reporting that the local police are coming up short on any meaningful evidence. They have already called in the Collier County authorities, and my friend in the FBI assured me that his people didn't find anything when they arrived."

"So, Mr. Delasandro, let me see if I have this correct. You had a team in place doing reconnaissance on a person of interest who was also on our short list. Out of nowhere, a stranger appears and abruptly ends the life of Mr. Sumner. Not a bad thing overall, as long as we have no exposure on this issue. Keep me informed if you ever find out the identity of this mystery man. Thank you and good-bye."

The phone fell silent.

# CHAPTER THREE

"Hey, Tina, I'm heading over to Starbucks to meet this Delasandro guy. Remember I told you he called regarding either flying lessons, or he's looking for some help in finding the right airplane for his business. I'll find out for sure when I get there. You feelin' OK? Do you need anything? Can I bring you something?"

"No, I don't need anything. Go. Have a good time; I'll see you later."

Marco Island's only Starbucks coffee shop was located on Collier Boulevard, the main road that runs the length of the island from north to south. Starbucks, just one of many stores, restaurants, and boutiques, was located in the Esplanade, a residential/commercial complex designed to mimic the colorful architecture found along the canals of Venice, Italy. The condominiums enjoyed a spectacular view of Smokehouse Bay, with a marina hosting everything from small fishing boats to mega yachts completing the picturesque scene. Prices for the residential units started at over a million dollars, while the restaurants and boutiques offered haute cuisine and couture targeting the rich.

"Mr. Delasandro? Hi, I'm Kyle Donnar. I understand you're interested in learning to fly airplanes." Kyle always liked to meet prospective student pilots away from the distractions of the local airport. Starbucks was the perfect place: easy to find, with ample seating, a quiet atmosphere accentuated with fantastic scenery, and good coffee, albeit a bit expensive.

The two men took their coffee to the harbor side, overlooking the idyllic setting of the marina and Smokehouse Bay. Being a weekday, most of the boats sat quietly in their slips, attached to the floating docks that gently rose and fell with the tides. Delasandro sipped his double espresso while Kyle Donnar nursed a large decaf coffee.

"Why the decaf?" asked Delasandro.

Kyle retorted, "I have enough stimulation in my life. I don't need to supplement it with caffeine."

"I think I understand what you mean," replied Delasandro. Subtly redirecting the conversation, he sympathetically offered, "It was sad news when your airline went out of business. I'm sure that was a major source of uncertainty and turmoil in your life, not to mention raising your blood pressure more than a few points."

Kyle briefly thought about asking his future client how he knew of his past life as an airline captain but let it go, deducing that whomever gave Delasandro his name also filled him in on the gruesome details and the abrupt ending to a dream career.

Kyle always liked to ask potential students the all-important and almost obligatory question: why do you want to learn to fly? Most people answered that it was always something they dreamt of doing. Others would acknowledge they wanted a career in aviation, but the majority eventually became weekend, fair-weather pilots.

Kyle had performed the next step of the interview hundreds, if not thousands, of times: outlining the requirements necessary to earning a private pilot's license as listed in the Federal Aviation Rules and Regulations. He quickly explained the importance and format of the thick reference book he laboriously dragged from his briefcase. The book was divided into sections known as parts, not chapters. The FAA always had to be different. Part sixty-one addressed the certification of pilots as well as flight and ground instructors. Part sixty-seven explained the medical requirements necessary for the different level of licenses—private, commercial, airline transport pilots—and part ninety-one outlined the general operating and flight rules. These were just three of the many parts contained in the FARs.

Kyle suggested, "Let's talk about part sixty-one of the Federal Aviation Administration rules and regulations. This is the part that deals with certification of pilots and flight instructors. With the information from this section, you can determine the minimum number of flight hours you'll need to log to earn a private pilot's license. From there we can break down the specific hourly requirements, such as cross-country flights, night flying, dual instruction, and solo practice flights."

Delasandro nodded in agreement and slyly interjected, "I'll bet it must have been a necessity to be well-versed in the rules and regulations when you were Chief Pilot for that charter flight department in Chicago, before your days with Universal Airlines."

"How do you know about that," asked Kyle.

Delasandro's grandfatherly voice reassured Kyle. "I always like to know who I'm dealing with, so I did a little background check on my future flight instructor."

Kyle replied, "Mr. Delasandro, you're starting to freak me out a little."

"Please, call me Joe. Mr. and Joseph are too formal. In fact, you can call me anything you like, but as the saying goes, just don't call me late for dinner. I know we're gonna be good friends."

"OK, let's get back to the Federal Aviation Rules and Regulations." Kyle impatiently nudged his new client.

Delasandro once again interrupted the thought process and asked, "Kyle, which set of rules did you use when you flew those middle-of-the-night, clandestine government charters into Central America? Or did it matter, considering the type of work you were doing? You had to have had a fairly high security clearance to fly those missions. If my sources are accurate, you had one of the highest security clearances issued to civilians."

"OK, who the hell are you? Which one of my asshole friends put you up to this? Since you seem to know so much about me, then you know I'm in no mood to play games," Kyle snapped.

"Easy, easy, Kyle. I'm just trying to get your attention," Delasandro said with his soothing, calm voice. I know more about you than you could ever guess. Just give me a few hours of your time. I'm quite sure that you'll find what I have to say is very interesting."

Piqued, yet curious, he replied, "Alright, I'll play along."

For the next few hours, Mr. Joseph Delasandro read his notes to Kyle Donnar. Going all the way back to when Kyle turned down a pro-baseball contract after his senior year of high school. A couple of emotionally tough years playing college football and baseball led to a period of self-doubt, second guessing, and frustration.

Kyle had worked odd jobs, from truck driver to fork lift operator, shipping and receiving clerk, service manager for a wholesale tire company, a sanitary engineer, otherwise known as a garbage collector, and, last but not least, joined the noble profession of firefighter.

"Kyle, I see you had all these jobs but I need to fill in the blanks. How did you go from job hopping to your dream career in aviation," asked Delasandro.

"During this period, I once again focused on the career I had always envisioned for myself: flying airplanes. I turned a blind eye choosing to ignore the bloody conflict in Southeast Asia. I spoke with military recruiters from the Marine Corp, Navy, and Air Force. Unfortunately, during the Vietnam War, only college grads could become flight officers, but I learned about a program where I could become a warrant officer and possibly fly helicopters. If I beat the odds and survived in one piece, I would at least be on track to reach my goals and the GI Bill could help pay for my education. To me this was a much better alternative to getting drafted into the Army and slugging it out in the jungles.

"I was within hours of signing the recruitment papers, much to the chagrin of my parents. My mother's opposition was understandable, but my father's attitude was confusing. My Dad was a decorated veteran with numerous beachhead landings to his credit, surviving under enormous enemy fire in the Pacific theater of operations during World War II. My father was like most veterans of that era. They simply fought for their country, never expecting special treatment or accolades upon their return. When badgered, my father would acquiesce and shyly recall the time he served in the Navy. The only experience he seemed to enjoy recalling was following the invasion of the island of Leyte in the Philippines. Halfway around the world from his home in Chicago, he ran into not just one but two of my uncle's- : his sister's husband, John, and his wife's brother, Jim. There wasn't a family get together where that story didn't eventually surface.

"The enlisting dilemma came to an abrupt end when President Nixon announced he would start to withdraw the troops from Vietnam. The draft soon became extinct, and the military no longer needed bodies."

"So, with the military options off the table what was your next move," Delasandro queried.

"I knew I would still have to finish a college degree, and did so while working on my pilot licenses and ratings supported by one of my many jobs. The degree was an absolute necessity if I hoped to compete in the job market. Miraculously, I completed my last two years of college, earned a Bachelor of Science degree in Finance, while working full time and completing pilot training, earning a commercial pilot's license as well as a becoming a certified flight instructor."

"I'm impressed," quipped Delasandro. "You couldn't have had much of a social life during that time."

Kyle nodded in agreement.

"Kyle, shall I continue?" Not waiting for an answer, Joe picked up where he left off. "Let's see, from there you did some flight instructing, some part-time flying, filling in at corporate flight departments, and then on to the charter airline in Chicago. Is this accurate so far?"

"Yep, you're doin' just fine," mumbled Kyle.

"OK, that just about brings us up to you getting hired by Universal Airlines. From this point on, we both know what happened to your career. Gross mismanagement is bad enough, but to witness incompetence to that magnitude while upper management rewarded themselves with stock options, bonus programs, and greedy salaries is beyond unconscionable. It's just plain amoral," Delasandro stated while shaking his head in disgust.

# CHAPTER FOUR

"You seem to know a lot about me. So what's this all about? You're obviously not here to talk about airplanes. So what can I do for you?" Kyle asked.

Delasandro quickly retorted, "On the contrary, I'm here to see what I can do for you. Let me explain. My company, Industrial Relations Consultants, is currently in need of someone like you. We need an articulate, intelligent, independent type, a person needing little or no supervision. Specifically, IRC needs someone to head up the flight department. Our chief pilot just retired."

"How did you find me," Kyle asked. "There has to be at least six or seven thousand qualified pilots on the street looking for work."

Always prepared, Joe Delasandro had just the right answer. "The aviation community, as you know, is a very small world. Multidimensional, socially adept, business-savvy pilots are few and far between. According to my sources, you've demonstrated numerous times throughout your career that you have the right combination of ambition, smarts, and physical attributes."

Flattered but not totally buying into the sales pitch, Kyle's pessimism and years of experience sent up red flags signaling something just didn't add up. Throughout his three decades of flying, Kyle had come to know many scammers, cheats, and downright thieves trying to score big in aviation. However, at fifty years old, Kyle reluctantly admitted to himself that there wouldn't be a lot of offers coming his way, so he decided to give this stranger the benefit of the doubt and let Delasandro continue.

"Why don't we set up a short trip to our home office just outside of Washington DC? I have one of the company planes parked at the local airport. How about tomorrow? A quick ride up to DC, we can have lunch, show you around, and have you back to your beautiful little island in time for dinner. Do you think your wife, Tina, would like to join us?"

"How do you know my wife's…" Kyle never finished the question. He looked over at Joe Delasandro and said, "Why wouldn't you know my wife's name? You seem to know everything else about me."

Joe Delasandro allowed himself a smile, or more accurately, a smirk of satisfaction.

The next morning, the two men met at Marco Aviation, a small fixed-base operation at Marco Island Airport. Marco Aviation sold fuel, had a small charter flight department—mostly offering trips to the Florida Keys and the Bahamas—and some seasonal flight instruction. The small general aviation airport sat at the dead end of Mainsail Drive surrounded by water on the north, south and east sides with a golf course on the west.

Standing in the waiting area of the one-story quaint terminal, the two men were greeted by Captain Tim Braden and his copilot Dirk Youst. After a quick safety briefing by the Captain, the beautiful Gulfstream V was airborne and headed to Washington DC.

The Gulfstream V is one of the finest corporate aircraft that money can buy, with a starting price of thirty million dollars, depending on the lavish interior accoutrements selected. Plush leather seats, state-of-the-art entertainment systems, and gold-plated sinks in the galley and lavatories came as standard equipment. The average person would only see a plane like this in the movies.

The two men helped themselves to coffee and pastries from the galley area. While Kyle was adding sweetener to his coffee, the copilot, Dirk Youst, turned around and dutifully inquired, "Finding everything you need, Mr. Donnar?"

Kyle, feeling out of place, nodded and said, "Thanks, I've got everything I need."

"Well, if there's anything we can do, just let us know," Youst replied as he rotated in his seat, getting back to his responsibilities.

Kyle turned to Joe and asked, "Why not one of those pilots; they seem qualified."

Delasandro tactfully avoided answering the question by quickly listing the other aircraft in the fleet. "In total we have two Gulfstreams, two Dassault Falcon Jets, and two Beechcraft King Air 350 turboprops. What do you think so far?"

Kyle answered, "There's no doubt you have some of the best equipment in the world of aviation."

The plane gently touched down on runway 19L (One-Nine Left) at Washington Dulles International Airport. After a short taxi, the Gulfstream came to a stop at Dulles Jet Center. In the world of general aviation, Dulles Jet Center was considered a world-class operation, familiar with the needs of aircraft of this caliber and the high-profile passengers usually associated with this lifestyle.. Delasandro and Donnar exited the tall, sexy plane and walked through the terminal building to a waiting limo. As they vanished, the two pilots began to prepare the aircraft for the return flight they knew they would make later that evening.

# CHAPTER FIVE

Exiting the airport, the limo ride took less than an hour. The route was scenic, winding through the foothills and farm country west of the Dulles International Airport. The limo eventually turned onto a road that was hardly visible from the main highway. Entering through wrought iron gates that opened and closed automatically, an antebellum-plantation-style home began to appear from behind a small grove of willow and ancient oak trees. As soon as the limo came to a stop in front of the main entrance, the driver scurried around to the passenger side of the vehicle to open the door for the two men. Approaching the entrance, Kyle couldn't help noticing an abundance of surveillance cameras and other security devices on the walls, doors, and entrance gates

The receptionist cheerfully greeted the two men. "Hello, Mr. Delasandro, how are you today," she asked.

"Just fine, Pam. How are you and the family?" replied Delasandro.

Starting the tour, it became obvious that the home office of Industrial Relations Consultants benefitted from the service of expert interior decorators as well as seasoned landscape architects.

The perfectly decorated interior, with its soft hues, beautifully stained woodwork, and strategically placed lighting, allowed for a serious but not rigid business-like atmosphere.

Most of the employees dressed professional yet casual. There was a sense of order. No one seemed to be rushing or shouting or displaying the typical controlled chaos you found in most businesses.

The tour ended with both men in Joe Delasandro's office. "Well, what do you think? I'm sure by now you have some questions," asked Delasandro.

Kyle responded, "You seem to have a fine organization here. The company is obviously doing well, judging from the fleet of planes and this beautiful office compound. What exactly is it you do here? Who are your clients? What is your main source of revenue?"

"I will answer all of your questions at the appropriate time," answered Delasandro. "I know that sounds strange; however, before I can divulge any information, I must ask you for a small favor. IRC requires you to sign a confidentiality agreement before I can address the questions of who, what, where, etc."

Before Kyle had time to formulate a response, Joe asked his secretary to bring the appropriate documents. He had barely finished placing the phone in its cradle when his Administrative Assistant, Mrs. Karen Mallett, (pronounced Ma-Lay), strolled into the office. Mrs. Mallett was a woman in her early sixties. Good family genes contributed to her young appearance, as did her hobby of running marathons. She was a widow, mother of four, and grandmother of eight. She had been Joe Delasandro's Administrative Assistant for over twenty years.

Mrs. Mallett handed the thick document to Delasandro and then turned to Kyle and said, "It's a pleasure to finally meet you, Mr. Donnar. I've been looking forward to this for a long time."

She left the room, and Delasandro passed the stack of papers to Kyle. Agreeing to terms of the confidentiality agreement required Kyle's initials on every page of what seemed like a never-ending pile of legalese. Finally, coming to the last page, Kyle had signed and dated the document. Delasandro asked Mrs. Mallett to sign the document as a witness and promptly sent the agreement off to the legal department to be stored in perpetuity.

"Now, on to your questions," announced Delasandro. As he had quietly breathed a sigh of relief that Kyle agreed to sign the documents. "What is your honest impression of what you observed today?"

Kyle answered, "If I didn't know better, I'd say you are an obscure section of The Government, or you do work exclusively for The Government. Having dealt with FAA bureaucrats and politicians most of my life, I sense the presence of Big Brother here."

Delasandro let out a quiet laugh. "I knew you would see through all of this immediately. I expected nothing less from you. However, we cooperate with many different governments not just the US. For lack of a better term, we like to refer to ourselves as a think tank.

"We really don't fall under the jurisdiction of, or report to, any particular authority. However, we do work for just about every branch of our federal government as well as numerous governments around the globe. Most of our work comes at the request of the many security organizations in the world. The CIA, NSA, FBI Interpol, MI6. You name it. We get calls from just about every well-known security organization and some not so well known.

We help them solve problems beyond their purview. We're consultants; we point out the obvious and charge hefty fees for the information—information the client already knew but needed an outsider to point out, clarify, and implement. It's like parents dealing with teenagers. Advice coming from the parents is automatically ignored. However, if the same advice comes from an outside source, like a coach or teacher or, heaven forbid, a rock star or celebrity, it's as if the words are etched in stone. Consultants are modern day snake oil salesmen, and the best part is that it's perfectly legal."

"Well, that explains very little. The more I hear, the more questions come to mind," was Kyle's initial response.

Delasandro continued with his explanation. "The more time you spend here, you'll get a better understanding and appreciation of our mission. The chief pilot position is vitally important and an integral part of our organization. We're tasked with transporting dignitaries around the world, and we're expected to do it with the upmost security and confidentiality. I'm positive you're the right person for this job.

"You haven't asked about compensation yet. Not interested in money?" jibed Delasandro.

Kyle said, "Of course, it's my favorite subject. I just thought it would be more appropriate if I let you bring up that subject. Besides, I didn't want to shoot myself in the foot by throwing out a lower number than you had in mind."

"I'm confident that you'll like what we have to offer." Handing Kyle a folder entitled compensation and benefits, Delasandro continued, "I'll hit the highlights, and you can read through the folder at your convenience. First, IRC will match your highest paid years as a Boeing 747-400 captain at Universal Airlines as your base salary. We offer a 401(k) plan with matching contributions. You and your wife will have full health insurance for the rest of your lives. Last but not least, when you retire, we will put together a very generous severance package, including a pension. Maybe not as good a pension as you would have had if your airline remained in business, but this pension will never disappear. We have the same plan as our senators and congressmen, and you know they won't be tampering with their benefits. Any questions or comments?" asked Delasandro.

Kyle couldn't believe what he was hearing. "That's extremely generous. I've never heard of an offer like this in the field of aviation. Usually it's just the opposite. Everyone wants to hire the best of the best, but they want to pay the least of the least. Everything sounds too good to be true, and in my experience it usually is, or it has a very serious caveat emptor attached in the fine print."

Delasandro responded, "Good, I'm happy you like the package, or at least find it interesting enough to give it a chance. I want you to study it, take some time and think about it, read through your information, and of course talk it over with Tina.

"By the way, are you aware of the etymology of your last name? It's just a little hobby of mine, something that takes us back to our roots. Knowing a little history about ourselves can shed light on who we are."

Kyle shook his head from side to side half-heartedly, indicating a negative response, and then offered, "I haven't given it much thought, but I'm sure since you seem to know everything else about my life, you're about to enlighten me."

"Your last name, Donnar, is the Americanized version of the old Germanic name Donar, which is a derivative of the Norse god Thor, the god of thunder. I wouldn't be the least bit surprised to find out you brought down the thunder from time to time during your life.

"Speaking of bringing down the thunder, your former CEO, Samuel Sumner, seems to have pissed off the gods. Someone brought down the thunder on his cozy little corner of paradise."

"Yeah, unfortunately it didn't happen sooner. It sounds like that prick got off way too easy. I would have liked to see him suffer for the irreparable damage he did to my airline, the employees, and all the families he destroyed with his greed. Maybe this will be the start of a new trend in this country. Start taking out the greedy bastards and their families, and see how they like it," responded Kyle.

"It looks like whoever did the deed was a professional. No useful evidence of any kind left at the crime scene so far. But you know the old saying that there's no such thing as the perfect crime, especially murder. Something, no matter how small or insignificant, will get the attention of a good detective, and the puzzle will begin to take shape," explained Delasandro.

"The way I hear it from the local cops, guys that are friends of mine, they have nothing to go on; the trail is already getting cold" Kyle replied.

Delasandro added, "A friend in the FBI said there might be a witness, a vagrant, some old guy who takes up residence in homes under construction, under bridges, and sometimes even in vacant lots. They're searching for him now but no luck yet. He has a weird name, probably not his real name, maybe you've heard it somewhere. I'm not even sure I'm hearing it correctly. It sounds like they're saying Speedy Calamaria. Does that ring a bell or sound vaguely familiar?"

Kyle closed his eyes and repeated the name to himself three or four times, each time changing the emphasis or accent on different syllables, when suddenly a quiet laugh emanated from his larynx and a smirk appeared on his face. The response did not go unnoticed by Delasandro.

"Just out of curiosity, where were you when your former boss got his brains scrambled?"

"Sorry to disappoint you, but I was with Tina in Chicago for a family reunion. I'm surprised you didn't know that too."

# CHAPTER SIX

The return flight to Marco Island gave Kyle the opportunity to observe the operations of the Gulfstream
V and its crew. He opted to sit in the cramped jump
seat in the cockpit rather than the luxurious leather
seats in the plush passenger cabin. He took advantage
of the time to speak with the pilots and get a sense of
how they felt about their employer and the degree of
job satisfaction.

This time the two pilots had switched seats. Dirk
Youst was now the captain, and Tim Braden, the captain of the first flight, was now the copilot. This was
unusual, and Kyle inquired about the swapping of
seats and responsibilities. Braden explained that all of
the pilots at IRC were cross-trained to fly at least two
different planes. The pilots would receive type-specific
ratings for the jets they would fly. However, they could
only act as captain on their primary aircraft. Any subsequent aircraft they flew would be as copilot only. In
this particular situation, both men held captain ratings
on the Gulfstream, so they swapped responsibilities
every other flight. Seat swapping was a practice the
airlines seldom followed. The airlines always wanted

one person to have the final word when the chips were down and time was of the essence.

After a quick climb to cruise altitude, the crew set the autopilot and settled in for the relatively short flight to Marco Island. The route of flight would initially traverse an area of the United States known as the Piedmont region, an area immediately east of the Appalachian Mountains converging with the Atlantic coastal plain, which eventually ended at the Atlantic Ocean.

Tracking on a southwest heading, leaving the Washington DC area, the sleek but powerful Gulfstream crossed the states of Virginia, North and South Carolina, and then down the coastline of Georgia to Florida. Air Traffic Control duties would start with Dulles Tower then transfer to Potomac Departure Control, eventually handing off to Washington Center for the high-altitude segment of the flight. Washington Center transferred authority to Atlanta Center and then to Jacksonville Center, and Miami Center. The latter took responsibility to coordinate the descent portion of the flight, directing the big jet to Ft. Meyers approach control, which then vectored the plane toward Marco Airport. The routing was essentially the same route followed by the major airlines flying down the East Coast to the south Florida area.

The pilots were anxious to talk about their aircraft and share information with Kyle. They were equally excited to ask Kyle what it was like to fly a jet like the Boeing 747-400, a plane with a gross takeoff weight of more than 800,000 pounds, ten times the size and weight of the jet they were currently flying. This exchange of information, or "pilot talk," was something pure aviators, pilots in love with flying, were always anxious to share.

The Gulfstream V cockpit had an impressive array of flat-screen computer monitors that projected the flight instrumentation along with vital systems, such as mechanical, electrical, and environmental support information. The standard "round dial" instruments were replaced with computer-generated icons. Moving map images on the navigation display depicted the aircraft's path as it passed over the earth. Overlying the map display, the pilot could request a multitude of information. The nearest suitable airports for landing automatically appeared on the screen, along with navigation symbols identifying the location of the ground-based navigation transmitters. The screen showed the position of other aircraft in the immediate vicinity and the corresponding altitudes. This was helpful to the pilots, allowing them more time to visually locate and see approaching aircraft, the electronic version of the "see and be seen" rule of aviation.

The primary flight display contained the artificial horizon, heading indicator, flight directors, airspeed indicator, vertical speed indicators, and altimeters—all these in one computer monitor versus five or more separate instruments.

System monitors for the fuel, hydraulics, oil (pressure, temperature, and quantity), bleed air systems for pressurization and air conditioning, along with the electrical systems, were located in the center of the instrument panel. Any information the pilots requested was at their fingertips. Kyle was familiar with most of the equipment in the cockpit from his experience as a 747-400 captain for Universal Airlines. The cockpit was quite a bit smaller, and the equipment had minor differences from the big Boeing, but overall Kyle anticipated no problems learning to fly this beautiful airplane.

The pilots seemed very happy with their jobs. Pay and benefits were well above national average, the quality of work life was excellent, and most importantly, the pilots enjoyed the respect commensurate with their experience, education, and responsibilities. This feeling of contentment was indeed rare in the aviation community. Most employers, regardless of whether a major airline or a small corporate flight department, looked at the flight crews as an unavoidable evil. The prevailing attitude from the bean counters is, "How dare these pilots ask for a livable wage? We're letting them fly our planes."

The sexy, sleek jet gently touched down on the five-thousand-foot-long runway at Marco Island. Landing on runway 17 (One-Seven; runway numbering corresponds to the direction of the runway in relation to magnetic north. In this case, runway One-Seven is aligned with 170 degrees on the compass so the aircraft landed facing predominantly to the south.)

Unfortunately Marco Island Airport only had one runway and no taxiways, so the plane had to roll out to the far south end of the airport where a large semicircle of asphalt adjoined the end of the runway, allowing enough room for the large plane to make a U-turn. Both pilots went on high alert as they began the almost mile long trek back to the terminal building.

Marco Island Airport had no air traffic control tower to coordinate aircraft movement, so the two pilots constantly monitored the VHF communication radios, announcing their position relative to the terminal while leaving all the strobe lights, navigation lights, landing and taxi lights on full bright, hoping to alert any aircraft trying to land at Marco Island that a plane was on the runway.

Stopping in front of the general aviation terminal, the crew shut down the engines and finished their after-landing and shutdown checklists. The door opened by pivoting on an extremely strong set of hinges down and away from the plane. The stairs were built into the door and automatically unfolded, allowing an effortless egress from the aircraft. Kyle exited the plane and walked through the small terminal building.

General aviation terminals, like the one on Marco, allowed passengers the convenience of not dealing with crowded gate areas, crying children, the odor of fast food restaurants, and the hassle of inept, undereducated security personnel. A person could come and go without anyone taking notice. A perk the rich and famous enjoyed.

Kyle was anxious to see Tina. Donatella Santina-Maria Angelina Valano, a classic Italian beauty, waited impatiently for her husband just outside the door. Her family was from the south of Italy. Her father's side of the family resided in Calabria, while her mother's people came from Sicily. Tina once personified every man's dream of the beautiful Italian woman. Statuesque with a perfectly proportioned and physically fit figure. Heads turned when she walked into a room. Despite her overwhelming beauty, Tina was one of those rare types: beautiful as well as a truly nice person, not a mean bone in her body. Unfortunately, months of treatment for ovarian cancer had taken its toll. Tina's skin appeared gaunt and her beautiful figure gave way to loss of muscle tone due to uncontrolled loss of weight.

She opted for the shortened version of her second name, Santina (little saint), because she wasn't comfortable using Donatella, a variation of a name from a long line of dead relatives passed down through the generations. An Italian custom.

The oldest of three girls, Tina Donnar inherited the duties of matriarch of the family with the untimely death of her parents. Her two younger sisters knew they could count on her in every way. Tina was the first female in her extended family to graduate from college. She attended a prestigious women's Catholic college in Lake Forest, Illinois, majoring in psychology with a minor in business.

Within months of graduation she found great success in the banking industry, eventually managing two dozen branches of a savings and loan company. Her prowess in the banking industry didn't go unnoticed. A headhunter showed up at her office one day and made her an offer beyond her wildest dreams.

The Bank Administration Institute (BAI) was her new employer. She managed the continuing education division for a couple of years before turning her attention to the marketing department. She revolutionized the way BAI did business. In the early days of desktop office computers, she taught herself, and most of the other employees, how to maximize their efforts with the use of this revolutionary new device.

Tina always went out of her way to help friends and co-workers. She volunteered her time to help with numerous charity events. Having no children of their own never stopped her or Kyle from participating in the myriad of school events involving their nieces and nephews. Kyle always felt that she was much too good for him and didn't deserve her. He never understood what she saw in him.

Outside the terminal, Tina greeted Kyle with a passionate embrace. They walked a few feet to their car and proceeded home. The drive took less than ten minutes. West on Mainsail Drive, South on Rt. 951, over the Judge Jolly Bridge, and around the west side of Marco Island on Collier Boulevard, paralleling one of the most beautiful beaches in the world. Kyle started to give Tina the details of the job as they pulled into the driveway of their picturesque old Florida-style home overlooking a small bay. Kyle suggested they finish the conversation inside. Tina agreed.

Kyle told Tina about the extremely generous offer; she didn't believe what she was hearing. She was concerned.

"I thought you would never take another flying job if it meant working for someone else," Tina said.

Kyle laughed and replied, "That was because I couldn't tolerate starting over at the bottom of the seniority system again, earning less money than if I flipped burgers at the local fast food restaurant.

"These young kids getting hired to fly the small regional jets for the commuter airlines have no clue as to what's in store for their future. They'll get a rude wake-up call when they have to qualify for food stamps. The salaries will continue to trend downward. The management at the airlines will replace them with someone who will work cheaper. I wonder if their parents are aware of their paltry salary and dismal future after dumping a hundred thousand dollars or more on a career in aviation.

"I never would have imagined that we would ever receive this kind of offer. What do you think? Do we take it or not?"

Tina hugged her husband, fighting back tears of joy. "I have one question, do we have to move to Washington DC and leave our island?"

Kyle responded, "Yes and no. We will have to move to DC. However, we can keep our home, and you can come and go whenever you like. As for DC, IRC has a beautiful house for us in the country, not far from the office or the airport.

"I don't see how we can pass on this deal. The compensation is great, and the benefits are fantastic. You always said, things would turn around and begin to go our way; you were right. Now we can work on your problem; we will be near some of the best medical facilities in the country. Joe Delasandro would like to have an answer from us as soon as possible," Kyle added.

The following morning Kyle waited to call Delasandro until he and Tina had a chance to talk more about the remarkable offer. Riding their bicycles, the pair pedaled over to Hoots Restaurant for breakfast. Tina's questions dealt more with the types of aircraft, the number of pilots, and the destinations, the typical who, what, where, when, how, and why questions. She was mostly satisfied with the answers.

But one question continued to gnaw at her. *What's the catch*, she thought to herself. *No one has ever helped us in the past.* It was always the other way around. Tina and Kyle were always there to support everyone else.

While Tina and Kyle struggled during the early years of his career, their families didn't have the resources to offer financial help, which was OK with them; they didn't ask for anyone's assistance. The one thing that did hurt and had always been a source of internalized ire was the total lack of moral support from family and friends. A career in aviation was foreign and hard to comprehend. Some family members tried to discourage them and even chastised them for not acquiescing to a more secure livelihood.

Returning home from breakfast, Kyle stood on the boat dock overlooking a bluish-green bay that lead out to the Gulf of Mexico. Every day something surprising or interesting appeared in the bay. This particular morning was special—a female manatee and her calf floated effortlessly at the surface, basking in the sun and seeming unconcerned about Kyle who stood only a few feet away on the edge of the dock. Tina walked up, wrapped her arms around his solid athletic frame, and whispered, "Make the call. Let's go to Washington."

# CHAPTER SEVEN

Delasandro was ecstatic about Kyle's good news. Trying to hold back his enthusiasm, he queried, "How soon can you be here? I'd like to get you set up as soon as possible."

"How's next Monday?" answered Kyle.

The following Monday, Kyle Donnar arrived late morning and stood in the lobby of IRC. Joe Delasandro met him, and the two men immediately headed off for a cup of coffee.

"We need to take care of some administrative paperwork. Get you on the payroll, set up your insurance, and, of course, take care of the ever-popular tax information so Uncle Sam can get his not-so-fair share. After that I'll take you to meet everyone and show you to your office."

After a busy morning and a quick lunch, the two men began the process of associating names and faces. Remembering faces was no problem for Kyle, remembering names was another story. The more time he spent with Joe, the more Kyle thought he looked familiar. Maybe it was the grandfatherly appearance, or maybe he resembled someone in the movies. It didn't really matter, Kyle was excited to begin this new and hopefully final job in his aviation career; nothing could distract him.

The tour from office to office introduced Kyle to the top dogs of the company and to the most important people—the secretaries, the true gurus of organization. Secretaries kept many a company and their executives on track.

Kyle met his personal assistant, Mrs. Diane Bishop. Mrs. Bishop was an attractive lady in excellent condition, thanks to her daily yoga practice, aerobics classes, weight training, and tennis sessions. She could easily pass for someone in her late thirties or early forties. In reality, she was a grandmother closing in on her sixties.

"Hello, Mr. Delasandro, how are you today?" asked Mrs. Bishop.

"Diane, how many times do I have to ask you not to call me Mister? Mr. Delasandro is my father. Diane, I would like to introduce you to Kyle Donnar, our new chief pilot."

"How do you do, Mrs. Bishop? I'm looking forward to working with you," Kyle said.

"The feeling is mutual. I've heard a lot about you these last few days," responded Mrs. Bishop.

"Diane, we are going to continue the twenty-five-cent tour. We will see you in a few hours."

The two men turned and walked away, leaving Diane Bishop to her duties.

"We have an advisory board here at IRC. The members of the board are normally only here for our scheduled meetings, but we do give them offices. I'm the Chairman of the Board. The advisory board meets once a month or as needed. We discuss how to handle projects that come our way from the other security organizations. At times, however, we reject projects. As much as we like the revenue, some requests come with, um, let's just say for lack of a better phrase, too much political baggage.

"Some members of the board come from other agencies and act as liaisons to their former employers. Other members come from academia, the military, and a few from private industry. Overall, and for the most part, it's a good group of guys," quipped Delasandro.

"You'll find most of these guys are straight shooters. They will tell you exactly what's on their minds. They've all been around for quite a while." Delasandro continued the introductory walk with Kyle but cautioned him about their next stop. "You're about to meet Lieutenant Colonel Harold Sheppard. Sheppard comes to us from the Pentagon and is the only advisory board member who uses his office on a daily basis. He's been retired from the Air Force for quite a while but still uses the rank thing to try and impress the women. We inherited him because no one else wanted him around, and I thought maybe I could redeem this favor at a later date. He comes from a privileged background. His grandfather and his father were career military officers, and the whole family had money. His father used his clout to get Harold into the Air Force Academy in Colorado Springs.

"The old man was reluctantly forced into using the 'set aside' program to get his kid an appointment to the academy. Are you familiar with the set aside programs?" Before Kyle could respond, Delasandro continued. "They started so the academies could get better athletes for the sports teams. Generally speaking, the students didn't have the grades to compete for an appointment.

In the case of Harold Sheppard, he was neither an athlete nor a good student. His father really ticked off some people when he forced the issue. Many truly deserving kids found themselves left out. As expected, Harold Sheppard squeaked by and graduated last in his class. Does this sound a little familiar? Like one of our esteemed representatives on Capitol Hill? Same scenario, different academy," Delasandro mused.

Delasandro cautioned, "Watch your back with this guy. He's still smoldering over the fact that the board refused to give him flying privileges in our aircraft. If he says anything to you that sounds the slightest bit off key, or just plain weird, bring it to my attention immediately. There's more than one member of the board that would like to get rid of him."

"How did he end up in the Pentagon?" asked Kyle?

"After graduating from the Air Force academy, Sheppard's father pulled some strings again. This uncoordinated, academically challenged beneficiary of a clout system gone awry was given fighter-jet training. The training command had its arm twisted and was forced, extorted, and coerced into using extra resources trying to get him through the basic flight school. He eventually washed out after a now infamous training catastrophe. So, in the end, he had to go somewhere. A remedy to the problem was to bury him deep within the walls of the Pentagon.

"Following his usual patterns, he quickly became persona non grata at the Pentagon, and against my wishes, IRC was forced into babysitting him.

"Sheppard doesn't talk a lot about his days in fighter jet training, at least not to us. I understand he throws it out there when he's on the hunt for women at the local bars. I'll bet his pick-up line never comes close to what really happened out there in Del Rio, Texas. I pulled some strings of my own and was able to get my hands on a copy of the control tower tapes on the last day of his flying career. Would you like to hear it? You'll wet your pants laughing when you hear this."

Kyle shrugged his shoulders, nodded, and said, "Sure, why not."

Joe unlocked a drawer in his desk, reached in, and extracted a cassette tape.

"Let me set the scene for you. By the time this tape was made, Sheppard had taken more than three times the allotted flights just trying to get through his check rides. The instructor for this flight was the last in a long line that agreed to work with Sheppard to help him overcome a particular problem. The flight took off early in the morning, departing from Laughlin Air Force base near Del Rio in southwest Texas along the Rio Grande River.

"The instructor wanted to take advantage of the cooler, less humid morning. The summertime temperatures mixed with humidity can be oppressive. The morning's sortie was to be a three-ship flight, practicing formation flying."

"Do you know what type of trainer they flew?" asked Kyle.

"I believe it was the basic trainer T-37. Are you familiar with this type?"

Kyle nodded and described it to Joe. "The T-37, built by Cessna, has side-by-side seating, a clear canopy, makes lots of noise with very limited power, and has served as a good training platform. Very docile and safe. I think it's been around since the mid-1950s. Slow, as jets go, less than four hundred miles per hour, and it weighs in around six thousand pounds gross take-off weight. Unfortunately it carried a not so flattering nickname: The Screaming Mimi. Most people joked that it was great at converting fuel and air into noise and smoke." Joe proceeded to insert the tape into his stereo system and turned up the volume.

*Laughlin Tower, Mayday-Mayday-Mayday, this is TORCH two-one [21]/TORCH two-one.*

*State nature of emergency TORCH two-one. This is Laughlin Tower.*

*This is TORCH two-one, TORCH two-zero [20] appears to have suffered loss of control and has recovered from violent unusual inverted attitude. TORCH two-zero NORDO (no radio) unable to ascertain condition of pilots. Canopy obscured by unknown substance, possible bird strike, unable to see pilots. TORCH two-zero appears to be heading back to base, TORCH two-three [23] and TORCH two-one will escort.*

*Roger, TORCH two-one. The emergency equipment will be standing by, clearing the pattern now, cleared for emergency landing.*

*Roger, TORCH two-one, three flight-over and out.*

Delasandro looked over at Kyle and asked, "Have you figured it out yet?"

"Bird strike sounds plausible to me," Kyle responded. "The T-37 had a problem with bird strikes coming through the canopy until it was re-engineered by Cessna."

Delasandro, eager to reveal the answer, jumped in and said, "If you remember, I said Sheppard had a particular problem he needed to overcome. His problem was a case of severe air-sickness, followed by violent projectile vomiting. That unfortunate morning, Sheppard, being the idiot he is, got up early and ate a very large breakfast of oatmeal, eggs, bacon and sausage, with grits and wheat toast, washed down by numerous cups of milk. The unidentifiable substance on the canopy was his partially digested breakfast. Identifiable pieces of bacon and sausage adhered to the interior of the cockpit.

"He managed to short circuit the electrical system in the cockpit, causing the NORDO situation. He also managed to douse his instructor in the vile mixture when the plane inverted. The plane came to a violent and abrupt stop on the runway, blowing the tires because the brakes locked up. The instructor yanked back the canopy and leaped from the plane, begging the fire department crash truck servicemen to wash him down with their high-pressure fire hoses.

"Needless to say, the remaining base instructors refused to fly with Sheppard after that incident, even if it meant a court martial and dishonorable discharge. That was the last act as a pilot for 'Guard Dog' ..... Sheppard's, *nom de guerre*. He should have been called 'Puke Bag' Sheppard. Pretty funny, huh? He doesn't know that I have the tape. I'm saving it for the appropriate time. Now you know what you are dealing with in Sheppard.

Let's get this over with," mumbled Delasandro as the two men walked unannounced into Sheppard's office.

"Harold, I'd like you to meet Kyle Donnar, our new chief pilot."

Sheppard rose from his chair but never ventured out from behind the security of his desk. His eyes focused on Delasandro, indignantly looking past Kyle as if to demonstrate that the new chief pilot wasn't worthy of his attention. Eventually offering a flaccid, insincere handshake, the men exchanged the usual pleasantries. Delasandro ended the meeting quickly. "Kyle, let's get back to your office and finish some paperwork."

As the two men walked down the hall, Delasandro said, "Oh, I'm sorry, I forgot to add to Sheppard's list of qualities that he suffers from Little Man Syndrome. When he shook your hand, he was actually standing on an elevated carpet protector under his desk chair. He comes in a bit taller than your average jockey. I think that says it all, don't you agree?"

Shortly after returning to Kyle's office, they completed the required paperwork. Kyle Donnar was now an official member of Industrial Relations Consultants.

"Well, any questions or comments?" Joe inquired?

Kyle answered slowly, "No, not right now, but I'm sure I'll have plenty of questions in the next few weeks. One thing keeps gnawing at me; I can't help but think I've met you or have seen you somewhere before."

Joe laughed and deflected the comment by saying, "I just have one of those faces. Trust me, if we had met, I would have definitely remembered you."

# CHAPTER EIGHT

(One year later)

Delasandro knocked on **Kyle's office door.** "Good morning, Kyle. Happy Anniversary. May I come in?"

"Absolutely, have a seat. Can I get you a cup of coffee or something?" Kyle walked over to the coffee maker and poured two cups of decaf coffee. "Want anything in it, Joe?"

"Yeah, how about some real coffee, the kind with lots and lots of caffeine. I can't believe you still drink this tinted sissy water."

"Joe, like the first time we met, I told you that I have enough stimulation in my life. I don't need to supplement it, and what's with the anniversary stuff?"

"The reason I'm here today is to congratulate you on your one year anniversary with IRC. We're really happy with the way you stepped in and took over the flight department without a problem. Now that you've been here a year, is there anything we need to address? Any problems we have to fix? Any new ideas you want to discuss on operating your department?"

"Nope, not really. Everything and everyone in my department seems to be running smooth. I inherited a great flight department. I have the best aircraft money can buy, the pilots are the quintessential professionals, and, last but not least, Mrs. Bishop keeps us all in line. She always has the flight schedules and training dates posted early so the guys know when they will be off duty and can schedule things with their family and friends. What else could I ask for?"

"Speaking of home life, how's Tina?"

"Well, I'd like to say everything is great in that department, but I can't. Tina loves the beautiful home, the five acres of rolling countryside—it's everything we could wish for and more. The problem is that we are still battling with the doctors back home. They don't seem to be any closer to coming up with the correct diagnosis; it's starting to drag her down mentally and emotionally. The standard treatments don't seem to be working. We are coming up on decision time. The docs would prefer to continue with the noninvasive treatments, such as radiation and medications. They are cautiously optimistic because the tumors haven't grown or spread."

"So she's still being treated by her doctors in Florida, huh?"

"Yes, Tina didn't want to change doctors just yet. I'm trying to convince her to see Dr. Sandra Berman at Georgetown."

"Is she one of the doc's from the list I gave you," Delasandro asked.

"Yeah, she was on your list."

"I do recall that name," Joe said, slowly nodding his head. "Kyle, just keep me in the loop on this. Let me know if there is anything you or Tina need."

"Thanks, I appreciate it," Kyle said.

Kyle and Joe finished their coffee. "I'll keep my eyes and ears open. If I hear of any other doctors with good credentials, I'll let you know. Well, I should head back to my office and get a little work done today. Give that Italian honey of yours a hug for me when you get home."

"Will do," said Kyle.

Joe returned to his office to plan the agenda for the monthly board meeting, including a quick scan of the latest potential clients. Most of the inquiries contained the usual proposals requesting assistance in organizing and executing intelligence-gathering missions, nothing out of the norm.

Tight budgets, congressional oversight committees, and governmental accounting offices encouraged all of the other security agencies to work across jurisdictional boundaries and pass along intelligence reports on individuals and organizations that fell beyond their jurisdiction. With luck, the appropriate agency would end up with the correct file and complete the necessary protocol.

Unfortunately, due to the bureaucratic mentality, most of the heads of the other agencies felt it was an absolute imperative to withhold information. The prevailing wisdom was that cooperation was counterproductive. Information was power. Unfortunately, the world witnessed the aftermath of this archaic attitude when the 9/11 attacks aired live and in full color on our home televisions. The heads of the security agencies admitted, after the fact and under pressure and fear of prosecution, that they knew the terrorists were in the country and that they had intel that a few of the suspects were learning to fly.

Fortunately, Industrial Relations Consultants never found itself in a budgetary crunch or lacking funds. IRC received a very large annual endowment from an international group of private benefactors who deposited money into an offshore untraceable bank account, generous enough that IRC never needed or used tax dollars from the United States or any other governmental entity to operate. IRC enjoyed freedom from the scrutiny of nosy reporters and Capitol Hill busybodies, allowing the company to remain an enigma, the way Joe Delasandro liked.

Occasionally IRC would receive a request from its benefactors to oversee a delicate or sensitive situation that couldn't be addressed by any of the government security agencies. Fortunately this was rare, for IRC was not equipped to put people in the field. IRC's mission was mainly a cerebral function, a think tank to be used as a resource. When the rare requests appeared on Delasandro's desk, IRC would have to locate and contact its independent assets strategically located around the world.

Independent assets, or operatives, were primarily field officers formerly employed by a government. Military special ops guys like Navy SEALs, Delta Force, Airborne Rangers, and Green Berets. These guys had figured out quickly that real money could be earned as private contractors in the security industry. One contract, either from a governmental agency or a private citizen, would bring in more money for those mercenaries than they could earn in an entire lifetime as a career military officer.

Continuing to scan through the pile of requests on his desk, Joe mentally prioritized them. Of course, the board of advisors would have something to say about each of the potential contracts. At the bottom of the pile, Joe came across a medium-sized manila envelope marked: "Urgent, For Your Eyes Only." This one found its way through the back channels from IRC's benefactors to his office.

Joe carefully absorbed every word of the message. He knew this request would get the board's attention. They were going to have their work cut out for them. Joe had no choice but to put this one first on the agenda.

# CHAPTER NINE

Kyle took the day off to drive Tina to see her new doctor. She was about to endure another day of poking and prodding. After months of trying to convince his wife to see a different doctor, she had finally made an appointment with Dr. Sandra Berman. They settled in for a scenic one-hour drive into Georgetown University Medical Center via Route 66, exiting at the Key Bridge ramp taking the bridge into Georgetown. Tina checked out the domed roof of the Capitol building and the Washington Monument from the passenger side. Kyle knew how important it was to accompany Tina, for she would be in no shape to drive home at the end of an exhausting day of tests.

"Good morning, Tina, how are you feeling today?" asked Dr. Berman.

"I've had better days, Doctor," Tina replied.

"I'm sure you have. Are you in any pain or discomfort? Does everything seem to be functioning normally?"

"Everything seems to be OK, no pain or discomfort, and all systems appear to be operating 'normal,' as my husband would say."

"How about your monthly cycle? Any significant changes? Are you on a twenty-eight-day cycle? Any abnormal blood flow?"

"No changes; you could set your watch to my cycle. Everything appears normal; that's why I'm having trouble understanding why these tumors haven't disappeared."

"Tina, the stubbornness of these tumors has me concerned, too. I received the entire file from your doctors in Florida. The tumors just don't seem to be reacting like cancer cells usually do when we find them in the ovaries. They haven't shrunk, grown, or metastasized like anything I've seen. You probably don't want to hear this, but I think we need to start looking at the possibility that the original diagnosis you received might be incorrect. Since you don't appear to be in any immediate danger, I would like to start from the beginning. A complete physical, blood work, MRIs, mammograms, and maybe try to get a larger sample of one of the tumors to biopsy."

Tina wasn't happy with that news, and her eyes began to well up with tears. Kyle immediately put his arm around her for comfort. The doctor left the two alone to talk and digest the doctor's suggestion. Twenty minutes later, Dr. Berman stepped back into the room, this time with a colleague following close behind.

"This is Dr. Charles Clayton. Chuck and I attended medical school together. He specializes in unusual and rare strains of carcinomas. In my opinion, he's one of the best doctors in his field, and I want him on our team. I hope you don't object."

Tina glanced over at Kyle to check his reaction. Kyle nodded his head in agreement and thanked Dr. Clayton for wanting to get involved.

Dr. Clayton had an impressive résumé. He had attended medical school at Northwestern University in Chicago. He and Dr. Berman completed their internships together at Cook County Hospital, where they experienced just about everything the medical world could throw at young doctors. On weekends, especially during the mild weather months, Cook County Hospital resembled a war zone.

Located on the near west side of the city of Chicago, within minutes of some of the most treacherous housing projects and urban blight in the United States, new doctors quickly learned firsthand of the atrocities committed by humans onto other humans. Turf wars from the local gangs fighting over illegal drug distribution territories. Drunks battering each other over a bagged malt beer that escalated into knifings and shootings. Overdosed drug users found lying unconscious in gutters with the heroin needles firmly impaled into whichever part of their anatomy they could still find a useable vein.

A sad but necessary convenience for the hospital was that the Cook County Morgue was located approximately one hundred yards, or the length of a football field, from the entrance of the emergency room. Doctors would pronounce the not-so-lucky victims dead on the loading dock of the emergency room and then shuttle the bodies over to an elevator door leading to the morgue's reception area.

Every new doctor, policeman, and paramedic would eventually have to take a tour of the morgue. The first hurdle for the uninitiated came as soon as the elevator doors opened. A gust of air emanating from the bowels of the building would greet the rookies. The odor was a combination of dead, rotting corpses mixed with bodily fluids and combined with an overpowering aroma of formaldehyde. If the new recruits didn't vomit on the loading dock, it was only a matter of time.

The elevator ride to hell was a scene fit for the scariest horror movies ever produced. The floor of the elevator was perpetually sticky, and no matter how long you tried to hold your breath, it wasn't long enough. Most people resorted to breathing only through their mouths.

The agonizingly slow elevator would finally reach its destination: the receiving room. As the elevator doors opened, the living occupants were assaulted with a stench that made the initial aromas on the loading dock seem like a breath of fresh spring air. Those that didn't vomit at this point were tough hombres. The ones that did puke were handed a bucket and a mop and told to clean up their own mess.

The reception area was a busy place. Cops assisted the medical examiners in identifying the victims. Taking the fingerprints off a dead body in one phase or another of rigor mortis was no easy task. The morgue was especially busy during the time Drs. Berman and Clayton took their tour. The victims of mass murderer John Wayne Gacy had just started arriving.

Coincidentally, as a rookie firefighter- paramedic, Kyle took his first tour of the morgue at roughly the same time as the good doctors.

On-the-job training of this nature would either make or break the spirit of a new intern. The doctors who survived their internships at Cook County Hospital would be better doctors as they continued their education toward their specialties.

Dr. Clayton eventually proceeded to Sloan-Kettering Cancer Center in New York, while Dr. Berman went to work at Georgetown University Medical Center. There was no doubt Tina Donnar's life was in good hands.

Tina was a good patient. Like most people, she didn't care for needles, so she always looked away when the nurse drew blood. Kyle was able to stay with her for moral support during most of the tests. As the nurse tied the restricting band around Tina's arm, she gave Kyle the option to leave the room. Kyle stayed and held Tina's free hand. The nurse disinfected the inside area of the arm with an alcohol swab. A dark blue vein slightly protruded from the skin. The nurse quickly but gently inserted the small diameter needle through the skin and punctured the vein. As soon as she saw a positive return of blood, she placed a vacuum test tube into the receptacle attached to the needle. She effortlessly filled six vials, and on the last one, she released the restricting band from Tina's arm.

"I hope that wasn't too bad. Hold this gauze tightly against your arm," the nurse instructed. After placing a bandage over the small puncture wound, the nurse packed up her equipment and left the room.

Dr. Berman escorted Tina and Kyle to the MRI department. Completing the required questionnaire took about ten minutes. Tina's name was called immediately. The temperature in the changing area was comfortably warm as she slipped into the hospital gown selected for her.

The nurses and technicians were polite, professional, and caring. The nurse in charge described to Tina how the MRI worked and what she could expect to hear in the way of noises while she was in the tunnel.

"Are you claustrophobic?" asked the nurse.

Tina replied, "I don't like the feeling of being trapped in the tunnel, but I don't think it's claustrophobia. I can control my feelings. Thanks for asking."

Tina was helped onto the machine and received her last minute instructions. As she entered the tunnel, she tried very hard to stay motionless as the machine scanned up and down her entire body. Her eyes closed, she tried to think of happier times back on Marco Island. Images of the beautiful beach, the dolphins and manatees, and fish jumping into the air in the bay behind her home flashed through her mind.

As quickly as it began, this part of her ordeal was over. Tina changed into her own clothes and met Kyle in the waiting area. "Everything OK?" he asked?

Tina nodded and said, "It wasn't too bad." She was now off for a complete gynecological exam including a mammogram.

Dr. Berman selected Dr. Nancy Miller for this phase of testing. Dr. Miller specialized in obstetrics and gynecology and had twenty-five years of experience. A petite woman, with a figure that revealed her past as a collegiate gymnast, wore her blond hair pulled back into a ponytail. Dr. Miller worked hard at making her patients feel as comfortable as possible and made time in her busy schedule to personally perform the examinations.

For the second time in one day, Tina Donnar changed into a hospital gown. She found herself sitting on an examining table, anticipating one of her least favorite things to endure. Dr. Miller entered the room and softly spoke to Tina, explaining the procedure. At the completion of the exam, Dr. Miller escorted Tina to the mammogram facility.

The attending nurse brought Tina back to the changing area and told her to get dressed. By this time, she was tired and just wanted to go home. Drs. Berman and Miller met Tina and Kyle in the waiting area. Dr. Berman explained that the team would review the results of the day's tests to determine the next course of action. If the tests came back without a solid diagnosis, they would have to discuss the possibility of retrieving a tissue sample to biopsy.

Tina and Kyle thanked the doctors and started the drive homeward. Dusk had fallen over Washington DC. The lights of the Capital City were illuminated, and the entire area sparkled brilliantly. The sight of Washington DC at night was spectacular.

Tina settled in as close to her husband as possible and put her head on his shoulder, inadvertently letting out a loud sigh. "Please take me home; I'm so tired. I was just thinking how lucky we are that you're working at IRC. The medical insurance is truly a blessing. I don't know what we would have done if this job hadn't come along."

"Yeah, IRC was a lucky break for us, one of a very few. You know, I would've done whatever to get you the best care in the world. Even if it meant working twenty-four hours a day, seven days a week, you would have the best.

"Speaking of IRC, now I know where I saw the names of Drs. Clayton and Miller. They were on the list Joe gave us. The same place we found Dr. Berman. If I didn't know better, I'd say that Joe Delasandro and Industrial Relations Consultants have their own team of medical professionals waiting on call."

Tina fell asleep on the ride home. Slowly decelerating, bringing the SUV to a smooth stop in the circular driveway directly in front of the main entrance, Kyle placed the vehicle in park and turned off the ignition. He didn't want to wake her, so he carefully carried her up the stairs to their bedroom. Laying her on the bed, he stealthily removed her shoes and covered her with a large down comforter. Kissing her gently on the cheek, he whispered, "Good night. I love you."

# CHAPTER TEN

Early the next morning, Kyle was off to IRC headquarters. He had a full day of logistical planning for the coming month. His assistant, Mrs. Bishop, tentatively set the flight schedules, but Kyle had the task of assigning the pilots to the trips, assisting in arranging ground transportation at the destination, and if necessary deploying a security detail for the VIPs. The pilots would handle all of the flight planning the day before the trip. Weather problems and last minute changes to itineraries would dictate departure times and routes.

Mrs. Bishop helped the pilots with special requests, such as in-flight catering. Depending on the level of importance of the passengers listed on the manifest, Mrs. Bishop would order food: Sweet rolls and sandwich trays for passengers of mid-level or lower importance. Higher-level dignitaries, on the other hand, received full breakfasts, hot lunches, and gourmet dinners served by attractive flight attendants.

Aircraft maintenance was always a top priority. None of the aircraft would leave the hangar until all scheduled and/or routine preventative maintenance was completed. If an aircraft needed repairs, a team of highly trained technicians would swarm the planes and return them to pristine condition. Custodial and grooming teams kept the planes in original condition. Anytime a person stepped into an IRC aircraft, the plane looked, smelled, and felt brand-new.

Looking over the original itineraries, Kyle saw that one of the Gulfstream Vs was headed to a small town in southwestern Colorado, while one of the Dassault Falcon 50s was heading for northern Wisconsin.

The Dassault Falcon line of aircraft was equally as impressive as the Gulfstream. Falcon Jet had a full line of aircraft to fit the needs of any size corporation. The airplanes were made in France, using the latest technology found in the French Mirage fighter jets. Without question, the Falcon Jets were equipped with the latest in avionics and cabin accoutrements.

The Falcon 50 model had three engines, as compared to conventional corporate aircraft with the standard two engines, one on each side of the fuselage near the empennage or tail section. The Falcon 50 added the third jet engine above the fuselage, integrated into the vertical stabilizer. The three engines gave the Falcon 50 an enormous power to weight ratio that enabled it to fly comfortably out of small airports as well as high-altitude mountain airports.

Always the quintessential aviator looking to increase the margins of safety, Kyle decided to swap the Gulfstream headed for Colorado with a Falcon going to Wisconsin. Three engines coming out of a high-altitude airport surrounded by mountains beat two engines every time.

As the day wore on, Kyle couldn't help but worry about Tina and the wait to hear from the doctors about their findings. Keeping busy helped him deal with the situation. But for Tina, the waiting was almost intolerable. Neither Tina nor Kyle expected to hear from the doctors for a couple of days.

Kyle continued to plan for the scheduled flights when he noticed something out of the ordinary in the itineraries. The passenger manifest listed two persons per aircraft to be dropped off at the destinations and picked up one week later. This was unusual in that most passengers would utilize the aircraft for the convenience of traveling to their meetings in the morning and returning the same day or, in some cases, the next day. For longer stays such as these, the airlines became the preferred mode of transportation. The double round trip flights would be very expensive.

Assuming these must be very important people to have this kind of access to the IRC flight department, Kyle nonetheless decided to check with Delasandro, pointing out the planned itineraries. Joe reassured Kyle that all was OK and the board of advisors had approved the flights.

Quickly glancing at the itineraries on his desk, Joe looked up at Kyle and suggested that he and Tina take some time off and head for Marco Island. Everything was in order, and Joe would even authorize the use of one of the Beechcraft King Airs for their trip, which would be listed as a training flight, continued education and proficiency.

"It'll do you and Tina some good to get back to your island. Let her feel the warm white sand between her toes on that private stretch of beach while soaking up some of that Florida sun. A week away from here will do you both some good."

Kyle called Tina with the news, and she wasted no time in contacting her friends on the island. A quick check of who might be in town revealed that Susan, Carol, Peggy, Toni, and Patti would be there; Mary had just returned to her home overlooking Lake Michigan. Lunches and dinners along with securing court time at the local racquet club was all part of the plan. This little bit of happiness was enough of a distraction to take Tina's mind off of her problem.

# CHAPTER ELEVEN

The arrangements for her return trip to paradise firmed through hours of phone calls between Tina and her girlfriends. Restaurant schedules, shopping excursions, tennis, and even a trip to the day spa for some pampering filled in the itinerary.

While the ladies managed the social calendar, Kyle kept busy in his office at IRC. Planning flights, scheduling maintenance for the fleet of aircraft, and sending pilots off for their annual recurrent training were all part of the daily responsibilities of a chief pilot. Kyle personally reviewed the amount of flight time and the type of flights each pilot logged.

If a flight crew returned from a long international trip covering dozens of time zones, a mandatory stand-down period was required before their next flight. Ample rest could mean four or five days removed from flight status to readjust their circadian rhythms. Given proper rest, the brain always manages to readjust to the daily cycles of light and dark.

Thanks to the jet age, the modern traveler could wake up in the morning, fly halfway around the world, and actually lose or gain an entire calendar day, depending on which direction they crossed the international dateline over the western Pacific Ocean. After spending a week or so in the new time zone, your brain adjusts to the local time and rhythms. Of course, upon returning home you have to reverse the process.

The first few days at home were miserable at best. Your brain tells you that it's time to sleep, but the clocks on the walls haunt you with the reality of the local time. You try to function normally, but a general malaise overrides your ability to concentrate or stay focused. Physical reaction time is slow and the process of making simple decisions becomes a major endeavor, definitely not a good time to use power tools, drive cars, or fly airplanes.

This is a way of life for a few thousand professional airline pilots in the United States. Safety in scheduling takes a back seat to the almighty dollar. The price tag for safe scheduling is enormous, so the airlines, like many other corporations, choose to roll the dice and play the odds on safety.

One of Kyle's top priorities when he took over as chief pilot at IRC was to operate the safest and most professional flight department. Having worked his way up the ladder of aviation, Kyle had the opportunity—or misfortune, depending on your view—to experience the entire spectrum of the world of aviation.

The glamour of flying airplanes quickly tarnishes if your employer is unconcerned about safety. Jobs flying freight or cancelled checks for the Federal Reserve Bank were at the lowest rung of the industry. Young, inexperienced pilots would take those jobs just to log flight hours and gain valuable experience, with the hopes of selling their skills to a major airline one day. For a few lucky pilots, the long, hard days and nights flying in severe weather, operating unsafe aircraft, and always feeling fatigued would one day pay off. For the unlucky majority, their careers would come to a frustrating conclusion, or worse.

The pilots employed by IRC considered themselves the lucky ones. They flew wonderful, safe, modern aircraft and had a chief pilot who looked out for their health and welfare. Alert and content pilots were the foundation of a safe and professional organization.

Returning to the office after having lunch with Joe, Kyle's cell phone rang. Tina was on the other end, her voice trembling slightly, she asked, "Can you talk?"

"Hi, sweetie, is everything OK?" Kyle asked. "I'm standing here with Joe; do you want me to call you from my office?"

"Dr. Berman called. She wants to know when it would be convenient for us to come to her office."

"Let me get to my office and call you right back," Kyle replied.

Joe observed the concerned look on Kyle's face as he hung up the phone and quickly deduced that all was not well and reiterated his offer of assistance. Kyle thanked him and proceeded to his office. Before closing his door, Kyle politely asked his assistant to hold all calls. Mrs. Bishop, recognizing a change in Kyle's demeanor, nodded her head and quietly acknowledged his request.

Quickly sitting down at his desk, he pressed the number one on his speed dial. A breath later, his home phone was ringing. Tina answered promptly, waiting for Kyle's return call.

"Hi, it's me. I'm in my office now, and I left instructions not to be interrupted. What did Dr. Berman say? Does she agree with the diagnosis from the docs back home? What about treatment? When do we start? Where do we go?" Kyle fired off all of his questions at once.

Tina quietly giggled and said, "Kyle, please relax. I'm as anxious as you are to get the answers to those questions.

"Dr. Berman called to set an appointment so we can sit down with her and Drs. Clayton and Miller. I'm guessing it's routine not to discuss this stuff over the phone. She would like to see us tomorrow, if possible. The morning would be preferable."

"OK. Call her and set it up for tomorrow. I have things under control here, and Diane can handle anything that might pop up. I'll see you at home in a couple of hours. Love you."

"Love you, too," Tina said before hanging up the phone.

# CHAPTER TWELVE

Joe Delasandro called for an emergency meeting of the directors of Industrial Relations Consultants. The members sensed an urgency of the situation, considering the board had just convened the previous week. Asking the board members to readjust their hectic life styles on such short notice sent a clear message.

Arriving as ordered, the board members took their usual seats around the large, rectangular, dark-mahogany table. While the men were settling into their oversized, thickly padded leather chairs, two attendants from the cafeteria strategically positioned a cart with coffee and refreshments abutting the rear wall in the room.

"Welcome, gentlemen. My sincerest apologies for having you come back so soon. Please help yourselves to some coffee and make yourselves comfortable." Joe casually walked over to the door, as if he was following the cafeteria attendants. He thanked them as they exited the room and closed the heavy six-panel oak door. A loud KA-THUMP signified the mating of the heavy-duty bolt lock as it came to an abrupt stop inside the metal doorjamb.

Making his way back to the head of the table, Joe exercised his authority as chairman of the board of directors and called the meeting to order. "I'm sure you have already noticed that we will not have a stenographer taking notes at this meeting." The men sitting around the table understood completely the implications of having no record of today's discussions.

Sitting around the table, starting at Joe's right side was General Thomas "Buck" Buckwalter, a retired three-star general of the United States Marine Corps. Buck Buckwalter earned his reputation as a smart, tough marine serving in Korea, Vietnam, Grenada, and Desert Storm. The name Buck came from the shortened version of buckaroo. He had grown up on a ranch in west Texas and had worked as a cowboy until he enlisted in the Marine Corp.

Next to Buckwalter was Dr. David Levine PhD. Dr. Levine's specialty was international economics, and he lectured at a prestigious Ivy League university as a professor emeritus. Extremely intelligent with a genius I.Q, however, frail in stature, Dr. Levine was the complete physical opposite of Buck Buckwalter.

To the right of Levine, and at the far end of the table, was Harold Sheppard, a retired Air-Force lt. colonel on loan from the Pentagon. Due to the politics, IRC was stuck with him. Sheppard's position at the far end of the table was no accident; Delasandro liked to keep him as far away as possible.

On Sheppard's right was Frank Schmidt, a former CIA assistant director of foreign operations. Serving almost twenty years in the field before taking an office job, Schmidt cultivated and maintained useful contacts on every continent. If ever there was a need for contract assets, Schmidt was the man IRC called.

Last but not least, Mr. James McKay was the former CEO and President of Applied Technologies and Remote Sensing, a defense contractor. Remote Sensing was the technical term for remote or distant surveillance. McKay's company specialized in high-definition optics for satellites, surveillance cameras, and side viewing radar for aircraft. McKay liked to boast that he could read the label of a cigarette pack sitting on a table at an outdoor café from one of his cameras in space. McKay got his start in the business doing aerial photography from a single engine Cessna 210 high wing airplane, and he held numerous patents on equipment he designed during his years in the business.

Delasandro began. "Gentlemen, we have a very serious issue to discuss. First, I received correspondence directly from our benefactors, and I have authenticated the code sequence and verified the originator of the message. I'll pass around the envelope with the routing codes for your concurrence."

Each man took a few minutes to check the codes against his own personal list of authenticating data. James McKay was the last to check, and then he returned the envelope to Delasandro.

"We all concur on the authenticity and origination of the document. Next I will give you as much time as you need to review the details of the request." Delasandro proceeded to distribute sealed folders to each of the men. While the men began to read the information, Joe walked over to the refreshment cart and poured a large black coffee.

Raising the coffee mug to his mouth, Joe was about to take a sip when his cell phone rang. "Delasandro here," he answered. The brief one-sided conversation consisted of head nodding with an ample smattering of yesses and no's and a couple of I see's thrown in for clarification. Delasandro quietly said, "Thank you, Doctor, I appreciate your help and keeping me in the loop on this situation. Have you and the other doctors talked about the possibility of enrolling her in one of our clinical trials and test programs?" The answer was a definite yes. "That's great news, doctor, go ahead and make the necessary arrangements. Let's get her started as soon as possible. I'll inform the board at our next meeting." Joe was careful not to let on that the board was actually in emergency session.

Each man closed his folder as he finished reading. Over the years, the board of directors received numerous requests from security agencies around the world. Most of the requests were routine and mundane, but some were outrageous and shocking. For the most part, the board members developed the art for remaining stoic, almost poker faced when reviewing information put before them. However, this time the men looked around at each other in disbelief. Frank Schmidt finally broke the ice and asked, "Is this a joke? Did I miss April Fool's Day?"

"I assure you, it is not a joke," responded Delasandro. "They are serious about this, and we need to discuss the ramifications of this request. First, let's take a look at the reason for the request. The three names you have before you are personally responsible for destroying the financial security of more families than the Great

Depression and all the subsequent recessions since the 1920s.

Their actions have destroyed livelihoods, pensions, 401(k) retirement plans, and they have erased personal fortunes in the stock markets. Our benefactors have seen a sizable decrease in their portfolios due to the actions of these men. They accomplished this dubious record through greed, fraud, and personal agendas.

This request is before us for a couple of reasons. First, our benefactors don't like to be embarrassed. Initiating damage control to reassure their clients is not something they ever envisioned. Second, there is a total lack of confidence with the current administration in Washington to quell this type of behavior. Third, and most importantly, a subtle but very clear message that the actions of greedy, amoral, and unconscionable individuals will be addressed swiftly and permanently."

"What makes these guys different than the scores of greedy CEOs that have gotten away with this behavior in the past?" asked James McKay.

"The difference this time is that these guys can be directly connected to the current administration in DC, and as I said before, our benefactors took a financial hit, and we know how protective they are of their wealth, which equates to power. They can't ever be perceived as weak or vulnerable; their empire would crumble.

"Two of the names in front of you were prosecuted and found guilty in the lower courts. However, in the Federal Appeals Court, judges appointed by the current administration reversed the guilty verdict. There's lots of noise insinuating that large contributions to this president's campaign paid off. The third guy on the list is no longer in play. It seems that someone beat us to the punch and did our work for us."

"Any idea of the organization responsible for the hit or why?" asked General Buckwalter.

"Total blank so far. We had surveillance in place at the time. We have an actual play-by-play video of the hit, but the shooter wore a baseball cap and seemed to be a pro by his demeanor. Our tech guys are working the tape frame by frame, looking for the smallest clue.

"We all know someone who was negatively affected by the actions of these men. Some of us have seen the impact of their actions on our personal portfolios. There is one more thing to consider: the actions of these men seem to be isolated cases, but we have discovered they were all intertwined by the fact that they all served on each other's board of directors. We are currently looking at the members of all three boards to see if anyone is trying to pick up where these guys left off. As always, we need to remain objective in our decisions and not let personal feelings enter into this process. Having said this, let me remind you that this issue was brought to our attention by our employers."

# CHAPTER THIRTEEN

The ride to the hospital was uneventful. Tina gazed out the window of the car, admiring the natural beauty of the cherry blossom trees as they started to bloom on schedule, as they do every spring. Three thousand cherry blossom trees were a gift from Tokyo, Japan, in 1912. This particular variety of non-fruit-bearing trees produced spectacular pink-and-white flowers, attracting tourists from around the world. Without question, this was one of the most picturesque seasons in Washington DC.

Tina and Kyle sat in the reception area of Dr. Berman's office at 9:00 a.m. sharp. They were the first patients to arrive and sign in on the office logbook. Tina was surprisingly cool and calm, while Kyle was the exact opposite. Prior to sitting down, she picked up a tennis magazine from the stack of periodicals on the coffee table. The Williams' Sisters—Venus and Serena—Maria Sharapova, and Roger Federer usually graced the cover of the tennis journals, and that was just fine with her; they were some of her favorite players.

In contrast, Kyle was skimming through the *USA Today* newspaper, not stopping to read any particular article in detail. Fidgeting like a little kid, he was unable to sit motionless for even one moment. His movements didn't go unnoticed. After a few minutes, Tina looked over at Kyle, smiled, and reached for his hand. She gently guided his hand into her lap as she returned her magazine to the table next to her. Using both of her hands to control his calloused, muscular hand, she drew it tight against her thigh. Whispering in his ear, she said, "I know you're worried. So am I. No matter what we learn today, I know we are in good hands, and we will beat this." She caressed Kyle's hand and kissed his cheek softly.

Dr. Berman entered the reception area through the door of one of the examining rooms. "Good morning, Tina. Would you and Kyle step into my office please? I'm waiting for Drs. Clayton and Miller; they should be here in a moment."

Tina and Kyle made themselves as comfortable as possible on the green leather settee directly across from Dr. Berman's desk. Dr. Berman began to move three chairs into a semi-circle facing them. As Dr. Berman set the last chair into position, Doctors Clayton and Miller entered the office. Dr. Clayton joked that his timing was perfect; all the heavy lifting was done.

The three doctors sat in the chairs facing Tina and Kyle. They all carried thick manila file folders stuffed with papers. Dr. Berman started the meeting by asking Tina how she was feeling.

"Fine, I feel really good."

Dr. Berman opened up her file and began to orally review the history of Tina's problems, dating back to her initial routine gynecological exam in Florida and ending with the most recent battery of tests at Georgetown University Medical Center.

As Dr. Berman navigated her way through the chronology of events, she paused to elaborate on the findings of each of the tests. Dr. Berman deferred to Drs. Clayton and Miller when dealing within areas of their expertise.

The presentation lasted for more than an hour. During this time Tina and Kyle were proactive, interjecting questions whenever they felt the need, and the doctors demonstrated great patience and compassion in responding to their questions.

Dr. Berman was beginning her final summary when Kyle briefly interrupted. "Correct me if I'm wrong, but so far I haven't heard anything conclusive."

Dr. Berman replied, "Kyle, you're correct. The information thus far has not produced conclusive evidence. At this time, however, I ask Dr. Clayton to take over and review something that caught his attention."

Dr. Clayton began his report by giving Tina and Kyle a quick recap of his expertise. He specialized in treating cancers originating in the abdomen, including the reproductive organs. Dr. Clayton continued to set the foundation of his findings, explaining in simple terms but not condescending, so that Tina and Kyle could completely understand. Dr. Clayton explained that as he was reviewing the test results, nothing contradicted the original diagnosis. Surgical removal of the affected ovary would have been the logical course of action. However, in reviewing the blood work, something caught his attention.

Dr. Clayton explained. "I noticed an unusually elevated level of CA-125 in your blood. CA-125 is a protein found on the surface of ovarian cancer cells and in some normal tissues. However, CA-125 levels may be high in other types of non-cancerous conditions, including menstruation, pregnancy, and pelvic inflammatory disease. I can understand how the original diagnosis was ovarian cancer. Our lucky break is that the initial treatment protocol was also incorrect. For some unexplainable reason, the treatment you have been receiving did manage to inhibit the growth of the tumors. If the tumors had been surgically removed, which is normal protocol, we might not have been able to find the root of the problem.

"The levels of CA-125 in your blood are much higher than typical ovarian cancer. I remembered a conversation I had a couple of years ago with another colleague, where a patient had similar numbers to yours. After some research, I was able to track down the doctor and get his opinion.

"We believe that we are looking at a case of EOPPC. Extraovarian Primary Peritoneal Carcinoma, a close relative to Epithelial Ovarian Cancer. EOPPC develops in cells from the peritoneum, which is the membrane that lines the walls and organs of the pelvis and abdomen. These cells are very similar to epithelial cells on the surface of the ovaries. Because EOPPC tends to spread along the surfaces of the pelvis and abdomen, it is often difficult to tell exactly where the cancer originated. Women who have had their ovaries removed can still develop this type of cancer.

"Treatment usually includes surgery to remove as much of the cancer as possible, followed by radiation and chemotherapy. Information on prognosis is limited since it is a newly recognized form of cancer. To be perfectly clear, I am extremely confident you do not have ovarian cancer.

"I know this is an enormous amount of information for you to digest, so I would like to suggest that we schedule a day when we can formulate our action plan."

# CHAPTER FOURTEEN

The board members continued to discuss the merits of this assignment. During discussions, the members tried to keep their personal feelings in check, which proved difficult. Everyone on the board knew someone negatively impacted by these three men, not to mention the enormous press coverage vilifying their actions.

Questions began to dominate the conversation. It was becoming obvious that the men sitting around the table would require additional information in order to arrive at an intellectual decision.

Dr. Levin questioned whether completing this assignment would have the desired impact. Frank Schmidt, remembering his days as a CIA field operative, was searching for answers on the location of the men in question and wanted to know who would carry out the assignment. Buck Buckwalter's concern was not whether or not to accept the assignment, but how to successfully complete the mission.

Joe Delasandro interrupted the constant flow of questions by explaining, "I've already taken the liberty of scheduling two recon teams to work up dossiers on the assignees. They leave next week. We know how to find these guys. We know where they live. I'm sending one team to Durango, Colorado, near the four corners area. The other team will go to Door County, Wisconsin. We will have the necessary information when the teams return. In the meantime, we need to do some research of our own. Before we make this decision, we have to be sure not to fall face first into the laws of unintended consequences. In other words, if we carry out our assignment, will there be a ripple effect involving innocent people. I don't want this to blow up in our faces. Remember, these are high-profile people. If, or when, anything happens to them, the press is going to have a field day.

"I need volunteers to research these individuals," Delasandro stated. Dr. Levin was the first to volunteer to look into the first assignee. Harold Sheppard volunteered to research the other assignee.

"Are there any other questions or comments?" asked Delasandro. The men sitting around the table looked at each other and thoughtfully and slowly shook their heads. "Good. I'll schedule a follow up meeting two weeks from today. I hope that will give you enough time to complete your research. Before you leave, I have one more announcement. I have given our team at Georgetown Medical the green light to enroll a patient into one of the special programs, so please indulge me as I explain.

"You have all had the pleasure of getting to know and work with our chief pilot, Kyle Donnar. I am sure we all agree he has been a valuable addition to our team. A little over a year ago, Kyle came to work for us. At that time his wife, Tina, had a pre-existing medical problem incorrectly diagnosed as ovarian cancer. Fortunately, her condition never worsened, but on the other hand it didn't improve. I convinced Kyle to take Tina to our team of doctors at Georgetown for a second opinion. Our team came up with a different diagnosis, and they feel strongly that she would be a good candidate for one of our covert clinical trial programs. Due to the extreme confidentiality of these clinical trial programs, I know I should have put this request before all of you, but I felt time was of the essence."

A short discussion ensued and the general feeling around the table was to acquiesce as long as all precautions for discretion would be in place. Unfortunately, one member of the team objected. Harold Sheppard stood up and questioned the ability of Kyle Donnar to maintain a vow of secrecy. "This man is only a civilian. He's been with us for a year. Can he be trusted with this type of information? Joe, when you hired him, I was surprised by how fast you made the selection. You didn't confer with us during that process, and now you have overstepped your authority again. What guarantee do we have that he won't use this information for his own enrichment and to our detriment if things don't come out as he likes? All we know is that he was a civilian pilot who worked his way up and became a captain for a major airline, a glorified bus driver."

The other four men sitting around the table stared at Sheppard in amazement. After he finished his short tirade, the men refocused their attention on Delasandro. Frank Schmidt took another short glance at Sheppard, then turned to Delasandro, and asked,

"Joe, does Harold not know the whole story?" Joe Delasandro shook his head and said, "No, I didn't think it was necessary."

Dr. David Levin spoke with a quivering tone and asked, "What story, what whole story are we speaking of? I, too, would like to understand the entire situation. Are Sheppard and I the only two not privy to this information?"

General Buckwalter stood up as though he was running interference for Delasandro. "Listen, gentlemen, the reason some of us know the story and a couple of you don't is not a reflection on you. I learned the details as well as Schmitty and McKay because we were involved in a certain line of work. Don't take this personally." The general picked up his cigar, placed it in the corner of his mouth, and sat down. "Joe, I think it's time for you to educate these guys and give them the courtesy of knowing the whole story."

# CHAPTER FIFTEEN

Typical spring weather rolled through the Mid-Atlantic states the night before Kyle and Tina were to leave for their home on Marco Island. Powerful cold fronts swept down from Canada and clashed with the warm moist air struggling to make its way northward from the Gulf of Mexico. This volatile combination was the catalyst that frequently spawned spring tornadoes.

Gusty winds colliding with the house, accompanied by deafening claps of thunder, made it impossible for Tina to sleep. She understood the trouble this type of weather created for pilots. Surrendering to the cacophony of Mother Nature's storms, she quietly made her way to the kitchen to start the morning coffee about an hour earlier than usual. The storms, however, were only one part of her sleeping problem. Her mind teetered between the dread of her condition and the joyful anticipation of going home and being with her friends. She had been looking forward to this trip and had planned on doing everything in her power to relax and have a good time in the warm Florida weather.

Kyle awoke and immediately tuned the television to the Weather Channel, part of his daily routine. To his delight, his favorite weather person, Stephanie Abrams, was co-hosting the broadcast that morning. Abrams seemed to have an excellent understanding of the weather; he knew she had a Bachelor of Science Degree from Florida State University in meteorology and a second Bachelor of Science in Geography with a Minor in Mathematics from the University of Florida. At the very least she had the credentials to back up her prognostications.

Her presentation of the information was professional yet entertaining. As a bonus, she was also a beautiful woman with a playful, almost sassy, attitude. She made the weather seem interesting in a sensuous sort of way. This "big picture" forecast was just the first step of a detailed weather briefing that he would receive from the National Weather Service through the flight planning computers once he arrived in his office.

The Weather Channel supplied Kyle with just enough information to determine that by scheduled departure time, the severe weather would be out over the Atlantic Ocean. This didn't mean that the flight was going to be in the clear. On the contrary, rain and turbulence would remain on the backside of the cold front that moved through the area. The initial climb out would be challenging, but once the sleek Beechcraft King Air leveled off at cruise altitude, the remainder of the trip would be smooth.

Kyle and Tina arrived at the hangar a couple of hours before scheduled departure. The hangar and adjacent offices were buzzing with activity. The flight crews were busy with their preflight checks and weather briefings, while the flight attendant for each plane was securing the morning coffee, sodas, ice, and snacks. Pastries would be the only food for the flight that morning.

Kyle deliberately scheduled his plane to depart last. He wanted to make sure the other aircraft got off without a hitch. The first Falcon 50 departed for La Plata County Airport, Durango, Colorado, on schedule. The Gulfstream V ran a few minutes behind schedule due to one of the passengers arriving late, courtesy of rush hour traffic.

Kyle planned on flying the leg to Marco Island and then handing off the airplane to his favorite captain, Tim Braden. Tim's copilot for the day would be Greg Pettinger, a former Universal Airline pilot and a friend of Kyle's. Pettinger flew for Universal for ten years, logging thousands of hours in heavy jet equipment, and now he had a wonderful new career thanks to Kyle. One of the lucky few.

Tim Braden's credentials as a pilot were impressive. He gained extensive experience in the backcountry or bush of Alaska, flying helicopters in the early days of his career. Completing his contract in Alaska, Tim joined the US Customs Department patrolling the border. He savored flying the drug interdiction missions over the Arizona desert near Mexico.

Sneaking up behind an airplane, flying low over the desert, and eventually arresting drug smugglers was a pure adrenaline rush. According to Tim, there was nothing better than swooping in and blocking the escape of a drug-laden airplane.

Timing was everything. Waiting until the plane landed at a remote airstrip in the desert, he would watch from a safe distance for the smugglers to begin to unload their contraband. Swooping into position, he would place the Apache attack helicopter directly in the path of the plane. Occasionally, the opportunity presented itself, and he would fire a short blast from the choppers machine guns in an effort to convince the bad guys to stay put.

He married a beautiful girl, a former beauty queen from Tennessee; Laurie was a petite blonde with an adorable southern accent. She melted Tim's heart the first time they met.

Kyle, Tina, and Greg Pettinger were the only passengers on their plane. Tina took her seat in the spacious cabin. Kyle taxied the airplane to the active runway and waited for clearance from the tower for takeoff. Moments later, Dulles tower cleared the plane for takeoff on runway One-Nine left. The powerful turboprop accelerated and was airborne seconds later. The Bendix Avionics Corporation onboard color weather radar with integrated Doppler turbulence detection was searching the sky, displaying the remnants of towering cumulonimbus clouds left over from last night's storms.

"Towering Qs" as the pilots referred to the storm cells, routinely reached altitudes exceeding fifty thousand feet, making it impossible to safely fly over the tops of the weather. To be safe, towering Qs have to be avoided by at least twenty to thirty miles to steer clear of their destructive power. To fly through one would be disastrous, most likely ripping an aircraft to pieces.

Smoothly and skillfully circumnavigating the aircraft around the precipitous weather, the King Air maintained an impressive climb rate of 2000 feet per minute until leveling off at 28,000 feet. The weather was now behind and off to the port side of the plane; a smooth ride was expected.

Three hours and twenty-two minutes later, they touched down on runway Three-Five at Marco Island Airport. Kyle landed the airplane with such finesse that no one felt the wheels make contact with the tarmac. Tina had to be awakened from her morning nap.

Kyle thanked his friend Tim for his assistance, left the cockpit, and helped Tina with her carry-on bag. They made there way through the small terminal building and jumped into the waiting taxi. The ride to their home took less than ten minutes.

Opening the front door of her enchanting Florida-style house, Tina detected the fragrant aroma originating from a bouquet of flowers waiting for her on the dining room table. Their friends had prepared the house for their arrival.

# CHAPTER SIXTEEN

F acing the members of his board of directors, Joe Delasandro took a large gulp from his coffee mug, set it down, and rose from his chair. "I knew that one day I'd be faced with the inevitable. I'm just a little surprised I was able to avoid it this long.

Kyle Donnar has been with us for a little more than a year. Most people believe I found him by accident on my fishing trip to southwest Florida last year. I can tell you unequivocally that it *was* a fishing trip, but the end result was no accident or coincidence. I was there for one reason and only one reason—to try and snag the person I felt would be a perfect fit with our organization. I have known Kyle Donnar for over twenty years, starting prior to my employment with IRC. However, he believes that he met me for the first time last year.

"I'll try not to bore you, but I think a short history lesson might be in order. In the early 1980s, our government was deeply involved in the politics of Central America. We were supplying weapons and cash to the Contras, supporting their resistance to the *Frente Sandinista de Liberación Nacional*, a socialist political party in the region; its members are the Sandinistas.

Our Cold War adversaries were desperate to establish a communist government in the western hemisphere, our back yard so to speak. We looked for, or created, opportunities to destabilize any government leaning toward a socialistic agenda. In retrospect I think we were extremely effective.

"I made numerous trips to the region during that period. Sometimes on military transports other times via commercial airlines. On special occasions I needed something a bit more private to ship my cargo and not raise suspicions. This is where chartering a private jet proved to be very useful."

Harold Sheppard sarcastically quipped, "Well, that's just fine, Joe, but what does all this have to do with you bringing Donnar into our organization?"

"Sheppard why don't you just sit there, shut up, and listen? You might actually learn something," snapped Frank Schmidt. General Buckwalter flashed a noticeable smirk and nodded his head in approval of the former CIA director's comment.

"Gentlemen, if I may continue. I contacted a long-time friend—a person I knew could be trusted. We met many years ago when we became members of the Freemasons. My friend owned and operated a charter, on-demand airline. Already approved to carry politicians and foreign dignitaries and in possession of a very high security clearance, this small company was just what I needed to carry out my mission.

"Based at the world's busiest airport, O'Hare International Airport in Chicago, no one would be the least bit suspicious of an airplane taking off in the middle of the night. The set up was perfect. The company was located in the obscure northwest side of the airport, hidden among the airline maintenance hangars far from public contact.

"I contacted my friend and told him as little as I possibly could yet just enough for him to connect the dots and figure out for himself who would be paying the bills. Our story was that I was a courier working for the federal government, and his company would need to adhere to strict procedures limiting the contact of the flight crews with the loading and unloading of the aircraft. He was familiar with the procedures and jumped at the opportunity when I told him how much the government was willing to pay for such a service.

"The typical trip started with a phone call a couple of days before my scheduled departure. This would give my friend plenty of time to make sure I had the aircraft and crew of my choice. I would show up at the hangar around eleven at night, where he would meet me and let my people load the aircraft. While we were loading the plane he would call the crew, usually waking them at home and advising them of a trip. The pilots arrived at the airport within an hour. The boss would have all the necessary flight plans and arrangements completed and would pour a couple of coffees for the boys. He would then go through a pre-flight briefing with the pilots explaining to them the nature of the flight.

"Based on my friend's recommendation, I had the same pilots fly me on every trip. They never questioned what or who was on board their aircraft. They were confident that they weren't doing anything illegal, so they just followed orders. When the plane was fueled and the freight loaded, I took my seat in the rear of the plane and dimmed the lights so the pilots couldn't see my face. The pilots climbed into the cockpit, closed the door, and took me to my destination.

"These charter flights were strictly used for transporting boxes of cash to be distributed to our allies in the area. Every trip went like clockwork. We would land at a remote military airport and our contacts in the region would meet the aircraft and quickly escort the pilots to get something to eat at the local mess hall while the plane was unloaded. By the time the pilots finished their breakfasts, the plane was refueled and flight plans filed. They always flew home empty. I would stay with the cash to oversee the correct distribution and then find my own way back to DC.

The trips were routine—until one night. I had just finished supervising the unloading of the boxes. Gunnery Sergeant Paul D'Amico, one of my hand-picked Marines in the region, and I hopped into a Jeep to follow the money to a secure location. Out of the corner of my eye, I noticed a flash of light. In the fraction of a second it took me to point in the direction of the flash, I realized what was happening. The initial flash and loud deafening explosion was so powerful that it lifted the Jeep completely off the ground and sent us rolling end over end. Thank God it wasn't a direct hit. The projectile impacted the ground a few feet away and exploded.

"Sergeant D'Amico and I were thrown from the Jeep, and we landed unconscious in a large pool of standing water created by the afternoon storms. D'Amico suffered some shrapnel wounds to his left arm and leg from the initial explosion. I was not injured, except that the force of the explosion knocked me out. D'Amico landed face up, while I was face down in the three inches of muddy water.

"From that point I can only tell you what was reported to me by other marines on the scene, so I will let General Buckwalter finish the history lesson."

"Buck, before you get started let me interject something here. Hey, Sheppard pay attention you're about to get a clear picture of this guy you referred to as a glorified bus driver," snapped Schmidt.

"Gentlemen, the rest of this comes directly form the base commanding officer, Colonel Mike Reyes. He reported that his insurgent team began to return fire in the direction of the attack. They had trouble suppressing the initial onslaught due to the enormous amount of ordinance fired in their direction and the strategic maneuvering of the enemy prior to the first shot.

"The firefight continued with neither side gaining an advantage. The explosion that took out the Jeep was the only alarm needed to alert everyone on the base, including Kyle Donnar and his copilot. This was Joe's lucky night. Moments before the attack, Kyle had been given the all clear and was walking toward his plane. He was far enough away from the initial fighting that he was able to take a moment to evaluate the situation, and then he sprinted over to the muddy pool of standing water and pulled Joe and Sergeant D'Amico to safety, preventing Joe from drowning in the muck.

D'Amico regained consciousness but couldn't move because of his injuries. Joe remained unconscious for at least an hour. Kyle assessed that their injuries were not life threatening and asked D'Amico what to do. D'Amico pointed to the wrecked Jeep and said, "Get over there and you'll find two M16s strapped to the roll bar. There should be extra ammo under the rear seat. Bring it all here, and we can set up an angle of crossfire and maybe take out a few of them." D'Amico was running on pure instinct but was fading in and out of consciousness. Kyle ran as fast as he could, hoping no one would see him.

"Kyle found the weapons and extra ammo as D'Amico instructed. Gathering everything together, he was about to make his way back when he started taking fire from the attackers. Kyle knew enough about guns to return fire from the relative safety behind the Jeep. Bullets were hitting the bent carcass of the vehicle and kicking up dirt all around him. Kyle later explained that he had a good view of the action from behind the Jeep, which enabled him to retaliate. Kyle fired his weapons and reloaded again and again. Apparently his crossfire created enough of a distraction that the attackers felt vulnerable and forced to make adjustments in their positions.

"Colonel Reyes sensed the shift in momentum and used the confusion to his advantage. He and his men went on the offensive and were able to flush out the attackers. As Colonel Reyes and his team advanced, it became clear that the opposing force was not a well-trained, cohesive fighting group. They fled back to the jungle, leaving behind their dead and wounded.

"Interrogating the wounded revealed that these men were mercenaries fighting for one of the communist dictators in the region. They were well equipped with Russian- and Chinese-made weapons, but they lacked the knowledge of effective tactics."

"Thanks, Buck, for filling in the blanks so to speak. You can see that I owe my life to Kyle Donnar. Had it not been for him, I would have died in the jungles of Central America that night. Colonel Reyes attributed Kyle's actions as instrumental in helping his men regain control of the situation. If Kyle Donnar was in the military fighting in a declared war, he would have been highly decorated for his actions. Instead, this small piece of history will forever remain secret. The US government was never officially in Central America at that time. Kyle and his copilot were thoroughly debriefed and understood the importance of silence regarding the event. His copilot unfortunately died a few years later in a car accident. He took the night's events to his grave.

"I hope this explanation will erase any doubt about the type of man we have as our chief pilot." Delasandro sat down and waited for comments.

# CHAPTER SEVENTEEN

Dr. Levin and Harold Sheppard remained quiet for a few minutes, digesting the information they had just received. Dr. Levin removed his bifocal glasses and began to clean them with a cloth napkin from the table and then began to speak. There was a slight hesitation in his delivery as though he was trying to formulate his thoughts. "Joe…I, ah, I have mixed feelings over this situation. First, let me say I have no problems with the trustworthiness of Kyle Donnar. I am quite sure he can be trusted with confidential information. I do, however, have a little problem with the fact that I, along with Harold Sheppard, have been deceived. I would like to know why you felt it was necessary to keep us in the dark." Before Joe Delasandro could address Dr. Levin's concerns, Harold Sheppard added his comments.

"Me too, I'm a little pissed off about being kept in the dark."

Joe started to answer Dr. Levin's question when General Buckwalter interrupted him. Chewing on the remains of his cigar, he quietly barked, "I convinced Joe that it would be in everyone's best interest if we brought Kyle on board without having to get caught up in lengthy and maybe incriminating explanations. Remember, the US didn't officially have troops in that part of the world at the time."

General Buckwalter's explanation didn't completely satisfy Dr. Levin, but he sensed that it would be in the best interest of the board to accept things the way they were. Harold Sheppard on the other hand wanted to continue the discussion.

"So, it appears the rest of you were aware of the circumstances surrounding the hiring of Kyle Donnar. I can only assume that your knowledge of the facts was due to the level of your respective organization's involvement at the time. I would have preferred to have some input in the hiring of Donnar, or at least been aware of his history. Just because he showed some guts over twenty years ago doesn't convince me that he's willing or able to take one for the team so to speak. I'm not so quick to give him carte blanche with all of our business here."

Dr. Levin was slightly confused with Sheppard's antagonistic attitude toward Kyle. He knew that Sheppard had wanted the position of chief pilot but didn't realize it meant that much to him, or was it something else entirely? After all, being a member of the board at IRC was more prestigious than heading up the flight department.

Dr. Levin tried to redirect the conversation. "I would have enjoyed being at the meeting when you contacted Kyle after all those years. Did he recognize you immediately or did you have to convince him of who you are?"

Joe Delasandro stared directly at Dr. Levin and reluctantly explained that Kyle didn't recognize him at their first meeting and hasn't put the puzzle together yet. "Kyle has mentioned that he thought he knew me from somewhere, but he hasn't figured it out. You have to remember that Kyle only saw my face once the night he pulled me out of the mud hole. Back then I had a full beard, long dark hair, and was thirty pounds lighter. It would have been a miracle had he recognized me. Bottom line, Kyle believes we hired him based entirely on his impeccable credentials. I want to keep it that way. I don't see any reason to bring up the past. Are we are all in agreement?"

Joe Delasandro addressed each man sitting around the table and asked if they agreed with his decision not to inform Kyle of the truth. "There is a time and place for everything, and I think this can wait a while longer." The members of the board acquiesced and deferred to Joe's wishes.

Joe continued, "Kyle and his wife, Tina, are going to spend next week at their home on Marco Island. Our team of doctors will enroll her in one of the clinical trials as soon as they return.

"By the time they return from Florida, our data guys will have completed the dossiers on the assignees. I would appreciate it if you could have your research complete prior to our next meeting. If there are no further questions, I'd like to adjourn this meeting."

As the men filed out of the conference room, Joe Delasandro made a subtle gesture to General Buckwalter asking him to stick around a little longer.

Buckwalter acknowledged with a nod and casually made his way to Joe's office.

Buckwalter began to make himself comfortable when Joe pulled a bottle of Jack Daniel's from his desk, filled a couple of glasses with ice, and covered the clear frozen cubes with the amber-colored whiskey.

"Well, Buck, what do you think of our little meeting?"

Buckwalter replied, "We've dealt with these special requests from the money guys in the past. This one should be no different. Let's get our facts straight, make a decision, and carry out the mission like we've always done. That's why we're here in the first place."

"I agree. My only real concern is how I handled the Kyle situation. I don't think David Levin is going to be a problem; he's always been a good team player. On the other hand, that spoiled jerk Sheppard still seems to be fuming over the chief pilot position."

"Don't worry about that reject flyboy. I'll handle him if it becomes necessary. His clout at the Pentagon died when they buried his old man. The proverbial silver spoon has been officially removed from his mouth, and I welcome the opportunity to replace it with my size twelve steel-toed boot.

Let's finish that bottle of Jack, and don't you worry about Kyle. When the time is right, I'll sit down with the two of you and bring him up to date. I've been looking forward to this for a long time. Don't forget, those marines in Central America were mine; my thanks to Kyle is long over due."

# CHAPTER EIGHTEEN

Seven days at home on her island was just what Tina needed. She shared her time with her closest friends—playing tennis, going to the spa for some pampering, and lounging at the beach. Marco Island's beach remained one of the best-kept secrets in Florida.

Most people thought of the beaches on the East Coast of the peninsula near Miami and Ft. Lauderdale, along with the beaches in the panhandle near the state capital—Tallahassee —and Panama City when looking for a vacation destination. However Marco's long and wide pristine snow-white sand beach and its incomparable variety of sea shells that washed up on shore with the daily tides put it in a class of its own.

The soft flour-like sand was groomed every night using a John Deere farm tractor with an attachment for sifting the sand. Removing debris and sea creatures washed up on shore, eliminated any fishy odor while simultaneously picked up litter left by careless tourists. This little corner of Florida was truly a hidden paradise that tourists hadn't discovered yet, and that was just fine with the local residents.

Kyle equally enjoyed his time away from IRC. He and his friends took day trips into the area south of Marco known as the ten thousand islands for some fishing. They always used the thirty-three-foot Grady White fishing boat owned by Randy, one of the guys in the group.

The identical twin, four-stroke, two-hundred-twenty-five horsepower Yamaha engines propelled the vessel with ease over the water at speeds reaching forty miles per hour. The guys fished for grouper, snook, sea bass, and tarpon. Tarpon were powerful game fish that could easily grow to over one hundred pounds. Hooking into one of these giants using lightweight fishing tackle was a fisherman's dream. The ensuing battle could last for more than an hour. Kyle and his fishing buddies always practiced the rule of catch and release, thus helping to preserve the fish populations.

The group of friends ate dinner in a different restaurant every night. The wives made a list of their favorites and made sure to visit all of them before Kyle and Tina returned to Washington. The evenings always ended with drinks and dessert at one of their homes overlooking the beautiful waters of the Gulf of Mexico.

The week passed too quickly for everyone. The ladies were all aware of the difficult times ahead for Tina. They avoided the topic unless Tina brought it up during conversation. The guys were equally sensitive and channeled their questions toward Kyle's responsibilities as head of the flight department at IRC.

Kyle managed to stay in touch with his assistant, Mrs. Bishop, at least once a day. She had no trouble managing the department in his absence. He often wondered why IRC needed a chief pilot as long as Mrs. Bishop was around.

The daily briefing contained information regarding the current flight schedule, pilot availability, and aircraft maintenance. Mrs. Bishop appreciated Kyle's dedication and professionalism, making her job easier.

The morning Tina and Kyle were set to leave, their friends took them out for breakfast at Hoots restaurant before heading for the airport. The ride to the airport was uneventful and only took only minutes.

For the ride back to Washington, Tim Braden and Greg Pettinger had brought the Falcon jet, which was fueled and waiting for them on the main ramp. Tim was emerging from the flight planning room with the most up-to-date information on the weather between Florida and Washington. All four strolled out to the plane at a leisurely pace led by Tim. Greg was finishing his preflight exterior check of the airplane and was last to climb the stairs into the luxurious cabin. Closing the door and securing the locks was Greg's last chore before climbing into the cockpit.

Tim gave the order to start the three large jet engines. Minutes later the big plane was ready and taxied to the runway for takeoff. Tim deftly maneuvered the jet, using minimum power so as not to damage any of the small aircraft parked behind him. The jet blast from those engines could easily overturn the lighter planes on the ramp. Tim and Greg completed the pre-takeoff checklist during the short taxi to runway One-Seven (17). Broadcasting their intentions over the Unicom two-way radio frequency and then listening intently for anyone else on the air, the big jet was ready to fly.

The two men scanned the surrounding skies for other planes. Marco Airport, like more than 95 percent of all the airports in the country, had no control tower, so the pilots were responsible for checking for other aircraft taking off or landing—a very important part of the "see and be seen" rule of safety. Uncontrolled general aviation airports operated safely and, in most cases, more efficiently than airports with FAA control towers.

No one responded when queried on the aircraft's radio, and the area appeared clear of traffic. Tim placed the nose wheel of the plane directly on the centerline of the runway and set the parking brake.

"Your airplane," Tim officially announced to Greg. With that, Greg acknowledged he was in control, released the parking brake, and pushed the three throttles forward, setting takeoff power. The jet accelerated rapidly and with such enormous power generated by the three jet engines everyone could feel their bodies pressed into the leather seats. Using only half the five-thousand-foot runway, the beautiful sleek jet was airborne, distancing itself from Mother Earth.

Looking out her window as the jet climbed, Tina watched her island drop away and eventually disappear from view. She wondered when she would see it again, or if she would see it again. A short while later, the plane completed its flight and taxied up to the IRC hangar. Kyle drove Tina home first and then headed for his office. She would use the rest of the afternoon to unpack and ease back into her daily routine.

Diane Bishop greeted Kyle as he entered the office. Everything seemed to be operating smoothly. Kyle felt fortunate to have Mrs. Bishop as his assistant. He sat at his desk and began to scan through the large stack of mail that had accumulated while he was away. Bishop had already opened anything appearing important and timely. Most of the mail on his desk consisted of advertisements and aviation magazines.

Relieved to see everything was under control, Kyle decided to grab a cup of coffee. Mrs. Bishop declined his offer to pick something up for her as well. Stealing a peek into Delasandro's office, he made the same offer. Joe was more than happy to join Kyle and hear all about his trip.

The two men sat at one of the tables in the cafeteria and sipped their coffee. Joe listened intently to the vacation details and said, "One day you'll have to take me on one of those fishing trips." After finishing their second mug of the afternoon, the men headed back to work.

Joe followed Kyle to his office and told him that the pilots would be busy that week. The board had scheduled another meeting, and Kyle's pilots would have to pick them up. Dr. Levin was at his home in Boston, while Frank Schmidt was in Bar Harbor, Maine. One crew could get those two while another crew could sweep through the southeast, picking up General Buckwalter on Hilton Head Island, South Carolina, where he was golfing, and James McKay at his hideout, the log cabin nestled in the hills of the Smoky Mountains overlooking a lake created from dams built by the Tennessee Valley Authority. Chattanooga was the closest airport for him.

"No problem. Just let me know the time and day you want them picked up. Something must be important if you're having another board meeting so soon."

Joe nodded his head and returned to his office.

# CHAPTER NINETEEN

The board members arrived at IRC headquarters on time and ready to get to work. Each man took his usual seat around the large mahogany table. They exchanged some small talk while waiting for Joe Delasandro to arrive. Everyone seemed prepared for the meeting, judging by the thickness of the folders sitting neatly on the table.

Entering the boardroom, his arms heavily loaded with papers and manila folders, Delasandro announced, "OK, gentlemen, let's get started." With his half glasses resting on the tip of his nose, he focused on David Levin and Harold Sheppard. "I trust you were able to come up with enough information on the assignees to help avoid embarrassing mistakes should we agree to the assignment." Simultaneously the two men nodded in the affirmative.

"Before I have you present your reports, let me bring everyone up to speed on Samuel Sumner III, the victim of the assassination on Marco Island. I'm distributing to each of you a short biography of Mr. Sumner. Given the fact that someone has already dispatched Sumner to a higher power, I'll try to keep this brief."

Delasandro continued his presentation, educating the board members on every detail of Samuel Sumner III. Lecturing groups of people was not Delasandro's forte. Forty-five minutes later he began to summarize his data. "You can see that Samuel Sumner III was obviously not qualified to take over the position of CEO at Universal Airlines. In my lifetime I have seen numerous situations such as this where a corporate board of directors failed to carry out their fiduciary responsibilities. Universal Airlines, unfortunately, is the largest failure of its kind. Samuel Sumner should never have been appointed CEO.

"The questions before us are simple. Did the actions of this individual contribute to or actually cause the demise of the airline? Unequivocally yes. During my research I stumbled across some information that convinced me that the demise of Universal Airlines was no accident created by incompetent management.

"Shortly after Universal liquidated its assets, a substantial deposit found its way to an offshore bank account in the name of Samuel Sumner. One hundred million dollars, to be exact, exchanged hands that day, and the money was not part of his overly generous golden parachute. It appears that Sumner was appointed and compensated for the sole purpose of destroying Universal Airlines and its powerful unions.

"We are painfully aware of the consequences of his actions. More than sixty thousand employees are now unemployed and have lost their pensions and assorted benefits. Many of the employees had been with the company for twenty-five years or more and are now filing for personal bankruptcies, hoping to save their homes. There have been countless divorces, medical emergencies caused by the stress, and ultimately suicides of employees unable to cope with a catastrophe of this magnitude so late in their careers.

"The money trail seems to be very complicated. I have not ascertained the source of the deposit; I have people working on it as we speak. It is my opinion, based on the actions of Samuel Sumner, that the demise of Universal Airlines was a deliberate act of sabotage. I will continue to concentrate my efforts and collect additional evidence to support my findings. Once again, someone did our work for us, and we are doing everything in our power to find out who the shooter was and why he did it.

"Next on the agenda is Russell Owen of Energy West. Dr. Levin, I believe you volunteered for this one."

"Thank you, Joe. I apologize for the brevity of my report, but I uncovered irrefutable evidence that should help us with our decision.

"Russell Owen started Energy West for the explicit intention of defrauding investors. The sole purpose of the initial corporation was designed as an elaborate Ponzi scheme. The early investors enjoyed reaping double digit returns unknowingly supported by incoming funds from subsequent investors. Russell Owen was preparing to pull the plug and fly off to the Cayman Islands with the investors' money when something unexpected happened.

"A group of our not-so-bright Wall Street types heard about this small privately held energy company and decided they wanted a piece of the action. The boys from Wall Street convinced Owen that he should put his company up for an IPO. Owen couldn't resist the temptation of selling stock in a worthless company. Overnight he would more than quadruple his cash while simultaneously thumbing his nose at the Wall Street snobs.

Owen is a master at producing fake documentation. The underwriters for the IPO scoured his books and found deal after deal, transaction after transaction, detailing numerous sources of income for the tiny company. The transactions were so complicated that the underwriters rubber-stamped the approval rather than ask questions and appear stupid in the eyes of this country bumpkin entrepreneur.

"Everyone shook hands, and the IPO was consummated. The sound of the closing bell on Wall Street that day greeted a new billionaire to a very elite club. Of course Russell Owen couldn't just take his money and run; he had to milk this thing for all it was worth. As with most crooks of this nature, greed got the best of him. Eventually people started to question the sources of revenue from this rising star of Wall Street. The initial underwriters continued to talk up this great company, keeping the stock price high while selling their personal shares in the fictitious shell corporations.

"As the smoke cleared, the house of cards came tumbling down, hundreds of thousands of people felt the negative aftermath. Financial managers representing pensions and 401(k) plans couldn't comprehend how they lost over fifty percent of the value in the funds they were supposed to nurture. In this case, millions of people suffered huge losses. Retirement programs and private pension funds were wiped out.

"The newspapers followed the trials of the culprits. Lawsuits, grand juries, and criminal indictments followed. Opulence Investments took the biggest financial hit, with fines in the hundreds of millions. Russell Owen was found guilty of fraud and sentenced to thirty years in a federal prison and fined three hundred million dollars. Unfortunately, he beat the rap in the appeals courts, citing illegal seizure of evidence, jurisdictional misconduct by the judge, and an assortment of other charges.

Russell Owen was smart enough to stash his cash in untouchable off shore banks. He has become an extreme embarrassment for this administration, spouting off that his generous contributions to the president's re-election campaign paved the way for his acquittal. Our people want any connections between Owen and the President severed immediately. They just don't feel this President has what it takes to make this go away."

"Thanks, David. I think we are all familiar with this case. If there are no questions, its time to put this one to a vote," Delasandro directed. Russell Owen was as equally distasteful and offensive as Samuel Sumner with the members of the board and received a unanimous vote in favor of the sanction.

"Last, we have Dr. James Morgan from Health Options. Harold you chose to run with this one; the floor is yours."

"Dr. James Morgan started his career as a research scientist and eventually created his own biotech research facility. The start up money came from a family trust fund. Dr. Morgan seemed content to discover or create new medicines as well as improve on some of the older medications no longer protected with patents. Morgan Labs was quite successful and was eventually purchased by Health Options, a giant HMO located in Madison, Wisconsin. The purchase price put Dr. Morgan on easy street and gave him a seat on the board of directors of Health Options. Dr. Morgan insisted on an appointment to the board to protect his closely held formulas for some of the more successful medications, procedures, vaccines, and patents.

"Health Options gained notoriety with their tight-fisted policies, refusing diagnostic coverage for many patients. Doctors were outraged that an insurance company had the audacity to challenge their judgment.

"Health Options tactics began to push corporate customers to seek other HMOs. Consequently, a revolving door was installed in the CEO's office at Health Options headquarters. Five CEOs came and left in as many years. While searching for a candidate, the board of directors appointed Dr. Morgan as interim CEO.

"Having a medical doctor at the helm of the company did wonders for the stock price. Health care providers around the country felt that this was a positive indication; they thought a doctor would understand the need for diagnostic testing for patients. Unfortunately, Dr. Morgan was more interested in his performance bonuses than providing health insurance to needy patients.

The heavy-handed tactics continued, and revenue once again began to slip, forcing Morgan into creative accounting methods. He simply "cooked the books" whenever he was coming up on a performance goal. He received his bonuses like clockwork. His demise started with the bean counters openly objecting to his methods. He summarily fired anyone questioning his actions.

The stock price remained elevated due to the fraudulent bookkeeping. Revenues and profits had been grossly overstated for years, until one day an accountant developed a conscience and decided it was time to become a whistleblower, arriving at the front door of the attorney general's office with documentation to back up his claim. The ensuing investigation rightfully placed blame on top-level employees in the accounting and finance departments as well as on Dr. Morgan.

"The government prosecutors had no problem finding defendants willing to turn over evidence in exchange for their freedom. The net effect of the fraudulent accounting was similar to that of Energy West and Russell Owen. The middle class of our country suffered through an all out assault on their livelihoods and retirements. Dr. Morgan walked away unscathed due to legal technicalities uncovered by his dream team of attorneys.

"Dr. Morgan inflicted physical as well as financial damage on the people of this country. He violated the Hippocratic Oath, harming patients by withholding treatments for monetary gain.

"I believe we got the call on this guy because of his very public connections to the White House. Needless to say, our people want this embarrassment removed from the front pages of the newspapers, and they want to protect this administration from its own incompetence."

"We appreciate your efforts Harold. Are there questions regarding Dr. James Morgan?" Delasandro asked the group.

"Yes, I have one concern," stated Dr. Levin. "Harold, you mentioned something about Dr. Morgan protecting the formulas, procedures, and patents for some of his medications and vaccines. Do patents protect his formulas, and if so can the formulas to be duplicated without the help of the good doctor?"

"Good question, David," responded Delasandro. "What about it, Harold? Are we sure that we won't be losing any breakthrough technologies or drugs if the doctor should go away?"

Harold Sheppard tried to hide his disgust for the "school teacher" to his left. Sheppard had very little respect for Dr. Levin. He believed Levin was a draft dodger for not enlisting while hiding behind a college deferment program until the war in Vietnam had ended. Sheppard thought to himself, *The audacity of this civilian to question a lieutenant colonel of the United States Air Force.*

Sheppard addressed the question by explaining in his usual condescending tone that the FBI had confiscated Dr. Morgan's files, including his lab reports. Everything was in good hands, and, as far as he knew, government labs were busy reviewing his procedures and duplicating the vaccines and medications.

The answer satisfied everyone around the table, and the vote to sanction the assignee quickly followed.

Joe Delasandro stood and thanked the men for their work and dedication. "That concludes this portion of our business for today." The men began to rise from the table when Joe's assistant, Karen Mallett, rang the buzzer on the intercom. Mrs. Mallett only interrupted a board meeting if something very serious needed attention.

"Mr. Delasandro, there is a call for you from Zurich. They say it's urgent."

"Thanks, Karen. I'll take it in here."

The board members immediately sat down and stared at each other in amazement. Their usual poker faces and stoic personas gave way to expressions of disbelief.

# CHAPTER TWENTY

Joe picked up the phone and answered, "Delasandro here." The voice on the other end quickly regurgitated a series of numbers and letters, leaving no doubt to his identity.

"Mr. Delasandro, am I correct that you are in the process of meeting with the board? If everyone is still present, please put this call on the speakerphone. I have something to add to your meeting." Without hesitation Joe did as he was instructed.

"Gentlemen, I know this call is completely out of the ordinary; however, something has been brought to our attention here in Zurich, necessitating a formal discussion with you." The voice emanating from the phone reverberated throughout the conference room in a god-like manner, deep base in tone with an unidentifiable European accent slightly quivering, revealing a person possibly in the twilight of their years.

"Mr. Delasandro, it has been brought to my attention that you unilaterally gave permission for our team of physicians in Georgetown to begin treating Mrs. Donnar. Is this true?"

"Yes, sir, it is," responded Delasandro.

"Mr. Delasandro, you neither have the power nor the authority to issue such instructions without concurrence with the board of advisors. Mr. Donnar's ability to retain confidential information vital to our existence has come into question. As you are all aware, we place a high value on our ability to be discrete. Do you have anything to say regarding this issue?"

Before Joe could say anything in his defense, General Buck Buckwalter addressed the question. Scanning the faces of the men sitting around the table he began. "Sir, we are all aware of the circumstances that brought Kyle Donnar to IRC. I for one strongly believe that since Kyle is the kind of man I can trust with my life, I can trust him with our involvement in these research programs as well as the dirty little secrets we all choose to live with on a daily basis."

The men sitting around the table completely agreed with the General, except for Harold Sheppard. "Well, Mr. Sheppard, you seem to be the only one in the room questioning Mr. Donnar's veracity. How do you suggest we handle this problem; what will it take to satisfy you?" inquired the caller. Now everyone in the room realized Harold Sheppard was the source of the information leak.

Somewhat embarrassed by his outing at the hands of the caller, Sheppard began his rebuttal by saying, "I agree with General Buckwalter but only to a certain extent. It's true that Kyle displayed loyalty and guts through his actions. That was a long time ago. I would like to know if he still has the same intestinal fortitude today.

The voice on the speakerphone queried, "Once again, Mr. Sheppard, do you have any ideas on how you would like to see this situation remedied?"

I would like to see a quid pro quo for the privilege of joining our ranks. I believe I have the perfect solution to this problem and may solve a secondary issue at the same time, killing two birds with one stone, as the saying goes. I recommend we put Kyle Donnar to the test, and if he's successful we will be guaranteed of his silence regarding any and all other issues or programs of IRC. The threat of life in prison, or worse, is good leverage, don't you agree?"

Joe Delasandro shouted, "That's totally absurd. You've got to be out of your mind! Kyle's a civilian, he doesn't have the training to do what I think you're suggesting. I wouldn't jeopardize his life nor the existence of this organization on such a hair brained idea."

"Joe, I'm a little confused. I did some research regarding the procurement process that was in place when you hired your fellow Mason's charter airline to fly your missions into Central America. The company as well as the employees had to pass stringent background checks in order to receive the necessary security clearances. Is that correct," asked Sheppard.

"Yes, I explained that at a previous meeting, what's your point" barked Delasandro.

"Well my point is: You claim Kyle doesn't have the proper training but I must disagree. In order to earn the security clearances the crew had to go through S.E.R.E training. You do recall that part of the process," stated Sheppard.

"Joe, what the hell is he talking about, what is this S.E.R.E. training," asked James McKay.

"Would you like to explain or should I," Sheppard prodded sarcastically.

Delasandro and General Buckwalter sat in silence, muscles protruding from their clenched jaws, glaring at Sheppard.

"Since no one seems to want to speak I'll give a quick synopsis of the training our boy completed, Sheppard gleefully stated. S.E.R.E. stands for Survival, Evasion, Resistance and Escape. Kyle and his co-pilot joined the ranks of an elite group of individuals. Mostly military types like the Navy Seals, Marine Recon, and a few CIA spooks in Warner Springs, California. There are four levels of training, A,B,C and D. Kyle and his partner only had to participate in the two toughest levels B and C. A and D is mostly military indoctrination.

"From the records I was able to dig up, Kyle completed this grueling training near the top of his class. Not too bad for a guy who was at least ten years older than the average trainee. Upon completion of the training his classmates demanded he join them in getting a tattoo of the S.E.R.E. patch as a show of respect. His personal information records describe the tattoo and its location on the outside of his right calf, just in case it would be needed for identification.

"I'd say Kyle Donnar is more than qualified to handle an assignment," said Sheppard.

Sheppard stood, closed his file folder, placed it on the table, and started for the door. "It's out of our hands now. I have an appointment with a cute masseuse at the health club." Sheppard firmly closed the door behind him as he exited the room.

The board members stared at each other in disbelief. Prior to Delasandro officially adjourning the meeting, the caller apologetically explained that Sheppard somehow got his hands on some incriminating evidence regarding Kyle and had convinced the associates in Zurich to back his play. His parting words addressed Delasandro. "Joseph, you must address the issue with Kyle and take care of your security leak, both serious violations of protocol." The meeting was adjourned, and everyone exited the boardroom except Delasandro.

Moments later Frank Schmidt returned pretending to have forgotten something. "Joe, I had a sixth sense that Sheppard was going to be a royal pain in the ass and eventually try to get even with us for not letting him take over the flight department. I didn't really trust him with this project either, so I took the liberty of contacting one of my assets. I think you remember her— Dr. Andrea Tortoricci. At the CIA we used her from time to time as a consultant when we needed an attractive yet highly intelligent operative with that certain talent of getting men to melt in her hands and start to blab. I asked her to get close to Dr. Morgan ASAP. What's this crap about incriminating evidence on Kyle?"

"Schmitty, I have no idea, but I will get to the bottom of this right away. Good move on bringing Tortoricci back to us."

As soon as he was completely alone, Delasandro placed a return call to Zurich, hoping to find out more about the so-called evidence regarding Kyle.

# CHAPTER TWENTY-ONE

The following morning Delasandro headed straight for the technical wing to speak with the techies working on the surveillance tapes from Marco Island. As he entered the lab unannounced, he was stunned by the lack of security and the laid back attitude of the entire IT staff.

Most of the guys working in the IT department were total geeks and nerds. Even though they were well paid for their talents, they were just happy to come to work every day and play with very expensive toys.

Jimmy Wooden, the department manager, casually strolled out of his office and was startled by the presence of Joe Delasandro standing in the middle of his lab. "Mr. Delasandro, this is a pleasant surprise. Is there anything I can do for you?"

"Jimmy, first of all I'm not happy with the cavalier attitude around here regarding security. Second, has Harold Sheppard been snooping around lately?"

"Now that you mention it, Bruce over there, working with the face recognition computer software, told me Mr. Sheppard stopped in a couple of days ago just to say hello. He asked what we were working on, and

Bruce went into his long winded lecture on how the face recognition software worked."

Switching his attention over to Bruce Goldstein, Delasandro asked, "Was there anything in particular Sheppard was looking for?"

"No, sir, Mr. Delasandro. I think he was just being nosy or scouting for useful equipment he could borrow to spy on his girlfriends. I purposely tried to bore him with my lecture on the face recognition software, hoping it would discourage him from coming around. I could see his eyes start to glass over, but then all of a sudden it seemed as though he saw a ghost or something and couldn't wait to leave"

"What were you working on at the time?"

"I was letting the face recognition equipment finish its final run on the shooter down in Marco. The baseball cap he wore was pulled down far enough to block any chance of seeing any facial features, but while going through the footage, I noticed a reflection off a glass cocktail table next to the victim's lounge chair."

"Is that what's coming up on the flat screen now?" asked Delasandro.

"Yes, sir, I'm trying to enhance the image, but I think this is the best we can expect."

Walking closer to the image on the screen, Joe could see the blurred face of the Marco shooter. Joe's face drained of all color; his skin seemed transparent. He looked ill enough that Bruce asked, "Are you OK, Mr. Delasandro?"

Joe nodded but didn't say anything in an attempt to gather his thoughts. "What's this number on the bottom of the screen, the 88 percent," Joe asked.

"The computer is telling us that it is 88 percent sure of the identity of the shooter," Bruce explained. But because we can't get a real clear picture of the assassin's face, four names came up as possible matches. Actually that's pretty good considering the enormous data base we have at our disposal."

"Did Harold Sheppard see this?" Joe asked.

"I think so," came the reply.

"Lock this operation down. No one is to see this information without my permission, and I mean no one," Joe ordered.

# CHAPTER TWENTY-TWO

Delasandro knew the day would eventually come when he would have to come clean with Kyle, but now there was a problem that took precedence over Joe's cathartic confession.

He rehearsed different scenarios over and over again, trying to come up with the best way to handle this disclosure. Joe was actually looking forward to the opportunity to finally thank Kyle for saving his life many years ago. He felt that repayment of this debt was long overdue.

Imagining a scenario where he and Kyle would chat over coffee or a couple of beers, telling stories and laughing at themselves, Joe figured he would eventually work into the conversation the topic of Central America and cleverly lead Kyle to the truth. Unfortunately, circumstances probably wouldn't allow for Joe's ideal version of this meeting.

Joe arrived at his office earlier than usual to meet with his close friend and mentor General Buckwalter. "Buck, I just want to make sure we are doing the right thing here. You know I always planned on coming clean with Kyle; I was just having trouble finding the right place and time. I'm almost happy that I'm being forced to do this now. I'm just really pissed off that I have to do it based on a schedule dictated by that jerk Sheppard."

"Joe, don't get crazy over this. If ya like, I'll join you guys for a beer, and you and I can both get a chance to show our gratitude. Don't you think Kyle has been suspicious for quite some time? He's smart enough to know that jobs like IRC just don't magically appear. My advice, see how he reacts to your little revelation and then decide if you want to take this to the next level."

"You're right, Buck, one step at a time."

Buckwalter headed for the airport and back to his golf game on Hilton Head Island. Joe spent the better part of the morning rehearsing his presentation. His phone rang a few minutes before noon, and the voice on the other end of the line inquired, "What are you doing for lunch today? I have to run over to the hangar and check out a few things on the planes. I thought I'd rescue you from office work, and we could grab something to eat." Joe was pleasantly surprised and told Kyle that he would be glad to sneak away. Kyle said, "I'll come by your office in a few minutes." Joe hung up the phone, thinking about the lucky coincidence and laughing at Kyle's offer to "rescue him"…again.

The two men hopped into Kyle's SUV and drove off to the airport. Kyle explained to Joe that it would only take a few minutes to complete his task at the hangar, and then they could grab lunch. Joe pretended to listen to Kyle's explanation of what needed to be done at the hangar, but the words didn't seem to penetrate; he was too preoccupied with the impending conversation.

As promised, Kyle completed his tasks quickly. Joe stood in the hangar admiring the beautiful, sleek, sexy jets tucked neatly into the large building. "Let's go, Joe. I'm so hungry my stomach thinks my throat has been cut." Joe laughed and the guys were off to the local hangout.

A couple of miles from the airport, Kyle pulled into a small restaurant. The small brick-and-frame building sat about one hundred yards off the main road and directly under the landing pattern for Dulles International Airport. A full-scale mock-up of a World War II fighter plane sat on the front lawn. Many of the local pilots and flight attendants stopped here at the end of a long day to unwind and share stories of their recent flights.

The flight attendants complained about the low class of people flying as compared to the "good ole days," while the pilots talked about their latest acquisitions, like motorcycles and sports cars, as well as the inefficient schedules they were forced to fly.

Entering the restaurant, the men took a table in the corner. The lunchtime crowd, consisting of mostly local business people, began thinning out as everyone headed back to their jobs. It was safe to bet that the majority of the patrons were airplane enthusiasts and pilot wannabes.

Within a few minutes, a waitress walked up to their table and greeted the guys. "Hey, Kyle, long time no see. Where you been hidin'?"

"Just working a lot. How have you been, Gina? Gina, this is a good friend of mine, Joe. Joe this is Gina Colangolo."

"Nice to meet ya, Joe," she replied with a smirk. "Can I start you guys off with something to drink?"

"Absolutely! How about a couple of Michelob Ultras in the bottle and a couple of those frosty mugs?"

"Coming right up, and I'll leave the menus with you."

"Did you notice the smirk on her face? Have you two met somewhere before?" Joe shook his head no and listened while Kyle gave him a rundown of the menu. "Everything is pretty good, especially the buffalo burgers—three quarters of a pound of lean buffalo meat and better for you than regular beef."

"Sounds good to me. Let's do it."

Gina arrived with the beer and Kyle gave her the order for two buffalo burgers medium well.

By this time the restaurant was almost empty.

Joe turned to Kyle and said, "We should do this more often. Get away from that office and take it easy." The two men exchanged small talk while waiting for their food. Gina delivered the burgers on huge platters lined with onion rings. A second round of beers quickly followed.

The walls of the restaurant were decorated with aviation memorabilia, mostly old photos from the golden age of aviation. Photographs of some of the most famous airplanes in history, and the pilots that flew them, hung on display like a small museum. Delasandro saw this as an opportunity to start reminiscing about the past.

Looking at the pictures of old planes, Joe was able to reconstruct his life during each of the eras represented by the photos. Joe was especially fond of the Viet Nam era war birds that flew over his head while he served as a marine in the jungles of Southeast Asia. Finally talking his way through the seventies and into the early eighties, he paused and mumbled about some interesting experiences he had in the early eighties.

Kyle caught the reference of the eighties and chimed in with, "Oh, yeah, the early eighties, I had some interesting times back then."

"Tell me about that time in your career, Kyle," Joe prodded. "Was that the time you were flying for the Charter airline out of O'Hare?"

Kyle looked over at Joe and said, "You know it was. There isn't much about me you don't already know. Hell, you can probably tell my life story better than me."

"Tell me about those flights you made into Central America. Was that exciting or just routine business?" Joe asked.

Kyle proceeded to explain the nature of the flights, briefly touching on the highlights. Kyle talked about the mysterious courier, the unknown cargo, and the red carpet treatment he always received after landing. "There was this one time, however," Kyle started and then stopped in midsentence. "Well, let's just say things got a little hairy and leave it at that. I'm not even sure I should be telling the story."

"Come on," Joe pleaded, "tell me about it. Like you said, there isn't much I don't know about you, so enlighten me."

Kyle reluctantly began to talk about that night when he abruptly paused and cautioned Joe. "No one knows this story, not even my wife. I've kept it from Tina all these years, and I see no reason she needs to know

now, agreed?" Joe nodded his head and motioned for Kyle to continue.

Kyle started the adventure by explaining how he and his copilot would be called into work late at night, greeted by his boss and an airplane already loaded and ready to fly. He continued with the details of the flight until the cargo was removed from the plane at the destination.

Joe asked, "Did you have any idea of what you were carrying?"

Kyle laughed and said, "It didn't take a rocket scientist to figure out it was probably money, cash and lots of it. Judging by the bulky boxes, not a lot of weight, along with the tight security when we landed, I figured it had to be cash. My best guess was that it had something to do with Colonel Ollie North and his money for guns program."

Kyle briefly spoke of the attack that night, completely omitting his actions. Joe asked Kyle, "Whatever happened to the courier? You said his Jeep was hit by rocket fire or something, and you never finished the story."

"OK, I'll tell you what happened, but you won't believe it. To this day it all seems like a dream, or should I say nightmare, like it never really took place." Kyle finished the story and gave out a little laugh paused and said, "I told you it was hard to believe. So what do ya think?"

Joe took a big gulp of his beer, looked directly at Kyle, and said, "I know one thing for sure; that courier is a very lucky man, and he really owes you a long overdue thank you. Both he and Master Sergeant D'Amico are alive today because of you."

Kyle froze for a second and said, "I never told you the sergeant's name. Hell, I barely remember it; how did you know?" Once again stopping short, Kyle stared at Joe. "I'm not very good at remembering names, but I'm damn good at remembering faces. The eyes don't change much over time. I've been looking at you for over a year now, and I have been saying that I know you from somewhere."

Before Kyle could continue, Joe put out his hand and said to Kyle, "The courier would like to finally say thank you for saving my life that night. You looked after me, and I've been trying to reciprocate ever since. I used my contacts to follow you and your career, hoping that one day I could do something for you."

The two men sat silently at their corner table. Joe continued to stare at Kyle, searching for any indication of emotion or reaction to this revelation. Kyle's initial reaction took Joe by surprise. Kyle started to shake his head from side to side, as if he was in disbelief, while letting out a muffled laugh. Kyle clasped Joe's hand and returned the friendly gesture. "I should have figured this out a long time ago. The signs were all around me; I just didn't put two and two together.

"The first day at IRC, you introduced me to the staff. Your secretary said it was a pleasure to *finally* meet me. I thought that sounded a bit strange, but in hindsight she really meant it. She's known about me for a long time, right?

"So I guess I'm a charity case. You hired me because you felt obligated. Don't get me wrong, I appreciate the opportunity, but I preferred to think I got the job because of my qualifications. Why didn't you just come clean the first time we met, what's with all this cloak and dagger stuff?"

"First and foremost, you are not a charity case. I hired you based on your qualifications. I never meant for this to go this long but I knew there was never going to be the right time for this conversation. You were brought on board for what you bring to the table which is more than IRC does for you. Your actions that night in the jungle spoke volumes about you. I only regret that I couldn't reciprocate sooner," Joe said reassuringly. "Are you okay with all of this?"

Kyle nodded and said, "Yeah, it's actually kind of nice to finally be appreciated for my efforts. God knows, the people at Universal Airlines only thought of me as a file number. Besides, if I ever decide to tell stories about my career, I'll have you to back me up." The two men laughed, chugged down their beer, and shook hands again.

# CHAPTER TWENTY-THREE

The ride back to IRC was enjoyable. Joe Delasandro had finally disclosed a secret that had been burning a hole through him since his reunion with Kyle. The relief and joy he felt was tempered by the thought of his next meeting with Kyle.

Arriving at IRC, the men stopped for coffee and then proceeded to their offices. Walking past Joe's office, Karen Mallett was waiting impatiently for them to return. Earlier that morning, Buck Buckwalter had tipped off Karen regarding Joe's unavoidable dilemma.

Seeing the expression on Joe's face, she knew all went well. She walked over and gave Kyle a hug and thanked him. "I started working for Joe immediately following your impromptu Rambo impression down there on the isthmus. I feel very fortunate to have worked for this man all these years, and it wouldn't have happened if not for you." Not accustomed to, or comfortable with compliments and praise, Kyle blushed, and silently returned to his office.

Kyle had wrapped up his work for the day and was checking his calendar to see what challenges faced him the next morning. Minutes before leaving his office, the phone rang. It was Joe. "Kyle, how's your morning schedule tomorrow? Can you block off some time for me?"

Kyle answered, "No problem. I'm free until eleven. How does that work with you?"

"That's great. Let's say about nine o'clock in my office? I'll have your wimpy decaf waiting for you."

The next morning Kyle was sitting in Joe's office promptly at nine o'clock. As promised, Joe had a steaming mug of decaf coffee waiting. Anticipating that the meeting was probably about the scheduling of future flights, Kyle had brought along his flight schedule planner, which contained all of the necessary information regarding scheduled maintenance for the fleet of planes and the availability of pilots.

Joe started off by pointing to the planner and saying, "You won't be needing that today. I have something much more important to discuss with you."

The serious tone in Joe's voice got Kyle's attention. Kyle closed his planner and sat it on the chair next to him. "OK, Joe, what's up?"

"How's Tina feeling? Has she been contacted by her doctors regarding treatment options?"

"Not yet; she's left messages for them, but still waiting for a return call. They don't seem to be overly concerned."

"Kyle, what I'm about to say to you can never leave this office. Do I have your word on this?"

"Absolutely, Joe. What's this about?"

"What would you say, or to phrase it more accurately, what would you do if you were suddenly given the power to guarantee Tina's chances for a full recovery?"

"C'mon, Joe, you already know the answer to that question. I'd do anything and everything to see that she beats this thing. I don't care what it costs; I don't care if we have to travel to the ends of the world. I'll sell everything—our home, vehicles, everything—in order to devote my life to seeing that she survives."

Placing his glasses on the desk, Joe sat back in his chair and asked, "Do you remember the list of doctors I gave you last year? Those doctors are part of a very special group, and I'm not just referring to their qualifications. All of the names on that list have been working for a very private consortium of investors on experimental therapies and treatments for many years. They have access to procedures, treatments, and medications that are not available to the general public. Quite frankly, I know for a fact that the cures for dozens of diseases are secretly stored away."

"Forgive my skepticism, Joe, but if we have a cure for cancer, why don't we use it? Think of all the needless suffering and the terrible deaths that accompany these illnesses."

"The only way I can explain this is to just come to the point. *Money*! Specifically the economy of the United States, which of course controls the economy of the world. How many times have you said or heard the phrase, we can put a man on the moon why can't we solve this problem or that problem? In truth, we have the solutions to many of the problems plaguing society today. For example, how many patents do you think are in existence for inexpensive synthetic fuels or mechanical devices that would increase the efficiencies of our vehicles by a factor of five or more? The answer is plenty.

"Whenever someone comes up with a new invention that actually presents a threat to the big oil companies, the device or the formula for the new fuel is purchased from the inventor for more money than that person could ever imagine. The inventor no longer has to worry about mass production or marketing or any of the other problems associated with bringing a new product to market. After signing contracts to assure confidentiality, the revolutionary product never sees the light of day."

"Joe, you're starting to sound like one of those crazy conspiracy theory nut cases."

"Yeah, maybe so, but let me give you another example: our war on illegal drugs. We know the sources of cocaine, heroine, and marijuana—everyone knows. We know the shipping routes and the people carrying it into our country. How tough do you really think it would be to take out the drug cartels and the people who run them? The answer: *no problemo, señor.*

"OK, I'll play along. Assuming what you are telling me is accurate, then why don't we do something about our addiction to oil, take out the drug lords, and cure every one with a disease?"

"Again, the answer is money."

"Mr. Delasandro, I'm sorry to interrupt but you have an overseas call on line two."

"Karen, is it our friends from Zurich?"

"Yes sir, I believe it is."

"Thanks Karen, I'll take the call." Switching over to line two, "Delasnadro speaking; yes sir I'm taking care of that right now. I'll contact you as soon as I have an answer."

Placing the phone back into its holder Joe continued: "If the oil companies were to be rendered impotent over night, the economies of numerous countries in the world would collapse. Any monetary advantage we would gain by cheap fuels would be short lived. Millions of people would be out of work, and from there the problems would spiral out of control.

"Unemployed people generally don't have the ability to continue their normal purchasing patterns, thus causing a ripple effect throughout the local economies. As more and more people collect unemployment benefits, fewer and fewer people pay taxes, putting severe strains on governments. You can imagine for yourself where this downward spiral could go. We are witnessing a smaller version of this scenario now. The United States has allowed corporate America to ship so many manufacturing jobs overseas that we no longer have a viable middle class to spend our way out of a recession.

"There's no arguing with you on that one. It seems no one has an answer on how to *jump start* our economy. Without the jobs the working class can't come to the rescue as they did in the past," Kyle agreed.

"Dealing with illegal drugs is just as tricky. If we put all the drug cartels out of business, the economies in the host countries would implode almost immediately. Those countries would then default on hundreds of billions of dollars in loans from the United States and the world banks. Just think of the chaos that would cause in our financial markets. The stock markets would crash; investor's portfolios would wither away, possibly creating another Great Depression."

"Sure, I can see things aren't always as clean cut as we would like, but where are you going with this? What does all of this have to do with Tina?"

"The situation involving possible cures for cancers and other deadly diseases causes me the greatest heartache. Somewhere, decisions are being made to withhold these miracle drugs, and the decision is primarily based on economics.

"The pharmaceutical companies who create these drugs would make billions but at the same time large sectors of our health care industry would become obsolete and unnecessary overnight. Think of all the industries created by the need to improve our health care system.

"Research and development firms, nuclear medicine, radiology, the entire field of oncology, the list goes on and on. What do you think would be the end result if all of the people associated with the treatment of cancer woke up one day and found themselves unemployed?

"The disgusting truth is that money, economics, finance, and the all-mighty dollar has the greatest influence in the decision-making process."

Kyle sat quietly for a moment and then responded. "OK, Joe, once again, what does all of this have to do with Tina?"

Joe looked Kyle directly in the eyes and answered, "Kyle, I do have the ability and authority to put Tina in one of our special programs, and I can assure you, her chances for a full recovery will be almost guaranteed. No, I take that back, her recovery is guaranteed. I've already given the order."

Taking a huge gulp of coffee from his mug, Kyle sat speechless trying desperately to make sense of everything he just heard. His mind raced. As if Joe's revelation in the restaurant wasn't mind shattering enough. His thought process was interrupted when Joe broke the silence. "I know I don't have to ask you whether you are interested in pursuing one of these programs; the answer is obvious. However, I do have to warn you that there is a down side to this offer. Everything has a price."

Kyle shook his head and responded with a cavalier attitude, "A downside? What kind of downside are you talking about? You know I'd do anything for Tina. Do I have to take a pay cut or even work for free? Do you want me to resign so someone else can have my job? Come on, Joe, where's the down side to me saving the life of my soul mate. I'd give my life to save hers."

# CHAPTER TWENTY-FOUR

"OK, Kyle, I'm about to ask you a question that will undoubtedly change your life and could possibly be the cause of your demise. I apologize for the dramatics, but I want—and quite frankly—I need your undivided attention. This is something we can't take lightly."

"Geez, Joe, I don't think I've ever seen you like this. Whatever you've got on your mind…just spit it out. Between the two of us we should be able to find the solution to any problem."

"Alright, Kyle, let's just dive in. I think at this point the best way to proceed is to give you a list of the players with a brief description, call it history lesson, and then I'll connect the dots. Hopefully when I'm done, you'll have a clear understanding of IRC, who we work for, and where we get our authority to exist.

"Much of what I'm about to tell you is going to sound incredible, farfetched, even border on a fairy tale. However, I can assure you that what you are about to hear is true and easily verifiable. All you'll need to do is spend a little time doing some research on any home computer."

"OK, go for it. I'm listening," Kyle skeptically replied.

"You've been a part of this organization for more years than you know or can imagine. Ever since your boss at the charter company, Don Royce, put you in command of our flights to Central America, you've been under the watchful eye of some very serious and dedicated men, all belonging to, for lack of a better word, a secret society. The funny thing is, the society in question is not secret at all and can be found all over the world. You've probably even heard of them: the Freemasons."

"Whoa, you had me worried for a second there. I was afraid you were going to say something like Specter, or Chaos, or maybe even Dr. Evil. Sorry, I don't mean to be such a smart ass, but you have to admit, this conversation is a little over the top," Kyle joked.

Inhaling deeply through his nose and exhaling from his mouth, Joe continued his lecture. "Your former boss Don Royce, Sergeant D'Amico, Colonel Reyes, and myself are all members. We were in Central America working for Colonel Oliver North and his program to finance the Contras of Nicaragua."

Reminiscing Kyle added, "It's kinda funny; I'm sitting here listening to you fire off all those names from my past, but it seems like it was just the other day. I do have to give credit where credit is due. Rather than bring down the Reagan administration in copping a plea to stay out of jail, ole Ollie fell right on his sword and kept his mouth shut. You don't see that kind of loyalty anymore."

"Kyle, if you remember your US history, many of our founding fathers belonged to the Freemasons, including George Washington, Thomas Jefferson, and Ben Franklin, to name a few. The Freemasons throughout history have been shrouded in mystery, rumors, and innuendos. A popular belief connects the Freemasons with the planning of the American Revolution as well as the French Revolution. The history of the Freemasons can be traced back hundreds and hundreds of years, all the way back to the Knights Templar and the Crusades. You with me so far?"

"Yep, you've got the floor, just lay it on me," Kyle answered.

"Let's start right here with IRC. First and foremost, let me tell you who we are not. We are not the CIA nor the KGB or MI6. We don't have any double O agents like James Bond on our staff. However, in a sense we are more powerful and cunning. We have the ability to topple governments by manipulation of the money supply around the world. Our bosses in Zurich have at their fingertips the power to destabilize any country's currency. They don't get involved in wars or any other problems between nations, unless there is a possibility the conflict will have a negative impact on our employer's fortunes.

"World leaders are very much aware of the situation and the power of our bosses, and throughout history they have attempted to usurp their authority only to be the recipient of their wrath. As the old saying goes regarding the golden rule: he who has the gold makes the rules.

"So let's get back to IRC and how we came to exist. I guess you could say we are a more subtle or evolved branch of an organization that was started in the mid-1960s known as *Propaganda Due*—Italian for the number 2—or P2 for short. Many of P2's members were also Freemasons, but some were also members of the Mafia. P2's membership included senior military personnel, high-level civil servants, politicians, newspaper editors, bankers, businessmen, and industrialists. At its height, P2's influence extended throughout Europe, the United States, and much of South America.

Speculation suggests the Mafia connection was necessary for the elimination of obstructionists. The organization's undoing began in 1981 when leader and founder Licio Gelli's Tuscany villa was raided, and a list of P2's members was discovered. IRC came into existence with the guidance of our benefactors around that time."

"I've heard you refer to 'our benefactors' from time to time. Are these the money guys you described?" Kyle asked.

"I'll eventually get there, but this might be a good time to discuss the Freemasons. To completely understand who we are, you need to be able to connect the dots, starting many centuries ago. The Freemasons are believed to be the direct descendants of the Knights Templar, which came into existence after the Knights were viciously exterminated on the order of King Philippe of France and Pope Clement V on Friday, October 13, 1307, thus starting the superstition of bad luck on Friday the thirteenth.

"Most of the Knights scattered throughout Europe and Scotland, taking with them the knowledge and secrets acquired in the Middle East during the Crusades. Their knowledge included sophisticated building techniques that have been utilized for centuries in the Muslim world. These techniques were coveted and only shared with fellow members of the craft of stonemasons. These masons traveled throughout Europe erecting many of the great cathedrals, most of which are in use today.

"As I said, the Freemasons are believed to have come into existence after the demise of the Knights Templar. Historians are equally split on the debate over whether or not the Masons are really the continuation of the Knights or a completely different organization. Quite a bit of time passed between the demise of the Knights and the first recorded existence of the Masons."

"Joe, I'm actually aware of most of what you have been saying thus far. The History channel on cable T.V. has run numerous programs covering the subject," Kyle added.

"Regardless of what the historians think, the Knights Templar played a very important role in history, and I'm not just talking about the Crusades. Upon their return to Europe from the Crusades, the Knights were given special status—call them the superstars of their day.

"In 1139, Pope Innocent II bestowed upon the Knights independence from all authority, be it religious or secular, except from the Pope himself. In 1161, Pope Alexander III not only exempted the Knights from paying tithes but also allowed them to collect tithes.

"Royalty throughout Europe gave the Knights Templar land and allowed them to collect rent on the lands. Over time the Knights became very powerful and wealthy, thus becoming the bankers of Europe.

Back then, and it's true today, no one liked bankers, especially bankers as powerful as the Knights Templar. You still with me, Kyle?"

"So far so good; continue."

"These warrior bankers owned businesses, sea ports, and even fleets of ships. They even developed a system of promissory notes, an early form of checks. For example, a person could deposit money or valuables with the Templar branch in France, receive a promissory note, and cash it at a Templar bank in Spain, relieving the traveler of the risk of losing his savings to robbers along the way.

"History has shown us that power and wealth bring enemies. Eventually King Philippe le Bel of France, who was deeply in debt to the Knights Templar, conspired with Pope Clement the V to bring an end to the Knights and confiscate their wealth. One problem faced King Philippe: the Knights had infiltrated the monarchies and theocracies throughout Europe, including placing key personnel close to the pope.

"The Knights were tipped off, and many escaped and managed to disappear with the loot. Overnight the fleets of ships owned by the Knights Templar vanished. I find it curious that almost 185 years later Christopher Columbus sailed for the new world bearing the Templar Red Cross on his sails. It appeared that the warrior bankers were back in business, only this time sworn by oath of death to keep a low profile. They remain in business to this day, serving anyone desiring a secret or numbered untraceable bank account.

"In the 1960s, British Prime Minister Harold Wilson was quoted as saying he could fight off many opponents, but against the "Gnomes of Zurich" he had no defense. The Gnomes of Zurich was his not-so-kind phrase for the bankers and financiers, who he accurately believed controlled everything.

"The GOZ, as I like to refer to them, are the generous benefactors you hear me speak of, and they are responsible for starting IRC. They control the money and exchange rates throughout the world and are not to be taken lightly. With the push of a computer key, they can destroy the authority of any government by rendering their currencies and buying power worthless.

"We rarely hear from the GOZ directly. In this case they've run out of patience with our current president and his cronies. In their opinion, nothing destabilizes monetary policy quicker than greedy politicians allowing the rich to get richer at the expense of the common man. Revolutions have been started over such things."

"Hey, let me tell you, I'm in favor of a little revolution in this country. It's time we got rid of all the dead wood on Capitol Hill. We have the best politicians money can buy. If it weren't for those crooks looking the other way my airline would never have gone through a bullshit bankruptcy. If the voting public would just go to the polls every election and get rid of the incumbent candid candidates we could have all new faces in Washington D.C. I'm sorry Joe, the wounds haven't healed yet and I get carried away. Please continue."

"No problem Kyle, I understand completely. However, by connecting the dots, so to speak, IRC is a continuation of the Knights Templar, with ties to the

Freemasons and the direct descendent of the now defunct P2 organization."

A somber pall over came Joe as he began to explain the conditions of his offer. "By now you are familiar with what we do here at IRC. Most of our work is on the intellectual side of the security business. Every now and then, however, we are asked to carry out actual fieldwork that doesn't quite fit the mission profiles of the other agencies. When this occurs, we find ourselves in an awkward position. We aren't staffed or equipped to handle clandestine operations. We are forced into using outside 'assets,' former military or freelance operatives making their livings basically as mercenaries. We are faced with this scenario as we speak."

"Joe, I don't like the look on your face. There's something eating at you, and I'm afraid I'm not going to be thrilled with the rest of this lecture."

"A request from The GOZ has come across my desk seeking our assistance. The board of directors met and discussed the merits of the request before we agreed to underwrite the mission. I'm sure you knew something was in the works when your guys had to go pick up the board members twice in one month.

"Just before the meeting adjourned, we received a direct call from one of our benefactors. It appears that one of our board members took exception to the fact that I unilaterally directed our physicians in Georgetown to start treating Tina. The usual protocol is for the board at IRC to take each case on an individual basis, discuss it, and make sure all necessary precautions are in order. By precautions I mean discretion, silence.

"One of the members was concerned with your ability to maintain your confidentiality and somehow contacted two of the three GOZ. He complained we didn't know you long enough, or well enough, to place that kind of trust with you."

"So where does that leave us," Kyle asked.

"At that point, I felt it was necessary to tell the board the entire story of how we first met. After hearing the account of your actions that night in Central America, the members agreed that they were confident you could be trusted—except one. He felt he needed some other assurances of your loyalty. The other members chided him for his antagonistic attitude.

"I know our bosses fairly well, and I don't think they would have cared about my decision if it had not been thrown in their faces. The world in which we exist cannot allow anyone to cast doubt as to the resolve of our benefactors. Their hands were forced into reprimanding me and acquiescing to the board member in question.

"That board member wanted a quid pro quo from you. In other words, he wants something from you before Tina is allowed to continue working with our doctors. He wants you to be directly involved in the current assignment. He feels your involvement will ensure your silence."

# CHAPTER TWENTY-FIVE

---

"Kyle, before we continue I have to show you something." Joe reached into his briefcase and produced a photograph that he held firmly in his hands, hesitating to show it to Kyle. Joe's head sagged, and his chin rested on his chest for what seemed an eternity, while the rage within him battled over whether or not to go through with his next move.

Exhaling with a much-labored sigh, he continued. "You're obviously aware of the demise of your former boss. As of now the local law enforcement in Collier County and Marco Island have absolutely no evidence to even start a meaningful investigation; the trail went cold, as they say on television.

"However, there is one piece of evidence—this photo I'm holding—that brings us together this morning. I need you to take a look at this photo and tell me what it means." Joe slowly placed the photo on the desk, facing Kyle, and waited for a response.

Kyle's eyes focused on the image and stared stoically for almost three minutes without blinking. Finally, taking a deep breath and exhaling loudly, almost snorting through his nose, he looked up at Joe. "What do you want me to say.?

"Is that your reflection in the glass table on Sumner's patio?"

Kyle's response took Joe by surprise. "It's not my reflection. I can honestly tell you that I was in Chicago the day Sumner got what he deserved. I wish it was me, but I wouldn't have let him off so easy. I would have dragged his lame ass into the Everglades and staked him down over the biggest nest of Fire Ants I could find. Hopefully it would have taken the ants two or three days to devour every bit of him, assuming the gators and other critters didn't join in on the smorgas-bord. Tina and I were in Chicago; her sister's son made his first Communion, and we had to be there for the event."

"If it's not you, why did you take so long to react? Do you have an idea, or do you actually know who that is in the photo?"

Kyle's face mirrored that of a person who was just informed that he has only a short time to live. Totally dejected, Kyle explained, "Does it really matter if I know who that is in the photo? It looks enough like me for your computers to give it eighty percent accuracy on the facial recognition. So, whether I did it or not, it appears that this thing is going to haunt me, am I cor-rect? Let me guess, this quid pro quo thing has more to do with this situation than with Tina's care, but we might as well throw Tina into the mix so both of my arms can be twisted. This has Sheppard's stink all over it; tell me I'm wrong."

"You're not wrong. Sheppard came across the image as it was being processed in one of the facial recognition computers downstairs in the tech lab. He was looking to purloin some small surveillance equipment, probably to set up at his apartment so he could record his sexual triumphs over some dumb drunk he picked up in a bar. According to the techie in the lab, Sheppard left with a piece of paper partially cupped in one hand. He had the audacity to leverage it with the guys in Zurich. They are not happy with this situation, and they despise being pressured by the likes of Sheppard.

"This now brings us back to the reason we are sitting here today. I have to ask you to be a part of this."

"Do I have a choice? If I say no, I'm sure a copy of that photo mysteriously finds its way from Sheppard to the authorities. The notoriety of a murder investigation is obviously something IRC can't tolerate. Tina's treatment would cease and we both know where that would lead. If the authorities sensed I was holding back information I could be charged as an accessory to murder regardless of my solid alibi. So, I ask you again, do I really have a choice? It seems Sheppard has painted us into a corner."

"I saw it in your face. You know who that is in the photo, don't you? Why can't you tell me who that is in the photo?"

"Joe, you're a Marine, you'll always be a Marine, and you live by a code of honor you adopted years ago. I was too young for Vietnam and too old for subsequent wars, but I too have my own code of honor. I need to be able to look at myself every morning in the mirror and know that I did what I felt was right.

"During the toughest times for Tina and me, before getting hired at Universal Airlines, I was offered lots of money and quick promotions if only I would cross a picket line of striking pilots from other airlines. I even turned down Universal the first time they offered me a job—my dream job, the job I wanted my entire life—but I wouldn't cross a picket line and become a scab. Scabs are the lowest form of humanity in my opinion, and I use the word humanity loosely. A scab is the crap you scrape from the bottom of your shoes. I didn't weaken then, and I won't compromise my ethics now. So, let's get on with this, what do I have to do?"

"I don't know how to say this any other way, so I will just spell it out for you, and then you can decide. This particular assignment is—to put it bluntly—a sanction, an assassination. I tried to convince the Gnomes as well as the other board members that this was crazy; you don't have the necessary training. Sheppard countered with the official record of your S.E.R.E. training, he even knows about your tattoo. We have been asked to hunt down three individuals. One of them was your old boss Sumner. All three men in question have caused great financial harm to innocent people as well as our benefactors, and they don't like losing money; it's bad for their reputation. If you accept this job, make no mistake, we are asking—no let me rephrase that—I'm asking you to put an end to their greedy lives."

Kyle sat with his jaw clenched tightly. He couldn't believe what he was hearing. He was being asked to eliminate two human beings in order to save the love of his life. Rage began to grow within every fiber of his body. The veins in his neck protruded to the point that a keen eye could identify a visible pulse.

Like a dormant volcano coming to life, Kyle appeared to levitate from his chair, tipping it over on its side. He threw his coffee mug in the general direction of a trashcan, careening it off the wall in an uncontrolled demonstration of total consternation.

Shouting in the general direction of Joe, Kyle expounded "This is just another chapter in my fucked up life, welcome to my world. So, I'm faced with a goddamn Hobson's choice. Do the deed or watch my wife succumb to a disease that according to you is completely curable. So basically I have no choice at all."

"This is entirely my fault. I was in such a hurry to do whatever I could for you and Tina I assumed incorrectly that no one would object to my actions. I've been racking my brain to try and figure out an alternate plan, but I've caused enough trouble already. Give me some time to work on this; I'm sure there's a solution to this problem."

"I've said time and time again that I would give my life for Tina; I never imagined I would have to exchange my soul for the lives of strangers, regardless of how much they probably deserve to be punished. I know this isn't your fault; I don't blame you. This is the story of my life. Every time I think I've finally reached my goal, something or someone cuts my feet out from under me."

"I don't want you to make up your mind right away. Go home and think about it for a while. Once you take this giant step, there is no going back. You will have to live the rest of your life with the knowledge you took a human life. Trust me; I know firsthand how hard it can be; the faces of the victims will live on in your psyche forever."

"I've already made up my mind. I wouldn't have had the opportunity to fly the big jets if it weren't for Tina. She supported me through thick and thin. Her emotional support kept me going. I've lived my dreams. If this is what I have to do to save her life, then so be it. I just want to know one thing: what guarantee do we have that after this is over that jerk-off Sheppard doesn't release the photo after all?"

Choking back his emotions, Joe stated emphatically that he would make it his mission in life to make sure Sheppard never got that chance.

"You've been more than fair with me. You offered me a great job at a point in my life when I was sure my career was finished. Now I have the opportunity to save the life of the most important person in my world. I don't want you feeling guilty, or whatever you're feeling, for putting me in this position. I know you would never have asked me to do this if there were any other options. I just want one thing from you. If for some reason I don't complete the entire assignment, and I think you know what I mean, will you see that Tina receives the care she needs?"

"Hey, don't even talk like that. Nothing is going to happen to you; I'll see to it. You've got my word on it. You and Tina will survive and live to an old age. I think I need to take the rest of the day off. We can pick this up tomorrow after you've slept on it. If you're still OK with this insanity, we'll work this out together."

# CHAPTER TWENTY-SIX

Kyle went home and spent a quiet night with his wife. Tina could tell that something was on his mind. He was physically home, but his mind was wandering elsewhere. Kyle stared out into space in a catatonic state. Tina became concerned; Kyle wasn't usually that quiet.

"Is everything OK? You seem to be preoccupied with something. Is there anything I can do? Are you feeling alright?"

"I'm fine babe; I'm just thinking about some scheduling problems that have surfaced. It's no big deal. In fact I've already sorted out the conflicts, and I'll reassign the pilots tomorrow."

Tina knew Kyle wasn't being completely truthful, but she had learned over many years of marriage to give him some room when he didn't feel like talking. Tina went about her usual routine and decided to go to bed a little early and finish reading her tennis magazine. Kyle stayed up and did a little research, discovering Joe's history lesson was dead on accurate.

The next morning Kyle was in his office reviewing the current travel schedule. Unsure of the future, he wanted to be certain that all was under control in his flight department, just in case someone had to take over his position. He was reasonably satisfied that anyone taking over his job would find an efficiently run operation. A knock at his door interrupted his thought process.

"Morning, you look surprisingly awake. I assume you slept better than I did. I'm still furious over this situation. I'm sorry I had to get you involved."

"I think I know you well enough. This must be the only way for Tina to continue under the care of your doctors. I just want to get the job done so we can get on with our lives."

"I brought you the dossiers on the assignees. Everything you need to know about these scum bags is in these files. The recon guys did a great job. We not only know where to find the targets, but we also have their daily routines and habits. We have people observing them as we speak. Do you want to go through the files together, or do you want to familiarize yourself with the data and then we can talk later?"

"Let me read through this stuff alone. I need to get a feel of what or whom I'm up against. I need to convince myself that this is for real and not some bad dream."

Joe slowly walked to his office. For the rest of the morning, he chastised himself for getting Kyle involved. He tried to rationalize his actions, but there was no way he could allow for self-forgiveness. He thought that maybe if he hadn't tried to help Tina, then Kyle wouldn't be in this position. That argument was quickly defeated by the thought of Tina dying needlessly. He felt he owed Kyle so much for saving his life, but what kind of way was this to show appreciation.

The day dragged on for Joe. He sat in his office trying to guess what Kyle was thinking. Around one thirty in the afternoon, Joe's phone rang. The abrupt but welcome interruption gave him a temporary reprieve from self-castigation. Answering his phone, he heard Kyle's voice. "Joe, it's me. I'm hungry, how about you? Wanna get out of here and get a burger or something? I've got some questions for you, and I thought we could talk without interruptions away from here."

The two men picked up some food at a fast food restaurant and drove to a forest preserve picnic area. Sitting outside and enjoying the beautiful spring day almost wiped away the shroud hanging over them. After inhaling his lunch Kyle began to talk about the information in the dossiers.

"Well, if nothing else, those files made for some interesting reading. I recognized the names immediately. Especially my former boss; I'm just sorry that I didn't get the chance to meet that son of a bitch face to face. He was the cause of so much pain for my coworkers. I watched numerous families break apart under the stress associated with the bankruptcy. While families were struggling to make ends meet, Sumner and his cronies took turns stuffing their pockets with cash belonging to Universal Airlines.

"I've started to think about the best way to complete this…what do we call it? A job? A mission? A hunting expedition? I have some ideas, but having never done anything like this before, I'll need your input on the technicalities of actually *executing* my plan." The men looked at each other and began to laugh at Kyle's Freudian slip.

"I'll share with you everything I've learned over the past four decades working in this environment. The US government spent a lot of money seeing that I received the best possible training. Even so, we wouldn't be having this conversation if you had left me face down in that mud hole. I guarantee that you'll be ready to do this thing."

"Thanks, Joe. I appreciate that. What's the typical weapon of choice? How do I get to the locations without bringing attention to myself? I just can't get on an airliner with a gun, and it would be a little conspicuous flying in on a private jet."

"The transportation is the easy part. You might even enjoy what I have for you. When was the last time you flew a single engine airplane? I have a nice little surprise for you tucked away in a hangar at a small airport out in the countryside. I earned my private pilot's license many years ago, but I just don't have time to stay current at the controls. I promised my wife before she died that I would only fly with a certified flight instructor, like you, at my side. Don't worry about the logistics; IRC will handle everything. You'll get untraceable credit cards and bogus identification. You'll be trained by the best to come and go without leaving a trace of evidence. You'll be a ghost.

"You'll have a choice of weapons, depending on how close you can get to the target. I personally prefer the old-fashioned revolver with a noise suppressor for close-in work. The old-style revolver has less chance of jamming compared to the semi-automatic pistols.

After that you can have anything you think you'll need. I'll have a support team at your service 24/7. If you need something, we will get it for you, ASAP."

The rest of the afternoon was spent discussing the finer points in the art of taking human life. By the time the sun was heading west, Joe was feeling a little more comfortable with Kyle's mental strength. He gave Kyle the directions to his airplane and told him where to find the hidden keys in the hangar. The plane had just returned from its annual mechanical inspection and was in perfect condition.

The two men spent a couple of days at the Quantico Marine Corps Base shooting range getting acclimated to a variety of weapons. Kyle was impressed with Joe's skill with firearms. Joe was definitely not the kind of guy you wanted to cross, especially during his days in the field. Kyle thought to himself, *Joe probably knows more ways to kill than anyone could possibly imagine.*

Kyle studied the dossiers every day. He presented different scenarios to Joe, looking for his input. Joe acknowledged that all of the plans had merit. The conditions around the target would dictate the final decision. Thanks to the marvel of Google Earth and some very secret satellites IRC had access to; Kyle could place himself virtually at the desired location, as if he were in the middle of his assignments. Every street, dirt road, tree, and river, down to the smallest detail, was there right in the middle of Kyle's computer screen. He had the tools, the skill, and the mental toughness needed to do what he had to do.

Knowing full well the chain of events about to begin, nausea hit Joe like a ton of bricks. As he recovered his composure, the phone on his desk began to ring. Reaching over to pick it up, he saw the phone extension beckoning his attention was the direct line from Zurich.

His mood quickly deteriorated from a little queasiness to a sense of doom and despair.

"Oh, my God, what have I done?"

# CHAPTER TWENTY-SEVEN

Unable to sleep, Kyle quietly eased himself out of bed and checked the weather. He was pleasantly surprised to find the entire East Coast dominated by a high-pressure system. Not a cloud could be found from Florida to Maine. Leaving his home early that morning, he gave Tina a kiss on the cheek as she slept. She was under the impression that Kyle was leaving for a routine day at the office.

Following Joe's directions, Kyle reached the secluded rural airport, found the keys to the hangar, and stood in disbelief. For a brief moment, he just stared at the beautiful airplane awaiting his expert touch. The plane, a thoroughbred of aeronautical brilliance, seemed to stare right back at Kyle, challenging him to saddle up for the ride of his life.

Expecting to find your typical high-performance single-engine private aircraft, Kyle was looking forward to putting in a couple of hours of basic air work to get comfortable with Joe's plane. To his totally unexpected surprise, Kyle's noble steed this day was a Socata TBM 850. A large single-engine turboprop, manufactured in France, boasted a powerful engine rated at 850-shaft horsepower. At first glance the TBM 850 imbued the sensuality of a perfectly proportioned lover glistening under the lights of the hangar. The pearlized paint highlighted with black-and-red pin striping gave the appearance that the plane was already flying. In this case, the beauty was not just skin deep. The interior was as spectacular as the exterior—leather seats, noise cancelling technology for a quiet cabin, entertainment systems from satellite communications, music, and a multichannel DVD player with a choice of movies.

The impressive passenger accoutrements paled when compared to the business end of the aircraft: the cockpit. State-of-the-art instrumentation came as standard equipment on this plane.

Engine and system information was displayed on a fifteen-inch Garmin 1000 multifunctional display. The multifunctional display had the capabilities of showing the engine gauges, pressurization systems, fuel monitoring, electrical and battery condition, flight controls, and crew alerting systems. Navigation and avionics included two primary flight displays, two digital air data computers, two navigation/communication ILS/ GPS receivers, a color weather radar, and terrain and traffic avoidance displays.

However, the pièce de résistance in this marvel of modern aviation technology left Kyle breathless. Nestled neatly into the lower left side instrument panel, just above the pilot's knee, was a small control panel labeled SVS. After staring at it for a few moments, the realization of what this device might be and its abilities forced Kyle into a frantic search for an operator's handbook just to confirm it was no mirage.

SVS, Synthetic Vision Systems, was a tool that allowed the pilot to "see" the runway and surrounding airport terrain, including obstacles, regardless of weather conditions. With SVS operating properly, a pilot could literally take off and land in fog, or any other weather situation, where reported ceilings and visibility was zero-zero.

The SVS display was integrated into the Heads-Up Display (HUD). The HUD projected a computerized display of all the essential flight instruments with the SVS onto the inside of the windshield directly in front of the pilot. Once the plane was started and ready to taxi, the pilot would never have to look down at the instrument panel again, all the information he needed was directly in front of him. An Enhanced Flight Visual System, or EFVS, completed the array of magic. The EFVS was especially handy at detecting debris or other traffic on the taxiways.

The SVS, along with the EFVS, were items on the wish lists of many avionics research and development companies. Numerous articles in the aviation journals and technical magazines occasionally touched on the subject, but no one was claiming a breakthrough on having actual working systems. As far as the general aviation public was concerned, SVS and EFVS were years away from production.

Kyle sat and thought to himself about the depth and breadth of Joe Delasandro's contacts. How did he get his hands on an aircraft this advanced? For a moment he allowed himself to not focus on his lethal mission.

Returning to the world of reality, Kyle located a small tractor tucked away in the rear of the hangar.

He attached a tow bar to the nose wheel and slowly extricated the plane from its nest. Returning the equipment to the hangar and locking the door behind him, he opened the door to the plane and began reading a detailed preflight checklist.

Unaware that the dangerous circumstances regarding his mission had now escalated, he went about his business as the quintessential professional.

Joe, on the other hand, was frantic and desperately trying to contact a trusted old friend. The phone kept ringing, and just as the voicemail recording began its computer-generated message, a female voice groggily answered with a guttural, "This better be important."

"Gina, Joe here, sorry to wake you. I have a serious problem, and as of now, you're the only one I can trust."

"What's goin' on? You sound like you're having a heart attack or something."

"I just received a phone call from the boys in Zurich. They're having second thoughts about a problem we're handling here. I know you like being retired and running your own show at the restaurant, but I desperately need you back on the team. Can you get your partner to take over for a while?"

"Anything for you, Joe, you know that. But what's so important?"

"I'll meet you at your restaurant in an hour."

Gina sat in complete silence as Joe brought her up to date regarding Kyle's situation. She couldn't believe what she was hearing. Finally breaking her silence, she asked in a disgusted tone, "This is all because of Sheppard? That SOB has always given me the creeps. I hate it when he shows up at my place with his little girlfriends, acting like a stud. So what is it you need me to do?"

"I need you to be Kyle's shadow. Watch him just like you used to do with some of our newer assets. Try to keep him out of trouble, finish the job if you think it's necessary, and, lastly, if everything goes to hell, don't let Kyle get arrested by the local authorities. The Gnomes are emphatic on this point."

"This makes me sick to my stomach. If the big mouth is who you say it is, I'll handle that one for you free of charge. You do realize this is shaping up to be a major FUBAR."

"I do, but I hope we're both wrong. Thanks, Gina. Here's your field kit. Everything you need is right there. Call me with regular updates and take good care of our boy."

Thirty miles from the IRC hangar, in the beautiful rolling hills of north central Virginia, Kyle completed his preflight inspection, secured the door, and strapped himself into the pilot's seat to begin the Before Start checklist. Moments later, the 850-shaft horsepower turbine engine roared to life. Inside the plane, the sound of the powerful engine was almost imperceptible. The noise cancelling technology utilized within the cabin of the plane made the use of heavy traditional headphones obsolete. Kyle attached a small boom microphone to the left side of his sunglasses, thus eliminating the need to fumble for a handheld one.

Repositioning the plane to the end of the only runway at the airport, he performed the preflight run-up of the engine and operating systems. Everything checked out to perfection just as the sun began to rise in the Eastern sky. The airport was deserted except for Kyle.

The communications radio in the plane sat silent; no other aircraft was in the vicinity. Kyle released the parking brake and started his takeoff on runway Two-Four (24). The Socata TBM 850 lived up to its reputation, lifting off the runway almost effortlessly. In a few seconds, the departure end of the runway disappeared beneath the nose of the plane as Kyle retracted the landing gear.

The streamlined aircraft began to accelerate. Passing through fifteen hundred feet, Kyle set the throttle and adjustable pitch propeller to a cruise climb power setting as prescribed by the flight manual. The plane climbed effortlessly to ten thousand feet where Kyle planned on doing some basic maneuvers like slow flight, stalls, and steep turns before returning to the airfield for a series of take off and landings.

Leveling off at cruise altitude, Kyle quickly checked the flight manual for the proper power settings and set up the plane for long-range cruise, trimmed the airplane for level flight, and turned on the autopilot. It did a great job of holding altitude and magnetic heading and was an important tool for reducing fatigue on long flights for the savvy pilot. He spent the next few minutes checking out the vast array of state-of-the-art avionics and enjoyed the spectacular view of the Appalachian Mountains before getting to work.

# CHAPTER TWENTY-EIGHT

The next morning, everything appeared normal following the daily routines. Tina was in the kitchen making coffee when Kyle came in from retrieving the morning newspapers. A low-pressure system overran the area during the night, bringing low clouds and rain showers. One thing that really irritated Kyle was finding his morning newspaper soaked through and through by rain. Kyle was talking to himself as he entered the house.

"How hard could it be to place the paper into a plastic sleeve and then place the sleeve-covered paper into a secondary sleeve, open side down, thus covering the entire paper with waterproof plastic?"

Tina tried not to laugh when she saw Kyle's face, but she knew this was one of his pet peeves. After pouring his coffee, she offered him a hair dryer for the paper. She couldn't hold back any longer and let out a giggle. As always her giggles, laughs, and teases made him smile. There was nothing Tina Donnar could do to make him angry.

Kyle asked, "Did I hear you say Dr. Berman called and needs to see you? What time does she get to her office? Let's call and set up that appointment."

Tina nodded and said, "I'll call right now and leave her a voicemail so she'll receive it as soon as she sits down at her desk."

"Since I can't read my newspapers this morning, I think I'll just head to the office and catch up on some paperwork. Call me if you hear from Berman."

Arriving at IRC, Kyle marched straight to Joe's office walked in and sat down. The expression on Joe's face was a combination of disgust, embarrassment, and sorrow for having to get Kyle involved in the ugly side of the business.

"What's wrong with you? Ya feeling OK? You look like you're about to lose your breakfast."

"Kyle, you know how much I hated getting you involved at this level. If there was any other way, anything I could have done, I hope you know…"

Kyle interrupted Joe and said, "Joe, it's alright! Things happen for a reason. The bottom line is Tina. She's all that matters."

"I can assure you, Sheppard is on thin ice around here. The other board members are extremely pissed off at the way he manipulated the situation for his own amusement. He'll get his one day."

The two men continued to fine-tune Kyle's mission. Joe asked if there was anything else they needed to discuss before concluding the debriefing. Kyle responded with one question.

"Where in the hell did you get that airplane? I've read about them for quite a while, but this is the first time I've gotten the chance to fly one. Let me tell you, that plane performs better than anyone could imagine; it surpasses all the advertising hype. Not to mention the avionics package with the SVS and the EFVS. I'm impressed."

"The plane was a gift."

"A gift? That's one heck of a nice gift, somewhere in the neighborhood of two million dollars, I believe. I wasn't aware you had rich relatives."

"I don't. You know I come from a similar background to yours, so give me a chance to explain.

"I was contacted by one of the Gnomes a couple of years ago, and he asked, hmm, well actually more like begged me to help him with a personal problem. This was extremely unusual considering it was the first time I ever spoke directly with one of the Gnomes of Zurich. When he told me who he was, I of course didn't believe him until he shared with me some intimate secrets about my professional life that only the Gnomes could know, as well as his verification code.

"He pleaded with me and explained that his daughter had disappeared from her dormitory and had not been heard from in over a month. The information I was able to get out of the local cops led me to think it was some kind of cult problem, not an actual kidnapping or worse. I got lucky, and one of my contacts in the area led me to a secluded estate off the beaten path in the countryside. The house couldn't be seen from the road. Sure enough the house belonged to a television evangelist who claimed he had a direct line to God.

"I staked out the place for a couple of days and noticed a steady stream of young, beautiful women entering the estate but not leaving. I decided to take a closer look for myself, so one night I disabled the security system and started to nose around. What I discovered was a processing factory brainwashing future disciples of the cult.

"I figured it was time to take some action, and I let myself into the house. I found the girl and tried to make a quiet, stealthy exit. Unfortunately, I wasn't as slick as I used to be and was confronted by a couple of security guards and the preacher himself. At that point, I did what I was trained to do, and let's just say I introduced the preacher and his helpers to their god. I returned the girl to her family, tipped off the police regarding the house, and returned to business as usual.

"The Gnome wanted to find a way to repay me and knew that I liked to fly small airplanes. So one day I received a phone call from the airport manager where I learned to fly, and he informed me that my beautiful Socata TBM 850 was just delivered and wanted to know which hangar I wanted for my new bird. Of course I thought the guy was drunk and playing games with me until a messenger simultaneously arrived at my office with the ownership documents and keys. So now you know."

Joe and Kyle concluded their business and headed for the cafeteria. They were about to sit down with their coffees when Kyle's assistant, Diane Bishop, barged into the room.

"Kyle, Tina is on the phone. She says it's urgent."

"Thanks, Diane; I'll take it on this extension." Mrs. Bishop stood next to Joe while they studied the expression on Kyle's face. "Hi, what's going on? What's wrong?"

"Nothings wrong, I'm fine. Dr. Berman would like to know if we might see her first thing tomorrow morning. She said to prepare for an overnight stay. She will fill us in on all of the details when she sees us. She assured me that we will be very happy with her proposal."

Kyle said good-bye and returned the phone to its cradle. "Joe, it looks like I'll need to be out of the office tomorrow. The doctor says she needs to see Tina." Mrs. Bishop jumped in and told Kyle not to worry about anything; she had everything under control.

Tina and Kyle arrived at the doctor's office promptly at 9:00 a.m. the next day. Dr. Berman was already there, along with Dr. Miller and Dr. Clayton, who was first to speak.

# CHAPTER TWENTY-NINE

"Tina, since our last meeting I've been researching your particular type of cancer. I've come across some very promising results from an experimental program. Please don't be nervous over the term experimental. The procedure I am about to recommend has actually been around for some time. Through research and technology, we are starting to see fantastic results. We would like to start today if you agree.

"In order to start the program, we need to remove some tissue from one of the tumors, a biopsy. Dr. Miller will handle that, and she will explain the procedure. Once we have the tissue, we send it to a biotech firm that uses the sample to engineer a vaccine, which will be injected, similar to a flu vaccine. The serum will teach your immune system to attack the cancerous cells, yet it won't harm the healthy tissue. We have seen remarkable results with this technique."

Concerned, Tina replied, "Why haven't we heard about this treatment? My doctors in Florida never mentioned or offered anything like this to me. I've researched cancer treatments and have never come across this or anything remotely similar."

"Well, Tina, all I can say is that we are extremely fortunate to be part of a great hospital in our nation's capital, where opportunities like this present themselves." Kyle broke in and politely suggested that Dr. Miller explain the first part of the program, the removal of cancerous tissue, before Tina could get off another question.

Dr. Miller explained, "This procedure will be minimally invasive. You'll be mildly sedated while I extract a tissue sample using a laparoscope inserted through a small incision in your abdomen. Following the surgery, I require you to remain overnight for observation. The procedure will be quick with a small level of discomfort. Laparoscopic surgeries are done every day; you have nothing to fear."

Dr. Berman joined the conversation by asking if Tina and Kyle had any more questions. If not, the three doctors would leave the room and let Tina and Kyle discuss the matter privately.

"What do you think? Is this for real? Why haven't we heard of anything like this before now?" Kyle could hear a slight tone of anxiety in Tina's voice.

"I think we need to focus on the facts. First, we are very lucky to be here with this great team of doctors on our side. We would be foolish if we didn't try this experimental therapy; nothing else has worked. Let's not get bogged down by the fact that we are just hearing about this for the first time. I say we should give it a try. There's no down side to this." Tina knew Kyle was right and agreed to start immediately.

The three doctors returned to the office to hear Tina's decision. Listening to her answer, the doctors seemed excited. Dr. Berman looked into Tina's eyes and spoke softly. "Tina, I know you've made the right decision, and we are going to do everything in our power to see that you live a long and happy life."

# CHAPTER THIRTY

Dr. Miller retrieved the tissue sample and promptly sent it to the engineers at the biotech facility to be transformed into the life-saving vaccine. The tissue was in the hands of the engineers before Kyle brought Tina home from the hospital the next day.

Helping her into the house, he made sure she was comfortable, having placed her favorite magazines, the telephone, and the remote control next to the recliner in the den. The third Grand Slam tennis tournament of the year was just beginning on the grass courts of Wimbledon, England. Tina never missed a chance to watch the matches.

"I'm going to the office for a few hours; if you need me, don't hesitate to call. I mean it. I know you. Don't wait around if you're not feeling right."

"Don't worry so much; I'll be fine." Kyle kissed Tina and left for the office.

Joe Delasandro was anxiously waiting for Kyle at IRC, ready to hear his version of how things went at the hospital. Kyle spent the next hour trying to answer Joe's questions, replaying everything the doctors had talked about in their meeting.

"Thanks for setting all this up for us. I feel more and more confident that Tina is going to beat this thing."

"No need to thank me; I'm the one indebted to you. I spoke with Dr. Berman while you were still at the hospital. She's very optimistic about Tina's prognosis. Why did you decide to come in today? You could have stayed home with Tina."

"I wanted to go over the information for my upcoming trip to meet Russell Owen from Energy West. I don't want to drag this thing out any longer than necessary. We need to get this behind us and get on with our regular business."

Kyle returned to his office where he spent the rest of the day learning everything he could about Russell Owen. In order to complete this sanction, he was going to have to become familiar with Owen's habits, daily routines, and, most importantly, the topography of the area around Durango, Colorado, where Russell Owen lived. Kyle felt that never having traveled to that part of the country was a serious obstacle.

The rugged terrain, the mountain roads, and the start of the tourist season were just a few of the problems he faced. The summer months in Durango were filled with travelers enjoying the majestic scenery, the great fly fishing in the Animas River, and the famous narrow gauge train that runs daily from Durango to Silverton, an old mining town high up in the Rockies. The old train was a favorite for the Hollywood movie studios, filming hits like *Butch Cassidy and the Sundance Kid* with Paul Newman and Robert Redford, the *Support Your Local Gunfighter* and *Support Your Local Sheriff!*

series with James Garner, and *Around the World in Eighty Days* with David Niven, and a host of others.

Getting into the area, completing the assignment, and leaving unnoticed was going to be challenging. Hopefully, if all went according to plan, Kyle calculated he could be in and out in three days. He would use the first day to get familiar with the roads, making sure he had numerous escape routes. He would observe Russell Owen on the second day and on the third day he would complete the sanction and try to get out of the area unscathed.

Diligently memorizing every detail regarding Russell Owen, down to the smallest minutia contained in his biography gave Kyle some insight into what he would encounter. Approximately ten years younger than Kyle, Owen stood six foot four inches, weighed in around two hundred and fifty pounds of solid defensive end, and was a formidable man. His massive chest tapering down to his waist forming the perfect "V" shape physique caused him to angle his way through most doorways. Selected in the second round of the NFL draft by the Denver Broncos, he was touted as one of the toughest defensive players to come along in many years. Unfortunately his professional football career came to an abrupt end shortly after it started due to a motorcycle accident rendering his right knee useless. This was not the kind of guy you just walked up to and pointed a gun at. Shooting this man and not killing him instantly would be like wounding a grizzly bear. It would just make him mad, and he would probably maul you to death with his colossus hands.

Owen's intimidating physical presence paired with his overbearing personality made it easy to understand why people would go along with his schemes rather than challenge him. His original plan was to play on the greed of the investors.

The Ponzi scheme was simple—promise and deliver extraordinary returns on investments to the original investors, and they would be sure to talk, or more likely brag, to their friends about their good fortunes. Owen had enough of his own money to start the ball rolling; he was liquid enough to pay out double-digit returns to the original investors through the first six months. The overly generous dividend was equal to an interest rate of 36 percent annually. True to form, the original investors began talking up this marvelous little energy company and its founder. The fact that the man in charge came with a marketable name from his football days was frosting on the cake.

Russell Owen's phone was ringing off the hook with prospective investors begging for him to take their money. A tidal wave of cash from new investors was used to pay dividends to the existing accounts; the plan was working like a charm. Each payout saw the interest rate drop just a few percentage points, but everyone was ecstatic with their return on investment. While all this was going on, Owen began to ship large amounts of cash to offshore banks, well out of reach of the US government.

The amount of cash thrown at Owen was staggering. He calculated that at the rate the money was coming in, he could leave the country before the next dividend payment was due with over one hundred million in cash. Owen was literally laughing all the way to his bank in the Cayman Islands. The greedy investors didn't realize they were putting money into a business that never existed.

The greed that hooked the original investors eventually hooked Owen. He couldn't resist the temptation of sticking it to the boys from Wall Street when he was approached about an IPO. They acquiesced to their egos and decided this ex-football player with his ursine features, good-old-boy drawl, and overall jovial quality just couldn't live without their expertise.

Owen created ghost companies that contributed to the income stream of Energy West—on paper. The elaborate paper shuffle was so complex that the experts from the investment communities either couldn't follow the paper trail or were embarrassed to ask the "Dancing Bear," as they referred to him, behind his back of course, for an explanation. The general thought process was that so many people were making money with the company that everything must be OK.

The first day of trading Energy West stock made Russell Owen a billionaire. Instead of taking his money and running, he opted to continue the charade. A few handpicked accomplices helped him create the illusion of a real company making money. Eventually, the scheme came crashing down when a few skeptical auditors began to scour the company's books.

In the end, millions of people were affected. Pension money invested by professional fund managers disappeared forever. Individual stock portfolios lost huge percentages of their total worth.

Russell Owen and his coconspirators were indicted and convicted of fraud and numerous other charges. They faced long prison terms; however, the appeals process turned out to be kind to Owen and his friends. The convictions were overturned due to technicalities, and Owen had alluded that his contributions to the campaign of the current president had bought him an understanding federal judge in the appeals court.

The hint of a scandal reaching all the way to the White House was totally unacceptable for an administration looking for a second term, not to mention the Gnomes of Zurich were still feeling the pain of their losses. Kyle understood the politics but didn't agree with the reason for the sanction. *This president was dirty*, he thought. The only reason he would complete the mission was for Tina's sake. He also rationalized that he empathized with the victims who had lost their retirements, just like Kyle and his fellow employees at Universal Airlines.

Kyle completed studying the possible scenarios for this mission and presented them to Joe. A few hours later, the men agreed on a plan. Kyle would need some special equipment for this outing, and Joe immediately got to work securing the necessary tools.

Arriving home late that night, Kyle told Tina that he would be filling in for one of his pilots on sick leave and flying some trips later in the month. The flight department was understaffed due to vacations and training requirements.

# CHAPTER THIRTY-ONE

Over the next few days, Kyle studied every detail regarding his sortie, in an effort to avoid any missteps. He replayed every scenario over and over in his mind; a mistake might cost him his life as well as Tina's.

Joe stepped into Kyle's office with a folder in hand.

"Kyle, can you spare a couple of minutes? I have a few notes regarding your trip that I'd like to go over." As usual, he didn't wait for an answer and began to read from his notes. "I've been going over the scenario, and I believe we can really focus on this particular plan. Looking over the dossiers on Owen, it appears that we might be able to take advantage of his two greatest passions, fly fishing and smoking expensive Cuban cigars.

"The first possibility is his love of fly fishing. Three times a week—every Monday, Wednesday, and Thursday—his wife leaves the house around nine o'clock for her tennis lesson at a resort ten miles down the mountain, along Highway 550 toward Durango. After her tennis lesson, she usually meets her friends for lunch and drinks and then heads home around three o'clock.

"Owen uses this time to indulge in his favorite hobby—fly fishing. He drives his Jeep a few miles down a dirt road to an area where the Animas River cuts through his property and offers an idyllic setting for fishing. The only vehicle access is by a private road on his property. However, you could park in a public scenic overlook off the highway and hike four miles uphill. Cars are left in the overlook area for hours while people picnic in the surrounding forest. Generally, no one ventures far off the road and into the mountains, so I don't think you'll encounter anyone around Owen's fishing hole.

"This guy still leads a dream life style. He seems to go about his daily routines as if he doesn't have a care in the world. If it was me, and I swindled a boatload of money from investors, I'd be looking over my shoulder all the time," Kyle added.

Continuing on, Joe explained, "The second possibility involves his passion for Cuban cigars. His wife won't let him smoke in the house, so he steps out on the deck overlooking the San Juan Mountains every night around eight o'clock with his cigar and brandy. Unfortunately, you would have to make your way to and from his house in the dark. I think these options are our best chances to get this thing done. Anything else would be too public."

"Whoa, did you say four miles uphill? At that altitude we're looking at a tough hike. I'm still in pretty good shape, but it's something we have to consider," Kyle lamented.

"Well, the way I see it, you can do the uphill walk during the day or at night, your choice. There is another option, but I think it leaves too many possibilities for a foul up. There is a secluded dirt road about a mile north of Owen's property where you can hide the car while you hike downhill to get into position. I don't like it because it opens up a window of opportunity for some local bumpkin with a badge to come across your car and call it in to the authorities. It all depends on whether you leave your car above or below the estate for a starting point. You make the call. Personally, I'd rather make my retreat down hill.

"I've taken the liberty of having some equipment assembled that you might find useful. I have an old friend at the Quantico Marine Corps Base, a weapons expert. We're going to see him this afternoon."

Before Kyle could respond, his assistant, Mrs. Bishop, interrupted with a call over the intercom system. "Kyle, I have Tina on line two."

"Thanks, Diane, put her through. Hi sweetie, what's goin on?"

"I just called to tell you Dr. Berman would like to see me tomorrow to start the series of treatments. I can't believe how fast things are moving."

"No problem, sweetie. I'll go with you."

Kyle placed the phone back in its cradle and looked at Joe. "Dr. Berman isn't wasting any time. She wants Tina to start tomorrow."

"Considering all this crap I have to put you through, I thought the least I could do was expedite Tina's care and try to ease your concerns. I decided to call in some favors due to me for some time now."

Kyle and Joe arrived at Quantico shortly after lunch. Gunnery Sergeant Bobby James Thibadeux met them at the front gate. The three men headed off to the target range to introduce Kyle to his new tools.

Sergeant Thibodaux was a career Marine with over twenty-five years in the Corps. Leather tough, with the overall appearance he was carved from a solid block of Cypress tree was raised in the bayous of Louisiana, where he honed his hunting and survival skills as a young kid.

Speaking with a noticeable Cajun accent, Sergeant Thibodaux began his lecture. "Kyle, Joe and I have been friends for many years, and he knows me as well as anyone. My philosophy is to use the KISS principle: Keep It Simple Stupid, especially when I have my life and the lives of my men at stake. I don't believe in fancy high-tech equipment that can't be repaired in the field.

"Staying with the keep it simple attitude, I put together a few things that Joe thought you might need. All of these items have proven themselves time and time again from the jungles of Southeast Asia to the deserts of the Middle East".

"With my luck I completely agree, let's keep it as simple as possible. Murphy's law controls my life," said Kyle.

"First, let's look at your primary weapon. I've put together a standard .30-06 caliber hunting rifle with a tactical optical sight. The rifle package is based on a standard survival design where the barrel detaches from the main body of the weapon and both pieces are stored in the waterproof synthetic rifle butt. The entire weapon can be carried in a backpack, completely undetectable. You should be able to assemble it and be ready to fire your first round with accuracy in less than three minutes. Breaking down the weapon and packing it away should be even faster.

"Joe and I decided on the standard .30-06 caliber because of its popularity with hunters. Your mission should appear to be the result of a stray bullet fired by a hunter. The telescopic sight I chose places a red dot on the target and is excellent in all light conditions, including the use of night-vision devices.

"As a backup for the rifle, I chose a .40 caliber semi-automatic handgun with a noise suppresser. Joe and I argued a bit over this because he prefers a standard revolver. I feel that if you need to reach for your backup weapon, you should have more firepower than just six shots. This weapon comes with a fifteen-round clip that can be changed out in seconds. This particular make and model has proven itself time and time again.

"The rest of the equipment is self-explanatory: binoculars, handheld GPS navigation device, and night-vision goggles. All of the items will fit into a standard hiker's backpack. You're going to look like a typical hiker taking a stroll when you step out of your vehicle.

"I think it's time for some practice. I expect to see you assemble the weapon, fire it, hit the target, and then disassemble it proficiently by the end of the day. Joe tells me you know a little about handling weapons, and I reviewed the file from your S.E.R.E. training. Pretty impressive for a civilian, now show me your stuff."

For the next thirty minutes Kyle practiced assembling and disassembling the rifle. The entire process took less than five minutes. Toward the end of the first half hour, Sergeant Thibodaux had Kyle prepare the weapon while wearing a blindfold. Satisfied that Kyle was comfortable with the rifle, he opened a box of ammunition and placed a dozen quick-loading eight-shot magazines of the high power cartridges on the table.

"The .30-06 is a popular caliber with hunters. The particular brand we will use is a standard over-the-counter cartridge that can be purchased anywhere in the country. The bullet will travel on an average of three thousand feet per second and deliver approximately 3500 energy foot-pounds of knock-down power at impact. You should be able to get close enough to the target to nullify any problems with wind and elevation. Over the first one hundred to two hundred yards, this shell has an almost flat trajectory. Wherever the red dot appears on the target, that's where the bullet will hit."

Kyle clipped the loaded magazine into the bottom of the stainless steel body of the rifle. The bolt action of the gun was smooth and quiet as Kyle chambered his first shell. Receiving the all clear from Sergeant Thibodaux, Kyle squeezed off the first round hitting the target dead center at a distance of one hundred yards. Thibodaux looked over at Delasandro with an approving nod and instructed Kyle to use the remainder of the afternoon getting more and more comfortable with his new tools.

Sergeant Thibodaux was extremely pleased with the level of skill that Kyle demonstrated that afternoon. He told Kyle to leave the weapons with him, and he would personally clean and check them one last time.

The two men parted company and headed for home. Entering the kitchen through the garage door, Kyle found Tina busy making dinner. He walked up behind her and gently kissed her on the cheek. To his surprise, she turned around with her nose curled up and said, "You smell like you've been around fireworks. What have you been doing all day?"

Momentarily stunned, Kyle was speechless. Quickly regaining his composure, he scrambled for an explanation. "I'm sorry. I didn't have a chance to call and let you know that Joe and I were leaving the office for the afternoon. Joe took delivery of a brand-new Italian made Beretta over/under 12-gauge shotgun used for skeet and trapshooting. He wanted to break it in, so we headed for the local gun club and shot at clay pigeons all afternoon."

"You shot clay pigeons all afternoon? This fits into which category of your job description? I don't ever want to hear you complain about working too hard. Go take a shower; you stink. Dinner will be ready in a few minutes."

# CHAPTER THIRTY-TWO

O n the road early the next morning heading for Georgetown, Tina was mentally preparing for the follow up testing necessary before receiving her first of what was going to be a long process of injections, monitoring, and more injections.

Arriving in Georgetown before the rush hour traffic started to congest the main roads in and out of the DC area, Kyle feared they would be so early that they would end up waiting for Dr. Berman. To his surprise the doctor greeted them as soon as they walked through the door.

"Good morning, Tina. Thanks for coming in early today. Before we start the regimen of injections, I would like to have a complete blood work up done, followed by an MRI. We want to have an accurate baseline from which to measure the effectiveness of the serum. We will start with one injection today, and you will wait here for a few hours afterward—just to make sure you don't have an adverse reaction. Over time we will increase the injections to three times a week.

"Let's quickly review the process. As you know, we harvested a tissue sample from one of the tumors. The sample went to a lab, and the cells were processed into a serum genetically programmed to attack only the tumors in your abdomen. The technique is similar to receiving vaccinations against polio and other diseases. If the treatment is successful, we should see positive results in approximately two to three months. Do you have any questions?"

Tina spoke first. "Do you know how much of the serum will be needed to complete the therapy, and what happens if you run out of the serum before we see results? Did you get a large enough tumor sample to manufacture the necessary quantities of the liquid?"

"To answer the first question, we don't know exactly how much we will need. That's why we need to have accurate measurements before starting the protocol. The biotech company we work with will manufacture the serum as needed. The shelf life of the liquid is short, so we have it delivered as required."

Cautiously satisfied with the answers, Tina and Kyle started off for the MRI department. The repeat tests went quickly, and they found themselves back in Dr. Berman's office around noon.

Drs. Berman, Clayton, and Miller were waiting for Tina and Kyle. Dr. Clayton spoke first.

"We all wanted to be here for the first treatment. We are confident that by this time next year you will be standing here in total remission." Drs. Miller and Berman nodded in agreement and asked Tina if she was ready.

Tina looked at Kyle with a tear in her eye and said, "I've been praying for a cure; now it appears that I might be the lucky one to have found the doctors that possess the miracle that I need. Let's do it."

Dr. Berman prepared the syringe. The bottle containing the life-saving fluid was stored under lock and key in what looked like a temperature-controlled wine vault. She expertly drew the serum into the syringe from the sterile bottle and measured it precisely, making sure not to waste one drop of the priceless liquid. "The first dose has to be small; we want to guard against any allergic reactions.

"Over time the doses will increase in size and frequency. So for today, it doesn't really matter if we use your arm, leg, or rump. As the doses increase, we will eventually have to move away from your arms to areas with more tissue to absorb the serum, such as your thighs and backside."

Tina opted for the arm and proceeded to roll up her sleeve. Dr. Berman gave her usual caveat: "You will feel a slight pinch and maybe a burning sensation. Nothing to worry about; the sensations will disappear quickly."

Dr. Berman swabbed the injection site with alcohol to sanitize the area. Confident the arm was as sterile as possible; she gently squeezed the back of Tina's triceps plumping up the muscle and surrounding tissues and inserted the hypodermic needle in a swift, unhesitating motion. The razor sharp tip penetrated the tissue without resistance until the needle was no longer visible.

Kyle watched Tina's reaction as the serum slowly oozed from the syringe into her body. The grimace on her face was a direct result of the burning sensation caused by the fluid seeping into the muscle tissue of her triceps. For Tina, the few seconds needed for the injection seemed to take forever.

Dr. Berman extracted the needle and rubbed the injection site with another alcohol wipe. Placing a small bandage over the tiny hole, the doctor completed the first step in Tina's quest to rid her body of a deadly intruder.

On the car ride home, Tina felt cautiously optimistic. She talked about all of the things she planned on doing once she got this stage of her life behind her. Kyle, having the advantage of knowing the success rate of these doctors backed by their generous sponsors, shared Tina's optimism to a higher degree.

"I have some work to do in the office tomorrow, but I'll be home early. I have to fly a trip the next day, and I'll be gone for four or five days. Don't hesitate to call me if you are having any problems or aren't feeling well. I told Mrs. Bishop to track me down if you call. She can reach me via the satellite phone in the jet if necessary."

"You worry too much; I'll be just fine. I'm sure the soreness in my arm will have disappeared by tomorrow morning, plus Dr. Berman asked me to call in once a day for an update on how I'm feeling. I'm in good hands. You go and play with your airplanes and keep your mind on your work. I don't want to hear about you on the evening news. You know I couldn't live with myself if I thought for one second that something had happened to you because you were too preoccupied with my problems."

# CHAPTER THIRTY-THREE

The morning passed quickly as Kyle dutifully checked the weather and flight planning. This was a flight Kyle wasn't looking forward to making. Flying more than halfway across the continent in a single-engine plane, attempting to maintain a tight schedule, and completing a grizzly task weighed heavily on him. Fortunately, Joe's TBM 850 was comfortable, well equipped with the latest avionics, flew very fast, and held enough fuel to cover a lot of miles on a tank of gas.

Checking the weather and winds aloft forecast for the altitudes from twelve thousand feet to eighteen thousand feet, otherwise known as flight level one-eight-zero, the overall prognosis was for fair weather across most of the country with light winds predominantly from the west-northwest. Kyle calculated the TBM 850 should be able to maintain a true airspeed of 275 knots at sixteen thousand feet, the most favorable altitude considering the velocity and direction of the winds at that altitude. Using his flight computer, he calculated that a headwind component of twenty-five knots would have only a slight impact and allow the sleek plane a respectable ground speed of 250 knots.

Planning one fuel stop in the Kansas City area, the entire trip would take a little over eight hours and thirty minutes. Durango's La Plata County Airport and its nine-thousand-foot runway was more than adequate for landing the TBM 850, but Kyle decided to bypass it for Cortez Municipal Airport in the southwest corner of Colorado. The drive from Cortez to Durango by way of Route 160 was normally less than one hour.

Landing at Cortez Municipal, Kyle would avoid any contact with local citizens from the Durango area. A second advantage would offer an escape route from Russell Owen's estate north through Silverton, then west to Telluride, and back south to Cortez along Route 145 if he felt backtracking through Durango wasn't prudent.

The plane was to be fueled and ready to go by 6 a.m. The owner of the airport acknowledged the request and said he would have the plane out of the hangar and waiting on the ramp. As Kyle was finishing his phone call, Joe Delasandro knocked on the door. "How are things going? Do you need any help with planning or anything else?"

Kyle shook his head and said, "Thanks, I think I have everything under control." He went on to brief Joe on the details of his itinerary.

"Before you head for home today, don't forget your *tool kit* is in the trunk of my car. Sergeant Thibodaux made sure that everything is in pristine condition." The two men walked out to the parking lot where Kyle picked up his package. Joe shook Kyle's hand and urged him to be extremely careful. Parting company; Kyle headed for home, while Joe picked up his cell phone and placed a call to Gina. After one ring, Gina answered the phone knowing it was Joe.

"Hey, Joe, what can I do for you?"

"Our boy is on the move; he's leaving for Durango tomorrow."

"Can you give me the details of his plan so I can keep an eye on him?"

Kyle drove home and spent a quiet evening with Tina. "You seem to be in one of those moods again. Anything you want to talk about," she asked?

"Everything's fine. I'm just thinking about the flight tomorrow. You should know me by now; I always go over the entire trip in my head before I sit down behind the controls. I don't like unpleasant surprises at 41,000 feet."

By six the next morning, Kyle was strapped into the pilot's seat of the powerful single-engine airplane. The engine roared to life and moments later catapulted Kyle into the early-morning sky. Climbing through three thousand feet, he contacted Potomac Departure Control and received his instrument flight rules (IFR), clearance to Kansas City Downtown Airport, and his first fuel stop.

Leveling off at sixteen thousand feet, he switched on the autopilot, setting the altitude hold and navigation functions. The morning sky was crystal clear with unlimited visibility, a perfect day for flying a small airplane.

The Blue Ridge Mountains and Shenandoah Valley passed beneath the aircraft and faded away from view.

The route took Kyle westbound over West Virginia, Southern Ohio, Indiana, Illinois, and Missouri before landing in Kansas City.

Passing over the West Virginia-Ohio state line, Kyle could see the Ohio River as it outlined the boundaries of Ohio and Indiana on the north side with Kentucky to the south. The large river continued to meander, mainly westward, until it merged with the mighty Mississippi at the southernmost point in Illinois. The view from this altitude allowed a spectacular view of the farmland melding gently into the banks of the river while the huge river barges slowly and steadily plying their way upstream to deliver their cargo.

Flying over southern Indiana and Illinois, the Ohio River slowly diverged to the south away from the TBM's flight path. Within minutes of crossing into Illinois airspace, the Mississippi River appeared on the horizon, dividing Illinois from Missouri. Crossing directly over St. Louis, the confluence of the Missouri River joining the Mississippi came into view to the right of the plane and the Ohio River mating with the combined Missouri-Mississippi Rivers to the south. From this vantage point, one could see why the early pioneers called St. Louis the gateway to the west.

Continuing westbound, the flight plan paralleled the Missouri River as if it was guiding Kyle directly to Kansas City.

"Kansas City approach, TBM/ONE Romeo Charlie one six thousand (16,000 feet altitude), with ATIS information Kilo."

"Roger ONE/Romeo Charlie, radar contact, descend and maintain eight thousand, turn right heading three zero zero, vectors for ILS runway One-Nine (19)." Switching off the autopilot, Kyle took control of the airplane and complied with the approach controllers' instructions.

The weather in the Kansas City area was good, and Kyle could see the airport from twenty miles away.

"TBM/ONE Romeo Charlie descend and maintain three thousand, turn left heading two five zero, the airport is at your ten o'clock position, report it in sight."

"Leaving eight thousand for three, turning left to two five zero, airport's in sight."

"ONE Romeo Charlie cleared for the visual to runway One-Nine, contact tower frequency 133.3."

"Tower, TBM/ONE Romeo Charlie left base for runway One-Nine."

"Cleared to land ONE Romeo Charlie," replied the air traffic controller. Kyle softly placed the airplane on the runway and allowed it to decelerate slowly, using most of the seven-thousand-foot runway.

Exiting to the left, he taxied directly to parking outside of Executive Beechcraft, the fixed base operator. Completing the parking and shutdown checklists, Kyle opened the door, stepped out of the plane, and stretched, hoping to rid his body of any kinks that had developed after sitting in one position for so long.

Placing his order for fuel with an attractive young girl working behind the counter, he then took care of certain physiological necessities. While the plane was refueled, Kyle asked the courtesy car driver to take him to the nearest restaurant for breakfast.

After quickly gulping down an order of steak and eggs with hash browns and rye toast, Kyle made his way back to the airport to continue his journey. Receiving his clearance from the ground controller, he taxied for takeoff. Stopping briefly in the run up area at the end of the runway, he completed the before take-off checklist.

"Kansas City tower, TBM/ONE Romeo Charlie ready for takeoff, runway One-Nine."

"Roger ONE Romeo Charlie, cleared for takeoff, leaving two thousand feet, turn right heading two seven zero."

The plane responded as expected and dutifully carried Kyle westbound for his appointment high in the Colorado Rockies. Flying over Kansas, corn and wheat fields stretched out as far as the eye could see. The terrain appeared flat; however, from this point on, the earth would continue to rise in elevation, finally reaching its apex at the Continental Divide in the Rocky Mountains.

Kyle chose to fly over northern New Mexico in order to avoid the fourteen-thousand-foot peaks near Wolf Creek Pass along Route 160 just west of Alamosa, Colorado. Just to play it safe, he climbed from sixteen thousand feet to flight level two zero-zero (twenty thousand feet) to get more clearance between his plane and the peaks below.

Tracking west toward the Farmington, New Mexico, VOR (Very High Frequency Omni Range), identified by its FAA designation of RSK (short for rattle snake), Kyle could see Durango, Colorado, directly to the right side of the airplane. Denver center was the air traffic control authority in this area. As the plane crossed over

Farmington, Denver Center began to descend the TBM for an approach into Cortez, Colorado.

Cortez Municipal Airport, elevation 5,914 feet above sea level, is over one mile high as compared to Kansas City at 760 feet above sea level. Although the indicated airspeed Kyle would use for approach would be the same for all airports, the actual speed of the plane though the air would be much faster due to the high thin atmosphere in the mountains. The plane needed more runway than usual to land and stop.

The landing was uneventful, and Kyle parked the plane at the Cortez Flying Service FBO. Before leaving in the rental car, he completed his fuel order in preparation for his departure; the only difference this time was that he only wanted the fuel tanks to be half full. Anticipating his departure from this high altitude airport, Kyle chose to limit the weight of the aircraft in order to enhance its takeoff and climb performance.

The short drive east to Durango took Kyle past the Mesa Verde National Park, the last known home of the Anasazi Indians, the "Cliff Dwellers," an ancient Indian tribe that occupied the area from around 100 to 1300 AD and then mysteriously vanished centuries before the first white settlers discovered the area.

Kyle checked in at the local Red Lion motel and began his orientation of the area. Feeling the effects of the long day of travel, he opted for an early dinner at a steak house and retired for the evening. He planned on an early start the next day for his rendezvous with Mr. Russell Owen.

# CHAPTER THIRTY-FOUR

A combination of jittery **anticipation and his inter-nal** body clock set for the Eastern Time Zone caused Kyle to wake up early—5:00 am local time. Poor sleeping habits, a result of awakening in different time zones, is the bane of a professional pilot's existence. Learning to overcome fatigue and continuing to function with perfection is what separates the great pilots from the others.

Using his time efficiently, Kyle studied the reconnaissance reports, memorizing every detail for the fifth and sixth time. The carafe of decaf coffee he brewed in his room was just enough to hold him over until breakfast. While sitting in a secluded corner booth at the motel restaurant, he poured over the local area maps, leaving nothing to chance.

The reconnaissance reports put Russell Owen at his favorite fishing hole between nine thirty and ten o'clock. Common sense dictated that it would be more advantageous to arrive on site before Owen in order to observe his routine as he prepared for fishing. After finishing his breakfast, Kyle returned to his room to pack his equipment. Along with the all-important *tool kit*, he included plenty of water and energy bars for his uphill hike to the estate. Having a Canon EOS T3i Single Lens Reflex 35mm digital camera hanging from a strap around his neck added a little extra weight, but it completed the façade of a hiker and nature lover.

The drive from downtown Durango north along Route 550 was the only major road in that direction. The early morning air was cool as expected, due to the elevation of the surrounding terrain. From Durango to the Owen estate, the elevation rose from approximately six thousand feet above sea level to eight thousand five hundred feet. Kyle was going to have his work cut out for him hiking at that altitude.

The sun's rays were just glancing over the peaks of the San Juan Mountains to the east. The town of Durango was nestled into a picturesque valley surrounded by the tall peaks of the San Juan range of the southwestern Rocky Mountains. Over eons of flowing southward from the snow-covered mountains north of town, the Animas River had carved the valley out of the rock.

The usual morning routine started as the town began to awake. The sounds of the Denver Rio Grande narrow gauge train rumbled and hissed as the engineers prepared their steam engines for another day of transporting tourists into the mountains, eventually stopping in Silverton for lunch. The train's steam-driven whistles reverberated against the sides of the steep rock walls every morning, as if announcing the start of another wondrous day in this tiny hamlet.

The narrow gauge track followed the Animas River northbound into the mountains where it mimicked

every twist and turn of the river. The early railroad construction teams were both clever and smart when they
surveyed the topography of the area. Following the
river gave the crews the option of utilizing the work
Mother Nature had started by carving out a natural
path through the mountains. The scenery along the
route was so spectacular that at some points the tracks
clung to the side of the mountain gorges with the
white water rapids of the river a thousand feet or more
below.

Driving on Route 550, the tracks disappeared from
view as the road began its assent toward the Purgatory
Ski Resort area and the top of the world. A few miles
south of Purgatory was Electra Lake, named and
owned by the local electric utility company for gen-
erating hydroelectric power. A private community of
expensive homes dotted the lake's shoreline. These are
the homes of the truly rich and famous, or in the case
of Russell Owen, the rich and infamous.

Each home was spectacular. Some were built to
resemble log cabins; only these cabins were a minimum
five to six thousand square feet, two or three levels of
living space, and with numerous fireplaces strategically placed for optimum heating, built with rock and
stone from the surrounding area. Wrap-around decks
of cedar with hot tubs and spas allowed for unencum-
bered views of the surrounding peaks.

The Owen estate was at the south end of the lake
where a waterfall cascaded down into the Animas
River. Kyle drove past the scenic overlook that was to
be the point of his embarkation. With some luck, his
trek into the area should give him a good look at the

prevailing terrain and possible alternative points of entry. The steepness of the sloping mountainside reinforced Kyle's concerns about his abilities to traverse a path to his rendezvous at the fishing hole.

Using the private dirt road entrance to Electra Lake, Kyle turned his car around and headed back down the road but not before recognizing that this was also the front entrance to the Owen estate.

Returning to and parking in the scenic overlook area, Kyle kept his distance from the other vehicles. Setting the parking brake and double-checking that all lights and accessories were off, he stepped from the car and scanned the area, hoping not to attract any attention.

Slowly but deliberately he made his way to the rear of the car and opened the trunk to retrieve his tool kit. Unzipping the backpack, he made certain that all of the *tools* were there and in good working condition. Satisfied that all was in order, he hoisted the pack from the trunk, slipped the straps over his arms, and tightened them to a comfortable fit, all in one smooth motion. As he closed the trunk, a deep guttural voice startled him from his fixation on the mission.

"Good mornin', sir. Looks like 'ur plannin' to do a li'l hikin' today."

Kyle's head jerked around to locate the source of the deep southwestern drawl. A towering La Plata County sheriff standing next to his patrol car. He was a huge rugged-looking cowboy who reminded Kyle of one of his favorite movie actors, Fess Parker.

Quickly regaining his train of thought, Kyle responded, "Yes, I thought I would take advantage of this beautiful morning and get a little exercise while taking in the scenery."

The sheriff replied, "You picked the right day, sir; the weather boys are forecastin' thunner storms and rain fer the next few days . Have a nice day now, and yawl be careful. Thar's some ornery critters up this way."

"I certainly will, thanks." The sheriff walked away heading for the picnic area with his lunch in hand.

Walking briskly away from the officer, Kyle mused that he was going to have to jumpstart his heart after that short encounter. Reaching into the side pouch of the backpack, he removed the hand-held portable GPS and switched it on. A few seconds later, the magical device came to life, displaying a moving map of the area with an arrow pointing directly at his current position.

A path through the grass trampled by countless tourists was coincidentally heading in the same general direction Kyle was walking. He followed the path as it winded its way into the mountains. Immediately he could feel the muscles in his legs straining as they propelled him slowly up hill.

The air temperature was a few degrees cooler than it was in town thanks to the added elevation. As a general rule, the ambient air temperature decreased by three degrees for every thousand feet of altitude. The benefit of the pleasant temperature was quickly dissipating as the effects of the thinner air began to take its toll on Kyle's breathing. Proud of always maintaining a certain degree of physical fitness, something he never relinquished from his college football days, he knew his body would eventually acclimate to the altitude, and he would get his second wind.

The path began to narrow about a half mile from the parking area and eventually disappeared completely. Checking his GPS navigation, Kyle determined it was time to veer to the left and head in a more northerly direction. The terrain was steep but not impossible to traverse. At the two-mile mark, as displayed on his GPS, he took a short break for some water and a couple of energy bars. The exertion had Kyle sweating despite the cool air.

Continuing his trek up the side of the mountain, he could hear the sounds of the rushing waters of the Animas River, reassuring him that he was on course. Feeling pretty good, Kyle marveled at how fast his body had adjusted to the altitude. "I must be in better shape than I thought," he said in a self-aggrandizing tone.

Rudely interrupting his self-admiration, an unfamiliar noise startled him. Looking through the branches of the Aspen trees, he saw a small group of mule deer. Keeping an open eye for the dominant buck that laid claim to the females in the bunch, Kyle proceeded along his predetermined path. Still admiring himself for his physical prowess, he allowed himself to lose focus of his present task, and his right foot slipped off a mossy rock, twisting his ankle. The injury was not serious, but it did serve as a wake-up call to stay focused.

Finally reaching the area near Owen's fishing hole, Kyle could see the dirt road that led to the estate. Everything was exactly as it was supposed to be, along with every rock and tree, according to the reconnaissance reports; it was almost as if he had been there before.

Taking a position in a thicket of brush and Aspen trees about twenty yards from the spot where Russell Owen would most likely park his vehicle, Kyle made himself as comfortable and as invisible as possible. His ankle began to throb, but the pain was manageable. However, the twisted ankle combined with the cowboy sheriff's weather forecast had made Kyle rethink his plan.

He carefully removed the .30-06 survival rifle with ammunition from the backpack, along with the telescopic sight and silencer. The assembly of the weapon went as smoothly as it did the day he practiced with Sergeant Thibodaux. Setting the rifle off to one side, he then removed the .40 caliber semi-automatic handgun with its silencer and inserted a clip of fifteen hollow point bullets. Now the only thing to do was wait and see if Owen appeared as scheduled.

The climb up the mountain was strenuous yet exhilarating. Kyle could feel his heart pounding as he tried to sit quietly out of sight. Drinking some more water and eating another energy bar helped pass the time. Adrenaline was pumping through his entire body, and he knew he had to rein in his nervousness and regain his overall composure.

Without warning, a white Jeep Wrangler appeared on the road. An old four-wheel drive coated with mud from its wheels halfway up the body, with the convertible canvas top retracted. Kyle spied his first look at the huge man sitting behind the wheel. There was no mistaking that this was Russell Owen. The massive ex-football player jumped from the driver's seat with surprising agility.

Owen spent the next ten minutes assembling his fishing gear and choosing the perfect fly for the day's lure. He slipped into his chest-high wading boots, reached into his Coleman cooler, and proceeded to chug down three cans of beer in quick succession. Kyle glanced at his watch in amazement; the man was chugging beer at ten o'clock in the morning.

Finishing the last drink, Owen tossed the empty can into the back seat of the Jeep, along with the others. Lumbering into the swift moving river, he began to cast his lure, hoping to entice a large speckled Rocky Mountain trout. The noise of the swift river colliding with the rocks in the stream gave Kyle the advantage of remaining undetected.

Carefully reaching for the rifle, Kyle raised the weapon and placed the padded end of the stock firmly onto the front of his right shoulder. The safety was still engaged to prevent any inadvertent discharges of his weapon. The tactical telescopic sight came to life with the flick of a switch. Focusing the sight on his intended target, he could see the image of a red dot positioned squarely in the middle of Owen's back.

Concentrating on the target, Kyle thought he saw something move off to his right. Snapping his head around to identify the source of his distraction, he discovered a branch of an Aspen tree swaying in the breeze. Returning his attention to Owen, Kyle swung his head toward the river, inadvertently jabbing a small branch into the corner of his right eye, his dominant eye, the eye he used for aiming. The initial pain was severe, and the eye began to tear profusely—everything was a total blur.

The minutes passed like hours as Kyle tried to relax his eye. Each time he raised the rifle and peered through the scope, his eye would water. He decided to attempt a shot using his left eye, something he only had practiced a few times. He brought the rifle up to his left shoulder and pointed it directly at the target. Looking through the telescopic sight, the image of the red dot was once again in clear focus and dead center on Owen's back.

Taking one last deep breath, he released the safety from the rifle and focused the red dot on the target. Only one more step was necessary—to gently squeeze the trigger. He briefly thought of the irony of shooting a human with a hunting rifle when he could never see himself as a hunter shooting a defenseless wild animal. Wiping his face, he placed the gun in its proper position on his left shoulder. Looking through the scope his target was in view again.

Russell Owen was midway into his cast; the small lure was just snapping forward from the backstroke, zeroing in on its landing zone. Quickly wiping the perspiration from his cheek, Kyle blinked one more time and took a deep breath. Refocusing his vision through the scope for the last time, terror shot through his entire being. The target, Russell Owen, had disappeared from view.

Resetting the safety, he lowered the rifle in search of his target. Russell Owen had vanished. Fighting back the myriad of emotions ravaging his psyche, Kyle listened and stared intently, trying to pick up any clue that would give away Owen's location. Slowly emerging from his seclusion within the thicket of brush, Kyle could not believe his eyes.

# CHAPTER THIRTY-FIVE

"Joe, something's not right. Kyle almost trampled me as he limped his way back to the overlook and his car. Thankfully, I had enough time to position myself under a pile of branches and leaves, and he walked right over the top of me. I couldn't see what happened to Owen; all I know is that Kyle wasn't having a good day."

"What do you mean he wasn't having a good day? What the hell is he doing out there?"

"I thought he was using the first day for reconnaissance? I followed him up the mountain, watched him take up a position, and the next thing I saw through my binoculars was Kyle preparing his weapons. I didn't take mine out of the car. I didn't think I'd need them today. I'm going to shadow him and try to stay out of sight. I'm on my satellite phone; I'll call you when I'm sure I have a secure line."

"OK, Gina. Take care of our boy and call me as soon as you can."

To Gina's surprise, Kyle casually strolled back to his vehicle and drove back down the mountainside to

Durango. He stopped at the local A&W Root Beer restaurant directly across from his motel.

Sitting in her rental car, Gina studied Kyle through her binoculars and watched in amazement as he downed a half dozen *taquitos* and a large root beer in a frosty mug. Completely befuddled, she figured nothing else would take place as darkness began to cover the valley, so she returned to her room. The parking valet greeted her at the front door of the Strater Hotel.

"Good evening, madam. Did you have nice day?"

"Yes, I had a very interesting day." Gina handed the car keys to the valet and then quickly walked through the beautiful lobby of the 1880s Victorian-style hotel.

Connecting her satellite phone to her laptop, Gina was able to scramble any conversations she might have that evening. "Joe, I'm back in my room now. I can see by the GPS chip you put in Kyle's tool kit that he's back at his motel. I'm sure we're done for the day."

"Good, get some rest and call me first thing in the morning."

"Will do, I programmed my computer's alarm to sound if he starts to move."

Rudely awakened by the sound of blaring sirens echoing off the mountains, emanating from the local fire brigade, Gina jumped from her bed. Startled but aware of her surroundings, she cleared her head and checked on Kyle's location.

According to the hidden GPS chip, he was still at his motel. Quickly showering and grabbing a cup of coffee to go, Gina joined the group of people standing on the sidewalk observing the actions of the local fire and police departments.

Rumors passed through the crowd that a body had washed up on the bank of the Animas River, right in the heart of downtown Durango. Confused and concerned, Gina worried about Kyle. As she tried to get a closer look at the action, she found it difficult to get past the police barricades.

Straining to look over the heads of the people in front of her, Gina felt a slight nudge on her left arm and heard the apologetic voice of the man who had bumped into her. She glanced up and watched the man continue down the sidewalk, making his way across the street to a motel. A heart-stopping fright ran through Gina. It was Kyle. He obviously didn't get a good look at her face in all the chaos.

Pushing her way through the crowd, she made her way back to her hotel. Unsure of what had just transpired, she decided to wait in her room and monitor Kyle with the GPS.

Suddenly the alarm on her computer began to beep. She watched the movement of the GPS chip as it made its way westbound on Route 160 toward Cortez, Colorado, Mesa Verde National Park, and the four corners area.

"Joe, what do you want me to do? It looks like he's heading back to his plane."

"Not to worry. Pack up your things and head on back. I just got off the phone with one of my contacts at the FBI. I guess our boy finished the job. The body pulled from the Animas River was Russell Owen."

# CHAPTER THIRTY-SIX

"Mr. Delasandro, this is Jimmy Wooden from IT. If you have a minute, could you please come down to the lab? Bruce Goldstein found something interesting on some of the footage we have from that incident on Marco Island."

"Sure, give me two minutes," responded Joe.

"Mr. D., I think we came across something that narrows down the field of possible shooters. Here, take a look at the very beginning of the sequence. We've been so interested in the main event that we completely missed this." Jimmy pressed play and the video began. "There it is—did you see that?"

Joe shook his head and said, "No. What am I looking for?"

Jimmy sequenced the footage back to the beginning. "Now watch very closely. Here's our shooter sneaking up to the Sumner estate. At first we thought he was having trouble walking through the soft deep sand on the adjacent property, but as he stepped onto Sumner's patio it became very clear…he has a definite limp. Something's wrong with his left leg."

"Oh, now I see it," said Joe.

"Mr. D., there's more. Our boy stands straight up, almost at attention, when he fires his final shot. This gave us a reference point on guessing his height. Based on the size of the hibiscus tree next to the patio, the height of the umbrella covering the table, and the dimensions of the sliding glass doors in the background, we figure the shooter is approximately six foot four inches, but no more than six feet six. Unless Kyle recently sprung up two inches and recovered from what looked like a serious limp, I think we can scratch his name off the list."

# CHAPTER THIRTY-SEVEN

C hecking with the Denver flight service station before taking off from Cortez Municipal Airport, Kyle requested a full weather briefing, including a winds-aloft forecast. A quick synopsis of the weather showed that high-pressure systems dominated the eastern two-thirds of the continent, and the prevailing winds were directly out of the west.

After takeoff, Kyle pointed the nose of the TBM toward the sky and climbed to flight level two-seven-zero, (twenty-seven thousand feet). Taking advantage of the strong westerly winds, the single-engine turbo-prop airplane comfortably settled in with an impressive ground speed of more than 300 knots.

Departing with his fuel tanks only half full, the climb performance of the plane was greatly increased due to the overall lighter weight of the airplane. The only drawback was that Kyle would have to stop for fuel sooner. However, the helpful tailwind put hundreds of miles between Kyle, the four corners area, and the dead body of Russell Owen before making his only fuel stop in Overland Park, Kansas.

While the fuel tanks were being filled, Kyle called Tina to tell her that his itinerary had changed and he would be getting home around three o'clock in the morning. He didn't want to startle her with an unexpected noise. "Don't wait up for me; it'll be too late. We'll talk in the morning." After grabbing a quick sandwich and a couple of candy bars from a vending machine, he paid for the fuel and was airborne, nonstop to Virginia.

His right eye and ankle were still sore, and he hoped Tina wouldn't notice anything when he arrived home. Unfortunately, he also knew that Tina was very observant when it involved him; she was intimately familiar with every square inch of his muscular frame. During the flight home, he tried to concoct a story to cover his injuries.

Arriving home as planned, he tried not to make noise and wake Tina, so he opted to sleep on the couch. She got up at her usual time and made her way to the kitchen to start the coffee. Seeing Kyle asleep on the couch, she tiptoed, trying to be as quiet as possible, to no avail. Kyle was such a light sleeper that he awoke with the first sounds of the hot water dripping through the coffee maker.

Sitting in the kitchen, Tina wore a big smile and very little else in anxious anticipation of seeing her favorite guy. The sash around the purple satin kimono she had purchased in Tokyo while on layover with Kyle many years ago was loosely tied, coquettishly concealing her sensuous figure.

Looking up from her morning paper, shocked by what she saw, she shouted, "What the hell happened to you?" Her smile transformed into a frown of concern. Her reaction caught Kyle completely off guard. Her expression was enough to startle him, but the use of the word "hell" really threw him for a loop. Tina seldom cursed.

Panicked and frantic to come up with something to say, Kyle stuttered, hemmed and hawed, and stalled for a few precious seconds, hoping to regain is composure. Recalling his concocted explanation from the night before, he said, "If you promise not to laugh, I'll tell you what happened.

"While I was doing the pre-flight exterior inspection of the plane, I momentarily got distracted by the sounds of a World War Two fighter plane taxiing for takeoff. It was my favorite plane, the P51 Mustang, D model. After watching it leap into the sky and disappear from view, I turned to finish the inspection and bumped into the trailing edge flaps of the wing. My eye began to water, and I then tripped over the chocks tucked in around the main landing gear and twisted my ankle."

Tina's shock turned into full-on laughter. "I'm sorry, I shouldn't laugh, but I wish I could have seen that. You must have looked hilarious. I hope you can work up a better excuse than that before Joe sees you. He'll have a field day with this one." It appeared that the story had worked; however, once again, Kyle felt a twinge of guilt for lying to Tina. He justified his actions by reminding himself that it was out of his love for her.

"I'm glad you're home. I have an appointment with Dr. Berman tomorrow. It's time for the second treatment. If all goes well with this one, she plans on increasing the dosage and frequency next week."

"OK, I'll make time to drive you to her office. I can be back at IRC by noon."

# CHAPTER THIRTY-EIGHT

After finishing his morning routine, he headed for the office. First thing on his agenda was to get a cup of coffee. Stepping into the cafeteria, he walked in on Diane Bishop talking to Joe's secretary, Karen Mallett. Kyle tried to act nonchalant as he made his way to the coffeepot, hoping neither of them would notice his blood-shot eye or his swollen ankle. The ladies said good morning and departed for their posts. He thought to himself, *They didn't notice a thing*. He couldn't have been more wrong. Within seconds Joe Delasandro stormed into the cafeteria bellowing, "Let me see that face. And why are you limping?"

Kyle proceeded to fill Joe in on the details of his trip. Hearing about the sprained ankle and the sharp stick in the eye, Joe could hardly contain himself and started laughing. "I'm not laughing at you; I'm laughing with you. No, that's not true, I *am* laughing at you. Regardless of all the trouble, it appears you completed the job."

"Yes and no," said Kyle. "The job is done, but I never fired a shot; albeit the end result was the same."

"But our people in that region reported that the La Plata County sheriffs found Owen's body as he floated into downtown Durango."

"I guess that's true, but I didn't do it. The fast-moving Animas River swept Russell Owen off his feet and dragged him downstream. His chest-high wading boots quickly filled with water, making it impossible to swim, and the three cans of beer he chugged probably didn't help much. My high school lifeguard training kicked in and my first instinct was to rush over and try to save him.

"Watching a man drown and not attempting to help was harder than shooting him." Kyle continued to describe the monumental struggle for life and his awe of Owen's strength. Finally, the powerful river won the battle and claimed its prize. I limped back to my car, my eye throbbing and watering and my ankle screaming at me."

"Well, that's one down and one to go, or more accurately, two down and one to go if you include your old boss Sumner. While you were gone, I had a slight run-in with that son-of-a-bitch Sheppard. Somehow he heard that Tina started her treatments with Dr. Berman. He cornered me and complained that he wanted both sanctions completed before Tina could enroll in the program. That was the only way he felt you could be reliable and trustworthy enough to join our inner circle. I quickly reminded him that the rest of the board members were not happy with his use of extortion, and if he was smart, he would keep his mouth shut from now on."

"Do you think he's going to be trouble for us?"

"He's always been a royal pain in the ass, but we have to live with him for now. He still carries some clout at the Pentagon."

"I have to take Tina to see Berman tomorrow; she's getting her second treatment. I'll be back to the office by noon. I'd like to start planning the job in Wisconsin if you have some time."

As planned, Kyle was back in the office by noon the next day. "How'd everything go with the treatment?" Joe asked.

"Perfect, no side effects or reactions of any kind. I think Berman is going to start increasing the dosages and frequencies next week. If all goes well, she wants to schedule a follow-up series of exams in about three weeks to see if the serum is having any effect on the tumors. We just have to keep our fingers crossed that it's doing its thing and training her white blood cells to attack those foreign tissues."

"Kyle, here are the files on Dr. James Morgan. I'm hesitant to give them to you because I'm considering going to the board and outsourcing this last sanction. Without question, you have fulfilled your end of the agreement."

"No. Don't do that. I made a deal with you and the board, and I always live up to my end of the bargain. Besides, I don't want to give Sheppard any room to complain or cause trouble for you. I'll see this through," Kyle answered.

"OK, but I wish you would reconsider. However, knowing you the way I do, there is very little chance of that happening. You're a rare breed, Kyle Donnar; there aren't too many people in this world that still know the meaning of the word integrity. One of these days, I need to figure out what makes you tick."

"Thanks, Joe. That means a lot to me."

"Well, about Morgan… our intel shows that he will be out of the country for another month. He's touring Europe with his latest girlfriend; I don't think the ink was dry on his divorce papers before he already had a sweet young showpiece hanging on his arm. I guess there really is a direct relationship between the size of a guys bank account and how attractive he is to the girls.

"Here, look at the latest reconnaissance photos. That's him—the guy with the horrible comb-over hairstyle and thick glasses; I guess you would call those six pubic hairs under his nose a mustache. I swear he must be cultivating the hair in his left ear to use in the comb-over."

"I just don't understand, with all his money you would think he might invest in a good toupee or maybe even a hair transplant. That comb-over has got to go," Kyle added.

Joe continued "his divorce was particularly nasty. His ex-wife raked him over the coals and received a hefty settlement. The two of them were overheard threatening to kill each other during the trial.

"When he returns from Europe, he'll be spending the rest of the summer and fall at his home on Washington Island, just off the tip of Door County, Wisconsin. He learned to fly a helicopter a few years ago and bought a Hughes 500 model that he uses to get on and off the island. The hangar on the island property is just large enough for the chopper. When in residence at his home in DePere, a suburb of Green Bay, he keeps his company jet and the chopper in a private facility at Austin Straubel International Airport.

The only way on and off the island is by boat or airplane. The island has a short grass runway, not ideal for the TBM, but there's a ferry that runs from Gills Rock, right at the tip of the peninsula. Unfortunately, it's very public, and it diminishes your ability to come and go unnoticed. I'm looking into alternate transportation to and from the island for you, something a little less obvious."

"Thanks for all of your help, Joe. I appreciate it. I'll use the time until Morgan gets back in the country to study up, and maybe between you and I, we can come up with a viable plan that doesn't injure, maim, or kill me in the process. The timing is good regarding Tina's treatment schedule, too. We should know if the serum is working before I have to leave. For now I'll just get back to my regular job trying to run this flight department." Kyle paused, but before Joe could respond, he added, "You know a lot about me, but I don't know anything about you. Before we start to explore what makes me tick, I gotta know how you got involved with all of this?"

# CHAPTER THIRTY-NINE

---

"Whoa, now that's a long story. Trust me when I tell you it's not very exciting so I'll try to summarize it so as not to bore you with the minutia. I grew up in the Italian North End of Boston. Like your beautiful wife, my parents came over from the Old Country with a few lire in their pockets and started a new life. I guess that's one of the reasons I feel so strongly about making sure Tina beats this cancer thing.

"The summer after graduating from high school, I was walking home late after my shift at a restaurant, when the local bully, Richie Columbo, and a couple of his stooges started fuckin' with me. I could tell they were either drunk or high on something, and I knew it wouldn't end peacefully.

"One thing I learned early on as a kid growing up in the city was that my best chance to walk away from one of these situations was to make sure I put down the biggest and toughest guy first. If you can do that, the other punks usually run for home.

"Well, that particular night ole Richie was really putting on the show for his buddies and stepped in a little too close for my comfort. You only have to be sucker-punched once in your life to know never to let anyone within arm's reach of you.

"Richie turned toward his stooges and made a face. I couldn't see his expression, but I learned later that he was sticking out his tongue, probably mocking me in some way. I figured he was goin' to sucker punch me as he turned back to face me. To his surprise, I didn't wait. I came through with an upper cut to his chin. I could hear his teeth breaking, and he dropped like a sack of bricks.

"Before his buddies realized what had happened, I had a one-hundred-yard head start and never looked back. Unfortunately, the next morning the cops showed up at my front door with a warrant for my arrest. I guess my upper cut did more damage than I thought. Not only did I knock out his front teeth but the punch caused him to bite off half his tongue, too. Ever since that night, Richie could never speak clearly, and the neighborhood referred to him as Richie "Mumbles" Columbo."

"You've gotta be kidding me, *Mumbles Columbo*?" Kyle repeated while laughing. "As the old saying goes, the truth is funnier than fiction."

"I appeared in court, accused of picking a fight with the three of them. The judge had no choice but to find me guilty of assault, but he was pretty clever. He knew about Richie's family ties with the syndicate boys and gave me a choice: pay a fine and take my chances on the streets of Boston or enlist in the military where the wise guys would have a harder time getting to me. I chose the Marine Corps and wound up in the jungles of Vietnam where the odds of survival were much better for me than in Bean Town.

"It turned out that I had a knack with weapons. I was very good with the standard-issue rifles and handguns. I tested extremely high on aptitude tests and showed leadership qualities. The Marines then gave me the opportunity to *volunteer* for special duty. I did some sniper work and actually got to work with some of the military's most famous snipers in Nam. Those guys racked up so many confirmed kills of high-ranking officers that the North Vietnam government put out bounties for anyone who could eliminate them.

"From sniping in the jungles, I was summoned for intelligence work, hence my work with the CIA after I mustered out of the Corps. I received an invitation to join the Masons, which led to the episode in Central America where you saved my ass and then on to IRC after Propaganda Due disappeared. So there you have it in a nutshell. Any questions? Oh and by the way, I don't know everything about you, like I said, one of these days I'm gonna find out what makes you tick. You still haven't told me anything about the face in the photo from the Sumner incident on Marco. You say it's not you, but you refuse to give up any info about the guy."

"Joe, you're just going to have to live with the fact that I live by my own code of honor—period!"

# CHAPTER FORTY

Two weeks had quickly passed since Kyle returned from the four corners area. Catching up on paperwork for the flight department, scheduling future trips, learning everything he could about Dr. James Morgan and his company Health Options, while continuing to chauffeur Tina to and from Georgetown for her treatments occupied all of his time.

Tina received her three injections per week, with ever-increasing dosages and no apparent adverse side effects. Dr. Berman felt it was time to schedule a complete exam: MRI, blood work, CAT scans, full gynecological exam, and anything else that might unveil any progress since the start of the therapy. Tina and Kyle impatiently waited for that day.

Reviewing the dossier on James Morgan, it became apparent that this sanction was going to be a challenge due to the logistics of getting on and off the island. The options were to use public transportation, such as the ferryboat, or find a suitable small airplane that could land and take off from the short grass runway, or even use a small boat like a kayak.

He quickly put to rest the thought of using a small boat due to the dangerous waters around the island. The narrow passage between the tip of the Door County Peninsula and Washington Island was only three miles wide, a slice of awe-inspiring beauty with Lake Michigan to the east and Green Bay to the west. The passage could be extremely turbulent because of the unpredictable currents and sudden gusts of wind from the Great Lakes.

The Native Americans from the region referred to the passage as the "Door of Death." Later, French explorers translated it to Porte des Morts. Legend has it that in 1872, the unpredictable currents damaged or stranded more than one hundred large vessels navigating through the Door. With the memories of his not-so-stellar performance in the Rocky Mountains still fresh in his mind, Kyle continued to research alternate forms of transportation.

Joe knocked on Kyle's office door and invited him to go to lunch. The two men decided to head for the usual place, the crew hangout near the airport. Opting for their favorite corner table, as far as possible from the crowd huddled near the bar. Gina, back from her trip to southwest Colorado, had previously received her debriefing from Joe and had a hard time not smiling at Kyle as she delivered two beers to their table as they settled into the chairs.

"Word has come down that our money people, the Gnomes, are pleased with the results of your work. They're especially happy with the end result of your recent adventure, making it look like an accident. They're confident the message has gone out loud and clear to the appropriate people. Anyone trying to connect this administration's willingness to obstruct justice, along with their pay-to-play politics, will quickly learn to keep their mouths shut. The Russell Owen thing, right on top of the Sumner assassination, has created quite a stir.

"The hypocrisies of this administration appear to have no boundaries. As far as we know, the courts and federal judges *did* intervene for these guys on orders from above. It wouldn't be the first time something like that had happened. We do what we're told, and in the end you and Tina will hopefully retire to your corner of paradise. This last one, whether appearing deliberate or an accident will definitely be headline news."

"So, what you're you saying is: Eliminating these guys is just a form of sending a message? Does it have to be a quiet execution or will bloody and gory be OK?" Kyle asked sarcastically.

"Our money people want to see this administration get a second term in the White House; the message has to be loud and clear: keep quiet or else. We got the lousy job of being the messenger. Now you see why I didn't want you to get involved at this level of our organization."

"Well, I'm in too deep to quit now. I have a job to finish. Let's talk about the first problem: how to get on the island."

The two men discussed different scenarios for getting on and off the island, weighing the pros and cons of each method. Nothing was as safe and reliable as the public ferryboat. The ferry schedule this time of year allowed for numerous opportunities to transit the dangerous waters. Kyle could blend in with the other tourists and even rent a bicycle for transportation on the island.

The plan was beginning to take shape but would need refining before the actual trip. The next problem was the job itself. This one had to look suspicious enough to raise a few questions, essentially sending a message.

Pouring over his notes, Kyle seemed to think that he might have an opportunity if he could catch Morgan in the hangar behind the house as he tucked the helicopter away for the day. Joe agreed, so they concentrated on the hangar for scenario number one. Other scenarios just didn't seem to add up or make sense. The hours passed, and the men decided to call it quits for the day and head home.

The next day, while looking over the dossier on Dr. James Morgan, Kyle recognized a definite pattern in Morgan's daily activities. On the days when the weather was nice enough to fly his helicopter to work, Morgan followed a rigid preflight routine. The kind of routine Kyle had been teaching student pilots for decades. Here was the opening. Kyle knew without a doubt every step Morgan would take. The plan seemed to come together.

He needed to prepare for back-up scenarios, just in case the weather didn't cooperate and Morgan stayed at his home in De Pere. But Joe was satisfied with Kyle's planning and wanted a little more time to make sure they had covered all of the bases.

Kyle and Tina had a scheduled appointment in Georgetown early the next day. Before leaving IRC for home, Kyle stopped in Joe's office to hand him his notes and let him know about Tina's appointment.

"Good luck tomorrow. I'm sure that when the test results come back, you'll have good news."

"Thanks, Joe. I sure hope so. I'll keep you in the loop if there are any changes to my schedule."

Tina and Kyle were sitting in Dr. Berman's office by 9:00 a.m. Dr. Berman had arrived only a few minutes earlier. "Are you ready to get this day started, Tina?" Dr. Berman asked.

Tina nodded and replied, "Let's get it done."

Kyle followed Tina through the hospital as she made her way from test to test and exam to exam. By the time she was finished, Tina was exhausted and wanted to go home and cuddle up on the sofa with Kyle.

The ride home took longer than expected; rush hour traffic had all of the main roads clogged, and the sea of cars barely moved. Tina fell asleep in the reclined passenger seat of their SUV. With no one to talk to, Kyle's thoughts bounced back and forth between his assignment and the grueling wait for the results of Tina's tests. Would he hear the results before he left for Wisconsin, or would the delayed results cloud his mind and cause him problems?

Arriving home, Tina felt the car come to a stop and opened her eyes before Kyle had to wake her. They walked into the house and exchanged their clothes for what they referred to as their uniforms—a pair of sweat pants, an oversized tee shirt, and flip flops. Taking up their usual positions, the television came to life. One of their favorite movies—*Casablanca*—was just starting on the classic movie channel. Kyle hurried to the kitchen to microwave a couple of bowls of popcorn and returned just in time to catch the opening scene, popcorn and sodas in hand.

The next morning he stopped by the company hangar on the way to the office to help the flight crews prepare for the day's scheduled trips. To his surprise, Joe was just pulling out of the parking lot as Kyle drove in. This wasn't completely unusual; Joe would show up from time to time to greet dignitaries who took advantage of IRC's fleet of planes.

The beautiful machines with their high-gloss Imron paint reflecting the sun's rays partially blinded Kyle as they taxied away from the hangar. Departing right on schedule, Kyle marveled at the fact that this was *his* fleet of planes, this was *his* flight department. With nothing else to do, he got back in his car and headed for the office.

Joe was waiting for him with freshly made coffee. "Sorry I didn't have time to stay and talk at the hangar; I had to get back here to take an important call."

"No problem, I was just a little surprised to see you at the airport today." They quickly jumped into the planning of Kyle's trip to Porte des Morts.

Kyle noticed a file labeled "Icarus Protocol" sitting on Joe's desk. "What's the Icarus Protocol?"

Joe laughed and replied, "It's not what but who. The *who* is you. You should know by now that nothing in this line of work can exist without a code name. You can thank Dr. Levin and Buck Buckwalter for this one. The rest of the board agreed."

"Even Sheppard?" Kyle asked.

"No, we didn't ask him for his opinion. I think his days are numbered here."

"Icarus? Couldn't you guys come up with something better than that? Hell, in Greek Mythology, Icarus was the guy who ended up crashing into the sea with his father when the wax on their wings began to melt. I'm surprised you didn't use a name like Kiwi or Emu or some other flightless bird. Actually, dodo, a large flightless *extinct* bird would be apropos."

# CHAPTER FORTY-ONE

Impatiently awaiting the results of Tina's tests was shear torture for Kyle.

The hours ticked away slowly, feeling more like days. The days dragged on like weeks. Tina handled the wait much better than Kyle. She went about her daily routine of shopping and keeping the house neat and clean. When she wasn't busy with her usual jobs, she would call her friends on Marco Island and spend time catching up on island gossip. Finally, one afternoon, the phone rang. Dr. Berman was on the other end of the line. "Hello, Tina. It's Dr. Berman. How are you feeling?"

"Actually I'm feeling pretty good, thanks."

"We have just received the last of the reports from the diagnostics we performed. I'd like to go over the results with you."

"That would be great, Doctor. Do I have time to get Kyle on the phone so he can listen. I'll need just a few minutes to set up the three-way call."

"No problem. Take your time; I'll be right here."

A couple of minutes later, Tina had Kyle and Dr. Berman on the phone at the same time. "OK, Doctor. Go ahead; I've got Kyle on the phone."

"Good morning, Kyle. I called Tina this morning to give her the preliminary results of the tests we took last week. The MRI and the X-rays were the first results to come back. Drs. Miller and Clayton studied the images with me. Taking into consideration that you have only been on this particular protocol for about a month, realistically we weren't expecting to see much of a difference. We took special care to accurately measure the tumors, looking for the slightest changes in shape, size, or position.

"Dr. Clayton was the first to notice something. His measurements were showing a small but definite decrease in the tissue mass of some of the larger tumors. We checked and rechecked his findings and concluded that he was correct—some of the larger tumors have definitely decreased in size."

"That's great news!" Kyle couldn't help but interrupt the doctor.

"Yes, of course we were excited by the findings, but we really needed to see the results of the blood work. Unfortunately, due to a large volume of emergency patients admitted to the hospital, the blood work took longer than expected. It finally arrived late yesterday.

"I took the liberty of reviewing the results before contacting Drs. Miller and Clayton. I looked specifically for the results of the CA-125 cancer antigen levels. If you remember, this was the test that led Dr. Clayton to identify your unique type of cancer in the first place. The results showed a decrease in the levels of CA-125.

I called Drs. Miller and Clayton with the good news. Needless to say they were elated, too. I think we are off to a great start, but until we rid your body of these tumors completely, we are not out of the woods."

"Oh, Dr. Berman, that is the best news we've had in a long while," Tina gushed.

"There is no question that we definitely have to continue the injection protocol, and we will increase the frequency and dosage as discussed. We don't want to give these cancer cells any chance of regrouping and coming back stronger. With this type of therapy, if the cancerous cells reform, there is a possibility that they could mutate and render the serum ineffective."

Tina was elated and thanked Dr. Berman again and again. While Tina and the doctor discussed future treatments, Kyle sat quietly on the other end of the line, silently fighting back his tears of joy. There was no way he could so much as murmur a single sound for fear that they would hear the emotion in his voice. The two ladies continued their conversation long enough for Kyle to regain his composure.

"OK, that wraps up the good news and our future plans. Do either of you have any more questions for me?"

"No, thank you. I think I'm set," Tina said.

"Great. Then I will see you for the next round of treatment tomorrow."

After disconnecting the three-way call, Tina hurriedly recalled Kyle. They talked for over an hour, sharing thoughts and dreams and future plans, topics she had put on hold since receiving her original diagnosis.

Kyle shared the good news with Mrs. Bishop and made his way down the hall to Joe's office, keeping his promise to share any new information. Kyle didn't have the words to express his gratitude to Joe for getting Tina into one of the clandestine test programs. Joe reassured Kyle that thanks wasn't necessary, for it was he who owed Kyle.

While they continued to discuss the details surrounding Tina's situation, the phone rang, interrupting them in mid-sentence. Mrs. Mallet informed Joe that this was the call he had been anxiously awaiting. Kyle turned to leave, but Joe motioned for him to stay and wait. The conversation was one-sided, with Joe nodding his head and finally saying, "I see, thanks."

Joe looked up at Kyle and said in an apologetic tone, "I'm sorry to rain on your good news today, but I was just informed that Dr. Morgan has returned to his home in De Pere, Wisconsin. We have to finish our planning and get you on your way before he decides to take another vacation." Kyle agreed and returned to his office to finalize his itinerary.

As usual, the reconnaissance teams did a thorough job. The combination of their notes, photos, and satellite imaging of the area enabled Kyle to virtually put himself on Washington Island and memorize every rock, tree, and road leading to and from the Morgan estate.

The property around the estate had a perfectly manicured lawn, with beautifully sculptured shrubbery lining the walkways. A combination of oak and sugar maple trees outlined the perimeter of the estate, with stately blue spruce pines standing perfectly spaced apart, paralleling the driveway leading from the main road to the circular driveway in the front of the mansion.

You could access the compound from the main road through the thick growth of trees around the perimeter, or you could approach from the rear of the property, climbing up a thirty-foot embankment rising from the water's edge. Wooden stairs from the rear deck cascaded down the embankment to the rocky beach. Kyle would have to make his decision after observing the pulse of the island.

While he studied the layout of the island and all of the details of the estate, a photo of Dr. James Morgan attached to a short biography sat off to the side. Kyle glanced at it from time to time, as though it was daring him to take a good look into the eyes of his next target.

Succumbing to the power of the photo, Kyle picked up the biography and tried to understand what would possess a successful doctor to risk his life's achievements in order to become even richer. How much was enough?

Here was a man who had enjoyed a privileged childhood. His father was a renowned orthopedic surgeon in the Green Bay area and had treated many of the most famous football players in Green Bay Packer history. Morgan had attended private schools, had driven the finest automobiles, and had traveled around the world with his parents—he had wanted for nothing.

Obligated to follow his father's example, James Morgan attended medical school at the University of Wisconsin in Madison. Graduating near the top of his class, Morgan had the option to specialize in the medical discipline of his liking. His father, of course, tried to influence him into orthopedics, but he chose to become a research scientist. He wanted to be the first doctor to find the cures for all of the dreadful diseases that plagued the earth. The decision created a rift between his father and himself, one that festered beyond the death of the elder Morgan.

The younger Dr. Morgan spent his entire professional life trying to prove that his work was just as worthwhile and meaningful as repairing the torn up knee of a superstar athlete. Regardless of the numerous patents granted to Morgan for miracle drugs that improved the lives of people around the world, his father always dismissed his work as not practicing *real* medicine.

The only way Morgan could demonstrate his success was to flaunt his lavish lifestyle. He had become extremely rich through selling his patents to large drug companies. Unfortunately, the more money he accumulated, the more money he wanted. Money was his way of keeping score.

Taking control at the health care giant Health Options, Morgan used his brilliance to purloin funds from the corporation while falsifying the accounting. His scheme worked for a while—until an insider placed a call to the federal government.

The indictments that followed were based on violations of federal statutes, which conveniently put his trial in the federal courts. Hundreds of former Health Options employees attended the trial, hoping to see the tyrannical monster—the person responsible for the loss of the retirement accounts and pensions of hundreds of thousands of people—go to jail for the rest of his life. A former Health Options employee who was interviewed outside of the courthouse regretted that Morgan's wrongdoings were not capital crimes punishable by death. This employee had no way of knowing how prophetic his statement was.

To the disappointment of the employees, James Morgan eventually walked away a free man. The judge in the case hogtied the prosecutor's arguments, disallowing most of the damaging evidence. It became apparent that the fix was in, and there wasn't much anyone could do about it. As soon as the trial was over, Dr. James Morgan began to spout off about how a person with a few well-placed political contributions could literally get away with murder. Without saying, the administration in Washington DC had to shut this guy up before someone started to take him seriously. The Gnomes of Zurich agreed to take action not just because they cared about the current president in the White House and thought it would be good for their business if he got a second term but also because they had lost hundreds of millions of dollars after falling prey to Morgan's greed.

Getting ready to wrap things up for the day, Kyle reflected on how corporate greed was responsible for destroying and tearing apart families. The pathetic part was that the politicians on both sides of the aisle in Washington really didn't care, as long as they received their share of the pie.

Before leaving for the day, Kyle stopped by Joe's office to hand off his itinerary and proposed scenarios for accomplishing the mission. Joe interrupted Kyle's report, making one suggestion.

"I know you can get the job done using the same tool kit we put together for your trip to Durango, but I'd like to add one more item. Trust me; what I have for you will fit nicely into your backpack.

"Gunnery Sergeant Bobby James Thibodaux is on his way here. I hope you don't mind hanging around for a few more minutes. I think you'll like what he has for you."

"Sure, no problem," Kyle answered. "But while we're waiting, I just wanted to let you know that Tina is scheduled for another round of treatments tomorrow, so I'll be taking the morning off. If all goes well, I plan to leave for Door County the following day."

"Kyle, we've gotta talk. I'm a little concerned, no, let me rephrase that, I'm a lot concerned. I've dealt with many type A personalities in my life. Some real hard charging individuals while I was in the Corps, as well as some of the not so savory types we usually contract to handle situations like this. Never have I come across anyone like you."

"What are you talking about when you say someone like me? Have I done something wrong, is the flight department not being managed the way you'd like? Is there anything else I should be doing for IRC? Tell me, please."

"No, no, no, don't misinterpret what I'm saying. You're doing a great job here, we couldn't be happier, and by we, I mean the board of directors excluding Sheppard of course, our real bosses, the Gnomes of Zurich, and me.

"General Buckwalter and I have discussed this and we just can't come up with any answers. Starting with the night you pulled my carcass from a mud hole, picked up a weapon and started returning fire on the enemy as though it was just another day at work.

I know your professional history. You've faced adversity, disappointments, and the premature ending of your dream job and yet, you keep picking yourself up off the floor and

moving on. Thanks to that idiot Sheppard you're forced into a situation where most people would have run as fast as they could to get as far away as possible. But not you. After your initial flare up it's been business as usual. I've got to know before you leave for Door County, what drives you. What demons within you keep you moving forward, like a shark in the ocean that has to keep swimming for fear of drowning."

"Sergeant Thibodaux is here to see you Mr. Delasandro," Mrs. Mallet announced over the intercom.

# CHAPTER FORTY-TWO

All went well with Tina's visit to Dr. Berman. Kyle stayed with her the rest of the day, just to make sure there were no adverse side effects with the higher dosage she was now receiving.

Staying true to the plan, Kyle departed early the next morning for his rendezvous with Dr. James Morgan, just as the sun began its assent in the East. Morning fog blanketed the quaint towns nestled in the valleys between the Appalachian, Shenandoah, and Allegheny Mountains. The flight took off directly to the northwest, tracking over West Virginia and Ohio, crossing Lake Erie, and continuing on past Detroit to the northernmost tip of the state of Michigan.

The Mackinac Bridge connected lower Michigan to the scenic upper peninsula, known affectionately as the U. P. Kyle chose to cross Lake Michigan almost directly over the bridge to minimize his time over open water while flying in a single-engine airplane.

This route allowed Kyle a view of all five of the Great Lakes as he traveled along his predetermined flight path. As he crossed the western tip of Lake Erie, he could look to the east and get a glimpse of Lake

Ontario near Toronto. From there, as he flew through Detroit airspace, he could see Lake Huron at his two o'clock position. He would eventually make his way to the northern tip of Michigan and cross over the Straits of Mackinac. Seeing the enormity of Lake Michigan and Lake Superior from this vantage point was awe-inspiring. A person could easily see how early explorers might have thought they stumbled upon the Pacific Ocean.

Always staying within gliding range of the shore-line, Kyle turned to a southwesterly heading. At cruising altitude, he had a spectacular view of the Door County peninsula, and he flew a direct line to Sturgeon Bay, the home of Door County Cherryland Airport.

Taking care to properly secure the plane after landing, he followed his usual routine and left instructions to have the fuel tanks filled for his return flight. Moments later he was behind the wheel of his rental car, heading for the Porte des Morts.

A room at a quiet bed-and-breakfast in Ellison Bay overlooking Green Bay would serve as a base of operations. Anything Kyle needed was within walking distance, including a place to rent bicycles.

Using a bicycle to tour Washington Island gave him suitable transportation and enabled him to cover long distances in a short amount of time. Not having to make reservations on the ferry for an automobile allowed him to maintain a low profile; no one would think twice about another bicycle rider on the island.

Kyle had arrived early enough in the day to make his first reconnoiter of the island. Everything went as planned. The ferryboats ran on a precise schedule, something that could be very important when planning his post-sanction departure. The worst thing he could imagine would be waiting for his transportation off the island if things didn't go quite as planned on the Morgan estate.

The ferryboat docked on time, and all of the passengers embarked, making for an orderly departure. Checking his map, Kyle determined the shortest route to the Morgan estate. As he pedaled away from the docks, he marveled at how bicycles had improved over the years.

He chose a mountain bike made by Trek, an American-made bicycle manufactured in Waterloo, Wisconsin, as his rental. This particular bike had fifteen speeds and performed excellently on all surfaces from pavement to dirt. The entire bike didn't weigh more than twenty pounds, yet it carried his six-foot-two-inch, two-hundred-twenty-pound muscular body with ease.

Minutes later Kyle was gliding past the wrought iron gates guarding the entrance of the Morgan estate. Anchored to stone pillars, the huge gates stood at least ten feet tall. A three-foot-high wall constructed of local rocks and stones collected from the shoreline extended from each pillar, marking the street-side boundary of the estate. The gates hung in the open position with no apparent electronic surveillance equipment. Living on an island was security enough; where could an intruder possibly hide?

Deliberately riding past the estate, Kyle wanted to get a view of at least three sides of the property. Everything was in its place, just like the surveillance photos had depicted. Once again, Joe's reconnaissance teams had done a great job collecting the information needed for the mission; nothing was left to guesswork.

After pedaling past the estate, Kyle stopped, took a drink of water, and made a course reversal, riding past the estate to view it from a different angle. From this side of the home, he could actually see the hangar that housed the helicopter in the rear corner of the property. The home appeared empty; there was no sign of movement anywhere. Kyle could see how the thick wooded areas on both sides of the estate would allow a person to traverse the property from front to back undetected.

This area of the island was quiet, so Kyle decided to park his bike and take a stroll through the dense stand of trees. Using the foliage as cover, he made his way to the rear of the property. Standing behind a majestic oak tree, he had a perfect view of the rear deck, the hangar doors, and the stairway leading down to the shoreline.

The best way to approach the hangar would be from the opposite side of the property; from there he could remain hidden until emerging. Unfortunately, the side door to the hangar was visible from the main house but was usable under the cover of darkness. While Kyle was engrossed in planning his entrance to the hangar, a Hughes 500 helicopter swooped in for a landing on the portable landing platform sitting outside the front of the hangar.

Originally designed for the military, the Hughes 500 was to be used as a lightweight reconnaissance helicopter. It eventually found its way to the civilian market, offering impressive performance. The small copter boasted a gross takeoff weight of 2,250 pounds powered by an Allison 250 turbine engine.

Normal cruise speed was a respectable 125 knots per hour (144 mph) with a top speed of 152 knots per hour (175 mph). Seats for five people, including the pilot, the chopper could fly for 375 miles.

The sound of the whirling blades of the upper rotor startled Kyle. The chopper seemed to appear out of nowhere. Kyle was worried that the occupants of the brightly colored machine had seen him. He crouched down as low as he could yet still maintain a clear view of the landing zone. As the helicopter gently settled onto the portable platform, Kyle could see the weight of the machine transfer from the rotor blades to the landing skids, an impressive piece of airmanship, especially from a low-time pilot like Morgan.

The rotor blades slowly decelerated to a full stop while Morgan performed his after-landing and shut-down checklists. Exiting the helicopter, he placed tie down straps over the skids and secured the machine to its platform.

Stepping down from the wheeled platform now cradling the helicopter, Morgan walked to the hangar and pulled an electronic control panel from a weatherproof container fastened to the side of the hangar door. Activating a control switch, the giant doors of the hangar began to retract along stainless steel rails in the concrete floor. Morgan disappeared into the cavernous opening only to emerge moments later riding a small John Deere tractor. Fastening a tow bar from the tractor to the platform, he gently wheeled the helicopter into the hangar for the night.

Kyle waited for Morgan to enter the rear of the home before making his way back to the road and his bike. Before returning to the docks and ferryboat, he spotted a public access path leading to the rocky shoreline. Pedaling down the path, he found himself at the water's edge within seconds. Once again, Kyle parked his bike and walked the beach until he came upon the stairs leading up to the Morgan estate.

Taking advantage of the absence of people, he walked up the stairs to test if this approach was feasible. Arriving at the top of the stairs, he could see the main house and hangar yet stay hidden behind the structure of the rear deck. Returning to his bike, he headed to the ferry, eventually arriving at the B and B in time to get something to eat and finalize his plans.

# CHAPTER FORTY-THREE

The next morning Kyle was on the ferry returning to the island with dozens of other bicyclists out for an early morning ride. The only difference was that this time Kyle had his backpack and its lethal contents strapped to his torso. Departing the ferry, accompanied by a group of bikers, he made his way directly to the Morgan estate.

Electing to use the path through the thick wooded area to the side of the home, Kyle made his way to the hangar and was ready to leave the protection of the trees and attempt to enter the building when he noticed movement out of the corner of his eye. Coming out of the house was a formidable looking man strutting as though he was on a mission. His actions immediately gave away his purpose; the man was a bodyguard. He marched around the perimeter of the property and returned to the rear entrance. This was definitely not part of the dossier and reconnaissance information. Now faced with a choice, Kyle had to decide to abort the mission or try to work around the problem, all the while keeping in mind his not-so-stellar performance in the mountains of southwest Colorado.

Perfectionists and type-A personalities, like Kyle, are annoying to those around them, but generally they are harder on themselves and not so forgiving of their past mistakes. The sprained ankle and sharp stick in the eye haunted and embarrassed him to the point that this time there would be no mistakes, no matter how insignificant.

As he sat motionless contemplating his next move, Kyle had no way of knowing about the frantic barrage of phone calls coming and going from Delasandro's office.

# CHAPTER FORTY-FOUR

Practically shouting into the phone, Joe asked, "Where are you? I just learned we have a serious leak. The mission is compromised, and there's strong evidence Morgan knows about Kyle."

"How do you know this? Are you sure? If you're right, I've gotta get movin', no time to talk now. I'll call you as soon as I can. Don't worry; I'm only a few hundred yards behind him," replied the voice from the other side of the secure satellite phone connection.

Dr. Morgan exited his home alone, but within a few seconds, the formidable bodyguard drove up to Morgan in a beautifully restored 1930s vintage Rolls Royce limousine. The car drove off, heading in the direction of the docks and the ferryboats. Kyle assumed the men were probably crossing over to the mainland. This presented Kyle with an opportunity to use the newest addition to his tool kit.

He waited for a few moments longer, wanting to make sure the limo didn't return. He could actually see the ferryboat start its crossing to the mainland with the Rolls Royce secured to its deck.

Kyle used the cover of the brush as long as he could and worked his way along the side of the hangar away from the house. As he got closer to the front of the edifice, he could see the large hangar doors were open just far enough for a man to squeeze between them and gain access to the magnificent structure.

Quickly traversing the hangar floor Kyle made his way to the tail boom of the helicopter. If all went as planned, he wouldn't have to fire one shot yet still accomplish his goal. Reaching into his backpack, he removed a small item resembling the letter U.

Gunnery Sergeant Bobby James Thibodaux had added a very effective and, in this case, lethal device to Kyle's tool kit: a shaped explosive charge. Small but powerful shaped explosives were designed and used in the demolition of buildings and other structures where a very precise chain reaction of explosions was needed to surgically raze the building.

Once in position, the explosive would do all of the work automatically. Utilizing a Phillips-head screwdriver, Kyle removed an oval-shaped inspection panel from the tail boom of the chopper. Reaching in, he could feel the shaft that connected the tail rotor blade to a transmission in the engine compartment.

Severing the tail rotor from the transmission would make the helicopter next to impossible to fly. Without the force of the tail rotor to counter the torque of the main rotor, the chopper would spin like a top out of control until finally impacting the ground. A crash of this nature was almost always fatal to the occupants due to the violent twisting motion of the chopper as it dug a crater into the earth. In this situation, the detonation would most likely happen while the chopper was over the water. Unlike conventional airplanes, helicopters only float for a few seconds. Dr. Morgan and his toy would have to be extracted from a depth of over one hundred feet of very cold Lake Michigan water.

After securing the U-shaped explosive to the drive shaft, Kyle activated the triggering mechanism by simply removing a plastic cover protecting the arming button. This particular device was designed to be activated when it sensed a change in barometric pressure. In other words, when the helicopter reached a predetermined altitude, the shape charge would detonate, separating the tail rotor from the rest of the helicopter.

Satisfied with his work, Kyle began to replace the inspection plate and remove any evidence of his visit. Tightening the last screw, he placed the screwdriver in his backpack and began his retreat to the safety of the trees and eventually back to the B and B to wait for Dr. Morgan's next flight.

Turning toward the door, Kyle looked up. To his shocking surprise, a short, round figure of a man was standing in front of the open doors, blocking Kyle's exit. "Good morning, Mr. Donnar. You are Kyle Donnar are you not?"

Reaching for his pistol hanging in a shoulder holster under his left arm, Kyle instinctively pointed the weapon at the man standing directly in his path to freedom. Ordering the rotund man to move away from the door, Kyle directed him to stand against the wall. Dutifully obeying, the gentleman strolled slowly to the sidewall of the hangar, as if he didn't have a care in the world.

Kyle glared at the man, never losing contact with him. Satisfied that he was in control of this unplanned turn of events, Kyle recognized the man as Dr. James Morgan. Confused, Kyle stammered through his question. "What are you doing here? I saw your Rolls on the deck of the ferry."

"You are correct, Mr. Donnar. May I call you Kyle? It seems that I already know you. My vehicle was on the boat in the capable hands of my mechanic. He was kind enough to come over to the island and escort the car to his shop on the mainland.

"My chauffer and I decided to walk along the beach back to the house, hoping we would find you doing whatever it is you have planned. We have been expecting your arrival and your punctuality did not disappoint us.

"Would you please take your finger off the trigger and forget about this dangerous game you're playing?" Morgan asked. Kyle couldn't believe what was happening and continued to point the pistol at his target. From behind him, Kyle heard another voice say, "Drop the weapon NOW. I have a Smith and Wesson .357 Magnum aimed directly at the back of your head."

Kyle froze but did not lower his weapon. "Kyle, I still have very good contacts in Washington. I became aware of the premature deaths of Samuel Sumner and Russell Owen while I was in Europe. I don't believe in coincidences, and I don't plan to be the next victim of this ungrateful administration, and of course let's not forget about your greedy employers in Zurich. Those sore losers and their predecessors have been controlling monetary policies for what—centuries? They don't seem to like it very much when they get beat at their own game. My financial contributions reach deep within the Capital Beltway, deep enough that my sources were able to give me all the information I needed to protect myself. So, please, put the weapon down. Your mission has failed."

A combination of fear and loathing momentarily took over Kyle's emotions. Fear for his life and loathing for the son of a bitch that leaked the information. "If I lower my gun, you aren't going to just let me walk out of here."

"That's true. I just can't let you leave, at least not until I get all the information I need to secure my future safety. I need to have the facts so that I can ensure this won't ever happen again. Think about it for a moment; I'm sure you'll see it my way."

Kyle's mind raced, looking for answers. Nothing was coming to mind, but he never lowered his weapon. The deafening silence prevailed for the next few seconds, and everything seemed to move in slow motion as Kyle searched for a solution. Standing motionless, almost completely frozen, all of his senses were in overload.

The unmistakable sound of the person behind him cocking the hammer of the .357 Magnum pointed at his head broke the silence. The sound was eerie as the metallic cylinder of the pistol rotated, depositing the powerful cartridge in position for firing. Time was running out. One way or another, Kyle had to make a decision.

# CHAPTER FORTY-FIVE

"Mr. Delasandro, Jimmy Wooden here. I think, in fact I'm sure, Bruce and I have cracked the Marco Island thing. When you get a chance, we'll be waiting for you here in the IT lab. We have a positive ID on the shooter."

"Jimmy, I'm in the middle of a crisis. I'll stop down as soon as I can." As an afterthought Joe quickly asked if it was good news or not, but Jimmy had already hung up. With nothing left to do but wait for any information coming from Door County, Joe headed for the IT department to see what Wooden and Goldstein had uncovered.

Entering the lab area, Joe was a little surprised to see that none of the facial recognition computers were in operation, and Wooden and Goldstein were casually going about their daily routines, whatever that was. Not being a child of the computer age, Joe Delasandro left the computer business and its separate language to those more in tune with the culture. Joe was heard many times stating: "I wouldn't know a *byte* if it were to come up behind me and *bite* me in the ass."

Seeing Joe standing there and looking impatient, Wooden strolled up to the facial recognition equipment, started booting up the systems, and then handed Joe a large hard-covered book, a high school yearbook. Joe asked in a frustrated tone, "What the hell is this?"

"We know you're very busy, but give us a few minutes to explain," said Wooden. Bruce and I got together with some friends last weekend to see if we could duplicate, and maybe improve, the system those students from MIT used to count cards while playing blackjack in Las Vegas. Are you familiar with the incident?"

"Yeah, I know the story,, but what's it got to do with the Marco thing," Joe answered.

"Well, if you remember, the casinos were taken for millions of dollars over a period of years. The MIT kids would fly to Vegas, use their system, rake in the cash, and be back in Boston for Monday morning's classes. The casinos weren't even aware these kids had developed a system to even the odds. Nothing was out of the ordinary, so the security and surveillance systems in the casinos, which by the way make our equipment look like something Fred Flintstone used, never noticed anything strange."

"OK, so again, what does this have to do with our problem?" asked Joe impatiently.

"I'm sorry, Mr. D., but bear with me on this. You of all people, with your, let's call it, ah, your indifference to computers, will love the irony. On a regular basis, all of the casinos in Vegas invite an old-fashioned "mom and pop" team to evaluate and look over the security systems, specifically looking for flaws. The mom part of the team was viewing the main floor of a casino through the security cameras when she noticed something. At two different blackjack tables, at the far ends of the floors from each other, two players stepped away from the tables, and one new player sat down. Coincidence maybe, but she jotted down the observation in her notebook and went about the rest of her business. The next week, working in a different casino, she witnessed the same pattern. Now she had something to look for, and she noted that the action on the casino floor took place about the same time as the first incident a week before. She reviewed the surveillance tapes going back a few months, and to her surprise, the same faces showed up at the casinos following a regular rotation. Still with nothing illegal or questionable to go on, she decided to use some old-fashioned detective techniques. She followed the gamblers as they exited the casinos with their winnings.

"The players checked out of the hotels and headed back to the airport. Using her connections at the airport to circumvent security, she managed to catch up to the gamblers as they all boarded a nonstop flight to Boston. There they were—the two players who would leave the tables and the player who sat down and had unbelievable good luck. *Too many similarities to be a coincidence*, she thought.

After some brainstorming and thinking—these kids were all around college age—she got a list of all the colleges and universities in the Boston area, and one stood out above all the rest: MIT. Getting her hands on a current yearbook, it was like looking at a lineup of the FBI's most-wanted list. All mathematics and science majors, she figured these kids had developed a system to beat the casinos, and now she knew what to look for, thus the yearbook sitting in your lap, a low-tech solution to our problem."

Opening the yearbook to the page with the over-sized "Super Mario" bookmark in place, Joe gazed at the page with utter disbelief. He wasn't sure if he was looking at an old photo of Kyle or at a photo of someone who could pass for Kyle.

"Who is this guy?" asked Delasandro.

"His name is Peter Welter. He was, and is, Kyle's oldest friend. They've been causing trouble together since they first met in grammar school in the mid-60s," answered Jimmy, standing proudly with his chest out and his hands on his hips.

"OK, so if we know who he is, why did he take out Sumner?" asked Joe.

"I'm sorry, but we don't know the why part of it, just who, but now that we know who he is, we should be able to put the pieces of the puzzle together," answered Wooden.

# CHAPTER FORTY-SIX

A sound coming from the far side of the hangar startled both Kyle and Dr. Morgan. A familiar sound but not instinctively identifiable occurred in quick succession; the noise repeated itself three times. Kyle fixated on the face of Dr. Morgan as it changed from a look of confidence to total confusion.

Kyle heard his stalker fall behind him and the clanking of the metal gun bouncing off the floor. Spinning around, he could see the assassin's body lying motionless. An avulsion roughly the size of a baseball was excavated from the left side of the gunman's face. Bone, muscle, skin, and brain tissue hung from the gaping hole.

Kyle frantically searched the surrounding area, looking for the other person, but to no avail. Again the silence was broken, only this time by a voice calling his name. "Kyle, Kyle! Are you OK? If so just stay where you are and take a deep breath. I'm coming out, so please don't shoot me."

Not recognizing the voice, he had little choice but to listen and acquiesce. Whoever this person was, he was undoubtedly a master marksman, and Kyle wouldn't stand a chance against him in a gunfight.

"I'm OK; my gun is down. Who are you?"

The mystery man slowly stepped out from around the door with his hands up in the air and with no sign of a weapon. As the man walked closer, Kyle still didn't recognize him. The man was about six feet tall and had a very lean, fit physique.

"Who are you?" Kyle asked again.

The stranger's demeanor changed suddenly, and he yelled: "GET DOWN, GET DOWN!"

Glancing sideways, Kyle saw Dr. Morgan raising his arm, pointing a pistol in his direction. The weapon fired, and the bullet raced directly toward Kyle's head. Missing him by less than an inch, he could actually hear the lethal piece of hot lead zip past his right ear.

Kyle's guardian angel opened fire, striking Dr. Morgan twice in the heart, killing him instantly. Morgan was dead before his body hit the concrete floor. The life-giving blood that once circulated throughout his arteries and veins was now gushing from his torso into an ever-enlarging pool of red.

Standing motionless and confused, Kyle was still wondering, *Who is this guy?* The stranger began to walk toward him, gun in hand.

"You don't recognize me do you? Don't feel too bad. The last time you saw me, I was in and out of consciousness in a muddy pool of water in Central America—the night you saved my life, along with Joe Delasandro's. I'm Paul D'Amico, Sergeant D'Amico. Do you remember me now?"

Kyle was still speechless, although his heart pounded impatiently in his chest.

"Joe sent me to keep an eye on you. Your pilots got me here late yesterday, and I've been shadowing you. I just learned that the mission had been compromised; someone's been talkin' too much back at IRC."

Kyle slowly regained his situational awareness. "Now I remember you, but who sent you? How did you find me? Oh, man, I'm confused." Kyle shook is head and let his firing arm relax.

"Let's get the hell out of here, and I'll explain the whole thing as we get off this island. But first, lets remove your calling card from the boom of the chopper," D'Amico ordered in his customary sergeant's bark.

After removing the shaped explosive charge from the helicopter's transmission, Kyle followed D'Amico down to the water's edge, grabbing the rented bike. The two men made their way to the ferry and finished their conversation. Kyle checked out of the B and B and drove back to Sturgeon Bay. D'Amico rode with him, and the two men parted company as D'Amico climbed the stairs of one of the Gulfstream Jets and headed back to Washington DC in style and comfort. Kyle followed in Joe's TBM-850.

# CHAPTER FORTY-SEVEN

Arriving home late that evening, Kyle had almost five hours of flight time to think about how close he had come to dying. Worst of all, had he failed in his mission, he might have jeopardized Tina's continued recovery, a thought far more dreadful than his own demise.

Tina once again sensed that something was not quite right with Kyle, but she chose to let it go. She knew if he wanted to talk about something, he would. Kyle grabbed the first opportunity and called Joe. The conversation was mostly a series of cryptic phrases, essentially telling Joe that he would be in the next day around noon for their usual debriefing.

Overwhelming relief washed over Kyle when he saw that Tina felt fantastic both physically as well as spiritually. The continuing good news regarding her recovery kept her in an almost euphoric state of mind. Some doctors claim that half the battle in conquering an illness is maintaining an upbeat, positive attitude. Tina had cornered the market in the positive attitude department.

Arriving at IRC exactly at noon, Kyle headed straight for his office to check messages and address any immediate issues with his flight department. Satisfied that everything was under control, he walked to Joe's office to begin the debriefing and to try to figure out how the mission was compromised.

Paul D'Amico was waiting with Joe. More than two decades had passed since Kyle had seen these two men together. The scene was surreal; Kyle almost couldn't believe his own eyes. More than twenty years, and millions of miles traveled in a career as an airline captain, had come and gone. That distant night in Central America was a fading memory. Now, sitting in one small office outside of the nation's capital, three men bound together by a twist of fate stared silently at one another.

Joe broke the silence with his customary offering of coffee. Paul trumped the offer, "To hell with the coffee; let's get a drink. As Jimmy Buffett says, 'It's five o'clock somewhere.'" Joe agreed and broke out a bottle of Jack Daniel's with three glasses. They raised their glasses to a silent toast before taking the first gulp.

Joe asked Kyle to go back to the moment when he started to plan this sanction, hoping that something might become obvious as to how and where the informer got his or her information. Unfortunately, nothing seemed out of the ordinary. He continued, thoroughly describing every part of the mission right up to the moment that Morgan uttered his name. Paul took over and finished the report from his point of view.

"I guarantee that I will find the person who leaked the information, and that person will regret his or her indiscretions," Joe said with a firm but calm voice.

The three men wasted the rest of the afternoon reminiscing and sipping whisky. Joe took great pleasure in poking fun at Kyle's missteps on each of the missions. Joe and Paul laughed so hard they eventually had tears streaming down their cheeks.

"I hope you guys are enjoying yourselves at my expense," Kyle uttered, embarrassed by the ribbing.

"The reason we're laughing so hard is that the stories bring back memories of our early days and how totally inept we really were and how lucky we were to get back in one piece," Paul said in a self-deprecating tone of voice. Joe nodded his head in agreement and filled their glasses again.

"So what happens now? Do I just go about my normal daily activities as though none of this took place?"

"You completed the assignment; there is nothing else for you to do. Go take care of that beautiful wife and have some fun flying those expensive toys out at the airport. In a few months, this whole nightmare will fade away," Joe answered.

"I don't think I'll ever forget that I took the lives of those men," Kyle lamented.

"Ah, but you didn't. Russell Owen drowned, and from what I just heard, you never got off a shot at Morgan. Unfortunately, you *will* take to your grave the expressions on the men's faces as they died." Paul, half sober, stared at the floor, shook his head, and mumbled, "Ain't that the truth."

Kyle rose from his chair and suggested they call it a day. Joe and Paul agreed. Kyle stepped over to Paul to shake his hand and thank him for saving his life. Paul responded, "I told you before, none of us would be standing here today if you hadn't stepped up and dragged our butts out of the mud." Paul gave Kyle a firm handshake, followed by a bear hug that took Kyle completely by surprise. Who would have guessed that this tough marine had a sentimental side?

The days and weeks pressed on, and Kyle was amazed at how accurate Joe was with his prediction of the nightmare fading. He actually took time to fly a couple of trips while some of his crewmembers were away for training. It felt good to get away and only have to worry about flying.

Between trips and office duties, Kyle accompanied Tina for her weekly injections. The three doctors were extremely pleased by the progress, but they cautioned that she was not out of the woods just yet. The injection therapy needed to continue until the last of the tumors had disappeared, just to make sure her body maintained a high level of antibodies to fight off the possibility of a relapse.

Tina was required to have periodic exams so that the doctors could accurately measure the size of the shrinking tumors. On those long and tedious days, Kyle would take the entire day off from work so he could pamper her. If she weren't too tired, they would have dinner at one of the numerous five-star restaurants in downtown Washington before heading home. If she didn't feel up to going out, Kyle would cook her dinner and wait on her all night long.

Returning from a short one-day trip, Kyle stopped by the office before heading for home. Joe Delasandro was still in his office, so Kyle popped his head through the door to say hello. Shocked by the pale, gaunt look on Joe's face, Kyle asked, "What's up? You look like you've been through a meat grinder."

"I wish that were the case. I've got some news involving you. Please, please sit down."

# CHAPTER FORTY-EIGHT

———————

"We know about Peter Welter," stated Delasandro. "We just don't know why he took out Sumner. I was hoping you would save us some time and fill in the blanks."

"I knew it would just be a matter of time before you solved that mystery. I've got a pretty good handle on who we work for, thanks to your history lesson. Pete and I were inseparable throughout grade school and high school, and, yes, we played up the fact that we looked a lot alike. We used it to our advantage as much as we could, usually not for good things. Let's just say that when something out of the ordinary happened in school, we were the usual suspects," Kyle replied.

"Let me ask you this; That day in my office when I told you the trail was cold and the local cops had nothing to go on except a weird name, I think it was Speedy or Peaty Calamaria, you had a shit eatin grin on your face. You couldn't have known your buddy was the shooter, what was with the smirk?"

Laughing under his breath Kyle explained; "When you said that name it took me a while to put it all together but when I figured it out all I could do was smile. The local cops on Marco were screwing with your friends from the FBI. The first name, Speedy is really Speotyto and the last name Calamaria is actually Cunicularia."

"Okay, who or what is a Speotyto or however you pronounced it?"

"It's island royalty, Kyle answered. Speotyto Cunicularia is the Latin name for the Burrowing Owls of Florida. They're small Owls that make their nests underground. If they choose to nest on your property you don't dare interfere or else you face serious legal problems from the Department of Natural Resources. Cute little buggars, and they're a hit with the tourists. Like I said, the local cops were messing with the FBI that day, most likely one of those jurisdictional things between agencies."

"Let's get back to your buddy", Delasandro suggested.

"Pete is one of those guys born with an innate ability to fix or build anything," Kyle continued. "He built really cool cars from Junkers and, could create anything you could imagine. He took his talent to Universal Airlines where he became a licensed aircraft mechanic and eventually became an instructor sharing his knowledge with the young guys.

"I used to get a real thrill when I'd report for a flight and see that my buddy had signed off on all the repairs and updates. I knew I was in good hands. Pete married a local gal and started a family. We laughed at each other, reminiscing over our exploits as kids, every time we got together. Needless to say we both took it pretty hard when our beloved airline was stolen out from under us. Pete landed on his feet, working for himself, fixing cars in his garage. He made enough money to support his family but was pressed hard to pay for decent health insurance. The only way he could afford a policy for his family was to accept an extremely high deductible. He never skimped when it came to his wife and kids, but he ignored a lot of serious injuries to himself over the years. The one problem he ignored for too long was a pain in his abdomen that grew over time. By the time he saw a doctor, it was too late; the pancreatic cancer was too far-gone, and he was given a death sentence."

"I'm sorry to hear that. So many good people like your buddy Pete paid the ultimate price for a greedy few," Delasandro added.

"We would talk on the phone and commiserate, usually after having one too many beers. We would plan the demise of the greedy Wall Street crooks and the robber barons, like Samuel Sumner. Probably not a smart thing to discuss over the phone, but we didn't care. I just didn't believe we would really carry out our plans of bravado.

"Now look at what we've done. Pete's dying and could care less who knows what he did, and then there's me, actually getting a shot at the bad guys and screwing it up.

# CHAPTER FORTY-NINE

Looking directly into Kyle's blue eyes, Delasandro said, "I don't know how to begin. I'm just so sorry that I ever got you involved in this. I received a phone call today from Dr. Berman. I anticipated that it was going to be the typical update I requested regarding Tina. Berman was frantic and almost incomprehensible. I had to calm her down before I could make any sense of what she was trying to tell me."

"What did she say?" Once again Kyle sensed his whole world was about to come crashing down around him.

"She composed herself long enough to convey the details of her bad news. She was in the process of ordering a new batch of serum for Tina's therapy. As you know, the serum is unstable and has a short shelf life, so she places her refill orders frequently. This time she learned that her order could not be filled. It appears that the only person who had access to the entire process had died and didn't leave any instructions.

"I didn't understand how this could happen until she explained to me that these small biotech companies fear that their formulas will fall prey to industrial espionage and end up being mass produced by a giant pharmaceutical conglomerate. In order to combat this, one key person, usually the owner of the company has access to the entire formula and process. The other employees only work on parts of the process and then pass it on. In this case, Tina's serum came from a company based in Wisconsin—Health Options, Dr. James Morgan's company."

Staring at Joe in total shock Kyle said, "I'm sitting here listening to you, but I don't really want to hear what you are telling me. How could this happen? Why would we be doing business with a guy we're supposed to kill? Please tell me this isn't happening."

Joe replied, "This is entirely my fault. I never thought to ask Dr. Berman for list of the biotech labs she uses in these treatments. Why would I? I don't tell her how to do her job and she doesn't interfere with my work. To me Health Options was just another HMO screwing doctors out of money by reducing payments on approved procedures. As for Berman and her team, they wouldn't have had any cause for alarm. They didn't know the Gnomes ordered us to take down Morgan."

"So let me get this straight. My wife has all but beaten this cancer only to find out that just before she completes her treatments she stands a good chance that the cancer will return and possibly mutate to a strain that can't be cured?"

Joe looked down at his desk, as if he was searching for the right answer, when Kyle said, "So, you're telling me that by killing Morgan, I've probably killed my wife at the same time?"

# CHAPTER FIFTY

Kyle's rage continued to grow, building to a crescendo. Every moment of every day, Kyle faced the unbearable realization that his actions may have had the exact opposite results of his desired outcome. Instead of helping his wife with her illness, he may have stymied her recovery, or worse.

The fact that he came within seconds of dying on an island in northern Wisconsin was now an afterthought. Gone were the feelings of guilt that had haunted him since accepting this assignment. Time was running out. Tina was scheduled to continue the clinical trials of a miracle treatment that had all but saved her life. If her doctors couldn't break the code and manufacture the serum in time, Kyle would have to tell her the whole story.

While Kyle was living through his own personal hell, Joe Delasandro worked tirelessly trying to track down the sources of the leak that almost cost Kyle his life. Using every resource at his disposal, he called upon every available agent to gather information. It was only a matter of time before a small and seemingly unimportant piece of information would eventually unlock the clues and lead Joe to the perpetrator.

Dr. Berman and her staff worked overtime, putting in long days, hoping that they would get lucky in deciphering Dr. Morgan's formula. Joe offered Dr. Berman all the resources available though IRC, which included some of the most powerful computers in the world. He checked with her every morning for a status report, and every morning she gave him the same answer. "Sorry, Joe, no luck. But we're doing everything we can."

Joe could feel the pressure building as each day passed with no progress on either front. To compound his problems, Dr. Berman regrettably informed him that Dr. Clayton had disappeared and had not been heard from for a couple of days. Joe was ready to explode with the receipt of this news.

Pacing back and forth in his office like a caged lion, Joe was ready to pounce on whatever crossed his path. Suddenly a phone call interrupted him in mid-stride. The caller had accidentally come across some information while having lunch with a friend from the Pentagon.

"Mr. Delasandro, this might not seem like much, and not be very important, but I thought you should know about it anyway."

The caller was Kyle's favorite pilot from the flight department, Tim Braden. Tim was having lunch with an old friend from the Pentagon, talking about the usual things—airplanes, cars, sports, and of course beautiful women—typical guy talk. The friend mentioned that one of Tim's regular passengers had been sniffing around his department at the Pentagon, trying to impress a young GS Thirteen secretary.

"Well, who are we talking about?" Joe asked.

"Lieutenant Colonel Harold Sheppard," responded Tim. "Like I said, this might not be important, but I thought you would like to know."

"Thanks, Tim. I'm not so sure if this means anything, but I'll have it checked out." Joe made a few calls to friends within the Pentagon and found someone to keep an eye on the situation.

The hours and days rhythmically ticked away like a metronome on a piano. Unfortunately, this time the rhythm was to a dirge. Kyle felt the relentless pressure crushing him from within. In a few days, Tina would be sitting in Dr. Berman's office, waiting to begin the last phase of her therapy. The sense of total helplessness was a new and horrible feeling for him.

Joe's contact within the Pentagon was standing outside IRC's front door when Joe arrived the next morning. "Joe, I may have something for you. Do you have a minute?" Joe grabbed his friend practically dragging him through the doors and raced up the stairs. Finally sitting in Joe's office, the two men began to talk.

"This thing you asked me to keep an eye on, the thing with Harold Sheppard, well it seems as though he's been talking a little too much about some of the things going on here at IRC. The young secretary he's been chasing likes to share her sexual adventures with her co-workers while bragging about how her new boyfriend shares secret information with her while between the sheets. She never gives specifics but wants everyone to think she's in the know. I checked her background and discovered she graduated from the University of Wisconsin at Madison. That's the same school where Dr. James Morgan taught.

"Very interesting, coincidence maybe," Joe replied.

"I took the liberty of checking her phone records and found she had made a series of calls to Morgan at the school and to his office. Here's the list of calls with dates and times." Joe reached for the envelope containing the information and thanked his friend. "I've gotta go now. I hope this helps." Joe thanked him again and escorted him to the door.

Studying the phone records, Joe discovered the calls to Morgan began about two weeks after she started seeing Sheppard. Joe continued searching the list and discovered that this young secretary had spoken to Morgan just days before Kyle left for Wisconsin. Could this have been just a coincidence or was there more to the phone calls? Joe couldn't take a chance, so he made arrangements to have the girl picked up and interrogated by some friends over at NSA.

Unaware of the frenzy of activity regarding her welfare, Tina was relaxing at their home on Marco Island where she was spending time with her friends prior to starting the next, and hopefully final, phase in her treatments. She e-mailed her travel plans, including flight numbers and times to Kyle so he would know when to pick her up at the airport. The reality of her returning to Washington increased Kyle's already elevated level of anxiety. How could he ever explain to her what he had done?

# CHAPTER FIFTY-ONE

A fter a perfect "snatch and grab" by a couple of surly operatives, the young secretary was so frightened she was no match for the professional inter-rogators from the NSA. Before starting the questioning, the inquisitors allowed the young girl some privacy so she could change out of her wet undergarments. The terror of being kidnapped and thrown into a window-less van with a hood over her head was enough to trig-ger uncontrolled urination.

Very little prodding was necessary before she began to tell about her affair with Sheppard, includ-ing all of the details of their sexual exploits. With tears streaming down her cheeks, she begged them not to tell her husband. The agents took advantage of this request and promised not to say anything to her spouse if she would tell them about her relationship with Dr. James Morgan.

She went on to explain that she was once a student of Dr. Morgan, in both the classroom and his bedroom. She had hoped that one day she could rekindle her romance with him. She admitted that she would leave her husband for a chance to be with her first lover.

The agents continued the question-and-answer session, skillfully working their way towards her warning Morgan of impending danger.

Abruptly throwing a copy of her phone records in front of her, they inquired as to the nature of the conversation on the date highlighted by Delasandro. She sat back in her chair and thought for a while before starting to talk.

"I believe that was the day he was returning from a medical convention in Europe. I asked him how things went, and he told me that the convention was tedious and he was surrounded by a group of boring doctors."

The two agents looked at each other, trying not to smirk at the fact that he had forgotten to tell her about the knockout blonde hanging on his arm in the reconnaissance photos.

"He asked me about my affair with GI Joe as he called him. He seemed to delight in listening to me describe our tryst. He was always interested in the secrets Sheppard was sharing with me. I didn't think much of it, and I didn't think Harold was really telling me anything of great importance. I described the story Harold had told me of a mission where he sent out one of his agents to assassinate some businessmen. I didn't really take Harold seriously but told James anyway."

"Do you remember what Morgan said after you told him that story?" the agent asked.

"He asked me if Harold might have mentioned any names or places. I told him about an upcoming mission to some island around Lake Michigan. After that he seemed to be in a hurry and said good-bye."

The two agents wrapped up the interrogation and dropped the girl back in the shopping center parking lot where they had grabbed her. Joe's friend from NSA personally delivered a transcribed copy of the session for Joe to study. Looking over the data, it was obvious the girl didn't know what she was doing when she spoke with Morgan. She had no way of knowing whether what Sheppard said was accurate or just some false bravado in an attempt to separate her from her panties, which of course served her purposes, too. The big question was: how did Morgan deduce that he was the next target?

Regardless of how Morgan figured it out, the evidence clearly pointed to Harold Sheppard who had a big mouth to go along with his caustic personality. Joe was going to put an end to Sheppard's cavalier attitude.

Less than thirty-six hours remained before Tina Donnar's scheduled arrival at Washington's Dulles International Airport. For Kyle the time seemed to tick away faster and faster, while his plight grew more and more desperate. The feeling of helplessness was driving Kyle insane. All he could do was sit and wait, hoping Dr. Berman and her team would come up with a miracle.

Kyle arrived at his office, showing obvious signs of stress. As he made his way toward his office, he overheard a familiar voice coming from the cafeteria. As he looked through the door, he was surprised to see Paul D'Amico drinking coffee with Joe and General Buckwalter.

The three men acted cool and calm and invited Kyle in for some coffee. He accepted and joined the trio. Kyle could sense something important was in the works, but discretion taught Kyle not to ask too many questions. If Joe Delasandro wanted him to know what was happening, he would have told him. Kyle finished his coffee and headed for his office when General

Buckwalter stopped him and said, "Don't worry; something is bound to break any minute. We have an army of people working on this formula problem."

The three men retreated to Joe's office where they made the decision how best to handle the Harold Sheppard situation. Before parting, the three men agreed that from that moment on all communications regarding the issue would be through standard operating procedures, meaning no open discussions via telephones.

Kyle finished out the rest of his day, struggling to focus on his work. During the drive home, he glanced at his watch and realized that he had twenty-four more hours before Tina stepped off a plane, and then he would have to break the news. It was going to be a long, sleepless night.

Tossing and turning, switching the television on and off, watching the hands on the clock speeding toward the new day, Kyle was unable to relax enough to fall asleep. At five o'clock, the familiar thud of the daily newspaper hitting the front stoop forced Kyle to surrender to the new day and to get out of bed and start his routine. He brewed a pot of coffee and turned on the television in the kitchen to catch the morning edition of the Weather Channel.

Twelve hours was all that separated Kyle from the worst nightmare he could imagine. Tina's plane was scheduled to arrive at 5:00 p.m. He would have to leave his office no later than four in order to meet her outside the terminal on time. The day seemed to pass quickly; before long it was already noon.

# CHAPTER FIFTY-TWO

———————————

Harold Sheppard left his townhouse in Georgetown, headed for the health club. Sheppard maintained the same schedule day in and day out. He left home exactly at noon, drove to the same convenient store, and purchased a bottle of Gatorade to take to is daily workout.

From the store, he drove straight for the health club in his new Porsche Boxster. Pulling into the parking garage across the street from the club, he always raced up the spiraling ramps to the top level, away from other vehicles, hoping to protect his investment from careless drivers.

As Sheppard carefully parked his car, taking two spaces, he gently applied the parking brake and shut down the motor. Grabbing his gym bag from the rear seat, he opened the door and stepped out into eternity. A familiar figure was waiting silently behind a concrete pillar for this exact moment. Sheppard looked up to see a woman walking directly at him.

Before he had a chance to reason any further, the slender, attractive woman raised her silenced 9mm pistol and fired three quick shots, hitting Sheppard three times in an area the size of a silver dollar centered on his chest. His body lunged backward from the force of the impact of the bullets, slamming his torso off the side of his car.

Quickly approaching Sheppard's car, she struggled a little and placed his lifeless body behind the steering wheel and closed the door before disappearing into the shadows. Leaving the parking garage, the assailant sent a cryptic text message to Delasandro: "All's quiet. Goin' back to work."

Joe replied with a simple: "Thanks, Gina, I owe you."

Three o'clock had rolled around, and Kyle was preparing himself for his rendezvous with Tina. Sitting in silence, his depression was almost debilitating. Carefully organizing his desk, he was preparing to leave his office when Delasandro called.

"Kyle, can you stop by my office immediately? I need to see you before you go to the airport."

Kyle dutifully followed orders and made his way to hear what Joe had to say. Knocking on the door out of respect, Kyle waited for the invitation to enter. Stepping into Joe's office, Kyle was startled to see Dr. Charles Clayton sitting with former CIA security director and member of IRC's board of directors Frank Schmidt. "Come in, Kyle. Have a seat. Frank has some information for you."

"Kyle, you know Dr. Clayton." Kyle nodded his head. "Every now and then, something comes up where we need to confer with a scientist the caliber of Dr. Clayton. Over the years, he has consulted with us at the CIA on a number of issues. I asked for his assistance when the board ordered the sanction on Dr. James Morgan. I never trusted or had much faith in Sheppard, and the thought of him educating our group regarding Morgan led me to suspect there might be some complications with that assignment. Not knowing anything about the actual assignment or who was targeted, Dr. Clayton was kind enough to supply us with a colleague of his who was comfortable, pardon the pun, doing a little *undercover work*. I'd like you to meet Dr. Andrea Tortoricci."

Kyle turned around and was completely startled to see a beautiful woman standing by Joe's liquor cabinet. Even more amazing was the fact that Kyle recognized her. She was the hot young blonde photographed on Morgan's arm.

"Dr. Tortoricci has an MD with a PhD in molecular biology. She volunteers from time to time, handling a little fieldwork for us. She and Dr. Clayton worked together a few years ago; that's how we found her. Assuming Morgan was probably one of those totally insecure types who kept everything secret, I asked Dr. Tortoricci for help. The good doctor accidentally-on-purpose bumped into Morgan at a lounge near his home and quickly made friends. Morgan never knew what hit him.

"Morgan believed that she was a temporary worker from a professional agency. He took a liking to her and let down his guard. Over time Andrea discovered where Morgan kept his important papers and formulas and copied them without his knowledge."

"I'm sorry it took me so long to get the formulas back here, but he didn't label them, and it took more time than I expected to sort through them, copy them, and return them in their original order," Andrea said apologetically.

"As for Tina, I needed help to decipher Morgan's notes and codes. I called Dr. Clayton and explained my dilemma. He quickly put it all together and raced to my aid. He dropped everything, cancelled all appointments, and took off before he had a chance to inform Dr. Berman of his unplanned absence. We sent copies of all the notes to Dr. Berman and her team at the hospital as well as our cryptographers at CIA this morning." Kyle was speechless, tears welled up, and he sat slumped over in one of Joe's stuffed leather chairs, shaking his head.

The overall mood in the room was so dark and somber that Joe couldn't bring himself to share the news of tracking down the leak at IRC.

Cautiously optimistic, Kyle slowly stood and thanked everyone then headed for the door. He had an important rendezvous with the love of his life.

"Kyle, hold up for one second. Let me drive you to the airport, it won't do Tina any good if you don't get there in one piece," Joe commanded.

One last question flashed through his thoughts enroute to the airport: *How do I tell Tina that because of my actions she may not stay in remission, and I'm the one responsible for this catastrophe?*

# CHAPTER FIFTY-THREE

The drive to Dulles Airport was excruciating. No matter how hard Kyle tried, he could not stop himself of the thought of losing Tina.

"What are you thinking right now? Let down that perpetual suit of armor and tell me what you're feeling," pleaded Joe.

"You always wanted to know what made me tick, what inside me drives me on and on. Well here it is plain and simple: I've learned to live with hypocrisy, betrayal and disappointment even before I knew what the words meant. And let's not forget the constant presence of Mr. Murphy and his Law: *'Anything that can go wrong will go wrong.'*

"As soon as we moved from the inner city to the suburbs it started. My brother and I were known as "those city kids". The attitude around the neighborhood was we had no right to invade this quiet little town. We sensed we were not wanted immediately. However, I found it strange that every Sunday the same people who shunned us sat in the front of the church with a holier than thou look on their face. The same church going neighbors looked for any excuse to call the police and report our criminal actions."

"What kinda things were you doing that the police would be called?" Joe asked.

"Oh, we were hard core offenders. When we weren't playing ball in the park behind our house we did boy things like throwing rocks at each other and riding our bikes like crazy people and occasionally we would get our hands on firecrackers. Whoa, if that doesn't warrant the death penalty, I don't know what does.

"One winter we actually had the audacity to hide behind a manger scene during the holiday season and throw snowballs at passing trucks. That one got us dragged home by our collars by one of the uppity neighbors and scolded in front of parents. That particular neighbor later saw his kids get hooked on drugs and dropped out of school."

"Yeah, but that's generally part of growing up anywhere. You're always gonna have those types of people around," said Joe.

"That's true but the discrimination continued into our new public school. I was always the more mischievous one. I was totally bored and hated being there. It took until the seventh grade before anyone tried to find out why I didn't care about my grades. The real reason the principal started looking into my behavior was because he wanted a reason to send me away to a juvenile detention center.

"A psychologist was brought in and I was given a barrage of aptitude tests. The day finally came for everyone to hear the results and to the dismay of all the teachers and especially the principal; I blew the I.Q. tests off the charts. According to the psychologist the school was not creating enough of a challenge for me. I should have been doing high school senior work. Hence the boredom and getting kicked out of class."

"That was good news, wasn't it?" Asked Joe.

"You'd think, but in reality it turned the teachers more against me. It sort of highlighted their incompetence. One day I was standing on the playground after lunch talking with some of my fellow delinquents when the principal walked up behind me and falsely accused me of something. I stood my ground and denied everything until the principal got so frustrated he smacked me with a back hand that almost took my head off. Did I forget to mention most of the students referred to him as Lurch. He was huge and resembled Lurch the butler from the Addams family. He called my parents and explained to them what happened. His worried look for striking a student turned to a smug, gleeful smirk. I later learned that my parents took his side and assumed I deserved the slap. From that day on it was open season on me.

"I even got in a fight with the wood shop teacher at our eighth grade picnic. He was a total whack job. All the guys feared this nutcase. He took a cheap shot at me when I was rounding third base on what should have been a home run. I didn't let him get away with the elbow to my ribs. I said something, and the fight was on. He was bigger and stronger and I got my ass kicked but before it was broken up I got some good shots in on that bastard. He never laid a hand on me again."

"I can't believe this stuff went on. Didn't your parents get involved?"

"My parents were much older than the rest of the parents in the area. They never went to college and grew up during the tough days of the great depression. Both attended Catholic school where corporal punishment was allowed. A little punch from a teacher now and then was okay in their minds. They also didn't want to make waves because my dad worked for the City of Chicago and was not supposed to be living in the suburbs.

"High School was better because it turned out my brother and I excelled in sports and played on the varsity teams starting in our sophomore years. I focused on doing whatever was needed to get through and on to college. I knew to be competitive in the aviation field college was must."

Joe added; "Knowing your history the way I do you still took the long road with many a detour before achieving your goal to fly for a major airline. I have your biography in my file. Remember, I read it to you that day on the island at Starbucks."

"So Joe, you see that throughout my entire life I've had more than my share of roadblocks thrown in my path. Nothing ever went as planned. Just look at this situation we find ourselves in today. Mr. Murphy and his law are in control of this ultimate FUBAR. I learned to always have plan "B" and" C" ready to go when plan "A" fell apart. But not this time, no backup plans. I relied on IRC and all its resources to cover my back. Over time I have learned to expect family to let me down, strangers to cheat me, go behind my back, and just plain screw with me. If someone told me I couldn't do this or do that I would work ten times harder just to prove them wrong. I have been knocked on my ass both metaphorically and literally more times than I can count, but I always get back up and into the fight. My type "A" personality became a type "A" on steroids, so to speak".

The rest of the ride to airport Kyle sat in silence preparing himself for a full disclosure of his lies and cover-ups. No explanation detailing why he did what he thought was necessary to save her life would be adequate. Tina would never want Kyle to compromise his integrity in any way for any reason, including her well-being.

Arriving at the airport, Joe parked the car at the IRC hangar and asked one of the mechanics to drop Kyle off at the terminal. The van ride took only a few minutes from the hangar to the arrivals section of the terminal. "I'll grab a taxi for the ride back; no need for you to stick around any longer," Kyle instructed the driver.

The waiting area in the terminal was elbow to elbow with people. Family members, limousine drivers, boyfriends, and girlfriends, all anxiously waiting and straining to get a glimpse of their loved ones as they exited the secure area of the airport terminal building. The scene was controlled chaos, with passengers entering and exiting trams used for transport between the main terminal to the planes.

Ironically, even while standing in this mass of humanity, Kyle had never felt more alone.

# CHAPTER FIFTY-FOUR

Dr. Andrea Tortoricci headed back to her office just outside CIA headquarters in Langley, Virginia, as soon as Kyle and Joe departed for the airport. .

"I can't get anything done sitting here, so I'll be at my office reviewing my notes if you need me," she had announced as she left the meeting.

The short ride from IRC to Langley was a picturesque postcard image of the countryside of Virginia. The rolling hills and farmland looked similar to the farmland in Wisconsin where she had spent time with Dr. Morgan, participating in a very dangerous game.

Suddenly, as she was admiring the Norman Rockwell setting of a farmhouse, barn, and grain silo, it hit her like a ton of bricks. While staying with Morgan on his farm in Wisconsin, she remembered looking at an invoice for a delivery of feed corn to Morgan's silo. The strange part was that Morgan had no livestock on his property to feed.

The invoice was unlike anything she had ever seen. Other than the word INVOICE boldly imprinted across the top of the page, there was no dollar amount listed or company name to pay. The information on the invoice was a smattering of numbers and letters that made no sense at all. Even stranger was the fact that the invoice had been in the same stack of papers with purchase orders from numerous hospitals around the country.

Arriving at her office, she quickly started reviewing all of the documents in her possession, hoping beyond hope that she had made a copy of that single sheet of paper. And then she came across a document that caused every muscle in her body to freeze; she stared in disbelief.

Sitting in front of her was a copy of the invoice, displaying its random series of letters and numbers. Dr. Tortoricci immediately placed a call for help from someone in the cryptology department.

Within minutes the most powerful computers in the world fired through algorithm after algorithm, searching to make sense of the letters and numbers. Pacing back and forth, Dr. Tortoricci was uncharacteristically losing her patience.

A geeky looking young man, just returning from a coffee break, walked into the whirling dervish of activity, wondering what was happening with *his* computers.

"I'm Anthony from the puzzle factory. What can I do for you?"

"Your computers are working on this code. Take a look at this and see if you recognize any patterns or clues as to what this might be," ordered Dr. Tortoricci.

Sitting down next to such a beautiful woman made Anthony a little uneasy, but he ignored his feelings and began to examine the piece of paper. Using his index finger, he gently pushed his thick-framed glasses into their proper position on the bridge of his nose.

Seconds later, he turned to Dr. Tortoricci and asked, "Is this some kind of joke, or is it pick on the nerd day here?"

"What are you talking about? I assure you this is no joke," she responded.

"Well, Dr. Tortoricci, this code you have in front of you is probably one of the most widely published documents on the face of the earth. *Boys' Life* magazine, the magazine put out by the Boy Scouts of America, used this year after year when I was in scouting. It was a game for the readers to decipher a hidden message in each month's issue."

"Do you remember how it works?"

"Oh please! Dr. Tortoricci, your average twelve-year-old boy scout can crack this code. Who ever gave this to you is probably having a good laugh at your expense," Anthony replied sarcastically.

Tortoricci quipped, "I don't think he's doing too much laughing right now."

A quick explanation and a handwritten legend supplied by Anthony was all she needed. She gave him a big hug and a kiss on the cheek and thanked him for his help. Returning to his duties, Anthony felt a rush of hot flashes from head to toe, something he had never experienced in his life.

Utilizing the legend Tortoricci realized the letters and numbers corresponded to pages, paragraphs, sentences, and words hidden within each file of the formulas stored in Dr. Morgan's safe.

# CHAPTER FIFTY-FIVE

The secure phone in Joe Delasandro's office began to ring. "Please, please pick up," Dr. Tortoricci shouted into the phone. Finally, after about the ninth ring, she remembered Joe drove Kyle to the airport and immediately dialed his cell phone.

Her anxiety grew as his cell phone began to ring and ring and ring. Unknown to her Joe was in the hangar speaking with a mechanic while his phone sat alone in the break room.

With no one to answer it, his phone eventually switched over to voice mail. Andrea Tortoricci had hung up and had begun to dial all of the numbers in her possession. Joe headed back to the break room to refill his coffee when every phone in the building began to ring and his cell phone was vibrating on the table where he left it. Quickly reaching for the phone hanging on the wall he spilled his coffee soaking his left shoe and creating a puddle on the floor.

"Joe, Andrea Tortoricci here. I've got it. I have the code, and you won't believe me when I show it to you. Dr. Clayton and I are scouring the documents; we should have something to shoot over to Dr. Berman within the hour. Can you reach Kyle? We have to give him the news. Don't let him meet his wife with the wrong message."

"I'm on it. I know how to reach him. Thanks, Andrea. You have no idea the load you just took off my shoulders." Joe immediately called Kyle. Kyle's phone started to ring at the same time Joe could hear a faint but clear rendition of Beethoven's Fur Elise. Knowing this was Kyle's ringtone of choice Joe tracked down the source of the music. Sitting on the floor of Joe's car was Kyle's cell phone.

The mechanic who dropped Kyle off at the terminal sensed the urgency of the situation and offered to take Joe to the same entrance. Joe agreed but not before calling the airport and leaving a message with the airport paging service.

Kyle spotted Tina coming down the escalator. He was awash in mixed emotions—glad to see her yet dreading what he was about to disclose.

# CHAPTER FIFTY-SIX

Before Tina reached the bottom of the escalator, she was waving at Kyle. A huge smile on her face, it was obvious she was glad to be home. As he started walking in Tina's direction, he heard his name over the public address system, calling him to the nearest white courtesy phone.

Holding up his hand, Tina could see he was pointing at the phone attached to a support pillar in the baggage area. Tina waved back understanding Kyle's intentions.

Picking up the handset automatically dialed an operator. Hearing the voice on the other end Kyle identified himself and the operator read him the message.

"Kyle, Dr. Tortoricci has the answer; I'll be there in two minutes to explain, Joe." The operator politely asked if there was anything else she could do for him before disconnecting the call.

At the same time the phone went silent, Kyle felt the arms of his beautiful wife wrap around his solid torso while receiving a gentle kiss on the back of his neck. Turning to face her Kyle could see Joe rushing into view with the thumbs up signal. Unaware of the frenzied activity behind her she gave her favorite guy a huge hug and a passionate kiss. Returning the embrace Kyle saw Joe hold his index finger to his lips. Nodding his head acknowledging the message, Kyle fought to keep his tears in check.

*KEVIN JOHN DOHM* is into his fourth decade as a commercial airline pilot with close to 30,000 hours of flight time in all types and sizes of aircraft. As Captain for a major airline, he also held the position as Chairman of the Board of a large corporate airport outside Chicago and currently serves as a member of the Aeronautical Advisory Board to the Governor of Illinois. He has also enjoys success in business through his entrepreneurial spirit. He currently resides in Chicago and Marco Island, Florida.